Kate Boyle grew up in Essex before gaining a first-class degree in History of Art from Bristol University. After nearly a decade of working in London, a dogged desire to conquer her inability to roll her r's led her to Madrid. There she spent two and a half years spitting over strangers and teaching English to Spaniards, but she never grew accustomed to their regular comments on her pale skin.

Now back in London she wastes hours dreaming of the sunny skies of Madrid and persists with the irritating habit of dropping Spanish words into conversation at random. When she's not revisiting her adopted homeland or trying to perfect the art of the flawless Spanish tortilla, she can be found in a PR agency by day and writing her second novel by night. She regularly writes for an antiques magazine and has contributed to two architectural books. *Happy as a Partridge* is her first novel.

Happy as a Partridge

First published in Great Britain in 2018 by Puente Publishing

Edited, designed and produced by Tandem Publishing
http://tandempublishing.yolasite.com/

Cover design by Lena Yang

ISBN: 978-1-5272-1859-8

10 9 8 7 6 5 4 3 2 1

A CIP catalogue record for this book is available from the British Library.

Printed and bound in Great Britain by CPI Group (UK) Ltd
Croydon CR0 4YY.

"To have another language is to possess a second soul."

Charlemagne

1

Did that just happen? I stared into the same face I'd seen in the mirror for the last twenty-nine years and wondered if it really belonged to me. A typical Virgo, I found decision-making, let alone spontaneity, didn't always come easily, but in a brief moment of madness and extreme frustration I'd just quit my job. Had I really QUIT? Was I a…I couldn't even bring myself to say the word…did this make me a quitter? A failure? Oh god. I *was* a failure. After two and a half months of complaining about everyone in the madhouse masquerading as an office, was I, in fact, the mad one?

I'd been so flattered when the swanky PR agency offered me the position of Account Manager, along with a bumper salary. Deep down I had known it wasn't exactly what I was looking for, but I buried the niggling voice and focused on planning all the holidays I could now afford. On day one I had gone home and cried. I mean, sobbed. Not only did my overly botoxed sixty-five-year-old boss think it acceptable to wear white leggings with no underwear, it turned out the 'arts' clients she had promised me were property developers adding token sculptures outside their buildings to 'widen their appeal'. She genuinely expected me to support, promote and enthuse about their hideous luxury developments and modern art, and then and there, on day one, the blindingly obvious hit me like a truck. I couldn't believe it had taken so long to sink in. PR just wasn't for me.

I steadied myself on the cool porcelain of the basin. It hadn't been a dream. I really was now unemployed, single and rapidly approaching my thirtieth birthday. Thirty. Such a milestone, wasn't it? I'd nurtured so many wonderful plans for my twenties. A great job. A gorgeous and successful husband. A handful of cute and cheeky kids. Bloody hell, I'd been cheated – the years had all vanished, I'd accomplished little and now I was unemployed again and facing a return to the hell of job hunting. The day-to-day tedium of 'keeping my chin up' and faking enthusiasm every time someone asked how the search was going or offered well-meant but utterly useless advice. Help. I had to force myself to look on the bright side. At least I was going to George's for dinner tonight – I was dying for a friendly face and, more importantly, a big glass of wine. George was a sweetheart. We had met at an excruciatingly formal Scottish weekend at which I had developed one of my extreme teenage crushes. After an awkward, drunken snog and fumble at a party a few years later, an unspoken pact had been made – no more romance (much to the disappointment of my mother who had been eyeing him up as a charming son-in-law), but we'd become close friends. In fact, he'd become a bit like a brother and I really appreciated his presence in my life.

For the last year or so he'd been going out with tall, bubbly and brilliant Rosie. With her swish of luscious locks and her great designer wardrobe she was a serious hottie. Despite her being slightly intimidating on first impressions, fiercely bright and highly successful in something-I-don't-really-understand-in-advertising-but-which-I-don't-feel-clever-enough-to-ask-about, I had come to adore her upbeat personality. As chirpy as a bird, she was the one to transform this moment of chaos into something more positive.

"Evie! How are you?" Rosie enveloped me in a cosy cashmere hug and pulled me into George's home. "Come in, come in. It's SO good to see you. I've been dying to hear your news, tell me everything," she said as she busied herself opening a bottle of wine.

I suddenly had an overwhelming urge to cry. God I was an emotional retard. My shoulders slumped and I wondered how I was going to cope with the rest of the evening. Not only that, but I was having to bend over slightly to stifle an increasingly painful stomach ache. At the risk of over-sharing, my tummy hadn't been in the best of health for the last week or so and I felt so lethargic and bloated I almost looked pregnant.

There wasn't a wine glass or teaspoon out of place on the table when we sat down and tucked into a goat's cheese, rocket and red onion tart starter. I say tucked into, but I was just playing with it. It was delicious, but I didn't have space for a single pea in my aching stomach. As I gazed around the table my heart sank. George and Rosie were lovely, obviously, but I wouldn't have said any of the others were particularly close mates and to be honest they'd always made me feel a wee bit small.

To my right was the ruddy-cheeked and smiley army officer Charlie, bubbling with excitement at having recently proposed to his equally sweet girlfriend Louise. He was deep in conversation with Antonia, a dress designer, who, having recently got married in Spain, was relaying the trials and tribulations of organising a wedding abroad.

"I mean the Spanish bureaucracy is so long-winded, if we'd known about it I would have had second thoughts."

Charlie cooed, "Oh but it was so worth it. Your wedding

was incredible. You looked like royalty in that horse and carriage."

Moving on around the table, as wedding chat really didn't get me going, particularly when I felt so uncomfortable, I tuned into D chatting animatedly to Emilia. I'd never met him, but D was short for Duncan, and Dunc was a hunk, that's for sure. For some reason an initial rather than a name added to his allure. Tall, dark and handsome, he was every bit a Fulham cliché. Thick dark curls covered his head, a sweet dimple appeared when he grinned and an aura of privilege surrounded him. Clad in Diesel jeans, Adidas Gazelles and a blue sweater that matched his eyes, I had to admit he was pretty dreamy. However, he'd evidently had a few drinks and less than two minutes into their conversation his appeal was waning.

"Now Genevieve is up the duff she's become such a grump and decreed shagging is off the cards for at least the next five months. What's that all about? I was under the impression it was a wife's duty to always be up for it?"

He thumped his hand down on the table with a loud guffaw and continued, "But then again I suppose the filly is going to lose her looks as she piles on the pounds so maybe I won't even want a piece of her until the little critter arrives. A mini-me I hope. Can't bloody wait."

I couldn't believe people like him existed. Simply ghastly, to use my mother's expression. Emilia, who had the misfortune to be sitting at his side, meekly simpered at his banter, and flashed a massive red-stone engagement ring as she stretched for the water jug.

"It's a stone called Red Beryl," she confided. "I work for a jeweller in Hatton Garden and it turned up one day with a dealer. I had to have it when Eddie proposed to me – they are so rare and special, just like him." She simpered as she reached across the table to clasp Eddie's hand and I giggled as I caught Rosie's eye over the table.

"It was quite pricey so we had to settle for a house in Earlsfield, rather than Holland Park, but it was definitely worth it," she continued, oblivious to our reaction. Eddie grinned, nodded in agreement and bent his head to kiss her hand lovingly.

"Where do you live Evie?" she asked, not taking her eyes off him.

"Not far – just off the Munster Road. It's a lovely place but it's all falling apart." I sighed. "I feel like I'm spending all my time waiting for builders and plumbers to fix things, and writing endless cheques at the moment," I waffled on, unsure how to cope with the sudden attention.

"Oh poor you," she smirked, "that sort of thing is so dull. Particularly when you're single and have no one to share the hassle with. I know it's so much easier now I have Eddie and we sort all that stuff out together." More lovey-dovey gazing between them made me want to vomit.

Reality struck home. This was it, wasn't it? Life had become nothing but marriage, babies and mortgages. An endless cycle of tedious conversations. The smugness bothered me the most. I'd be quite happy to hear about their lives if I didn't feel they shoved their happiness down my throat at every opportunity.

Why do I feel second class because of my inability to hold down a boyfriend, let alone a job? Does it make me a lesser person? Because if it doesn't then I'd dearly like to know how to stop feeling like it does. It's as though I've somehow missed a boat I didn't even realise was leaving. Why had I been staring on from the sidelines rather than participating more in the game? Looking back, I ran through the boyfriends I'd had, or the guys I'd dated, and realised most of them were now happily married with a child, or one on the way, and I struggled to breathe as panic set in. Was this what I was going to have to face forever? A forced smile plastered on my face as I hung out with a stream of self-satisfied couples and feigned interest in their predictable lives? Something HAD to change in my life. I simply couldn't go on like this.

I couldn't go on like this physically, either. I excused myself and headed to the bathroom, trying to walk normally and not give away the discomfort I was in.

Perched on the side of the bath, I concentrated on taking deep breaths and trying simultaneously to ease my mind and the stomach pains. It was all just too much. Maybe yoga was my calling. In fact, maybe I could relaunch myself as a yoga teacher with a permanently Zen karma that would be the envy of everyone. My imagination drifted to images of my body, perfectly toned and lycra-clad, leading retreats on idyllic Mediterranean islands. Yep, THAT would be the life. A new Evie. Hot men would flock to my classes and I'd be whisked away on a constant stream of romantic dates. Sun, sea, wine and men. What more could anyone want?

I took my phone out of my pocket. Scrolling through emails from the local gym and penis enlargement companies, I spotted one from International House, the language school where I had been studying Spanish for the last few months.

Dear Miss Fuller,
Congratulations. We are delighted to inform you that you have been awarded second place in our recent online competition. Your prize is four weeks of full-time language lessons – in the language and school of your choice – at any of our ninety-six global locations.
Please get in touch at your earliest convenience to arrange

the details, and once again, many congratulations. The judges were most impressed with your entry.

Best wishes,

Helena Johannsen, Head of Marketing and External Affairs

Erm. What was going on? Had I really won a competition I had no recollection of having entered? Or was this simply an odd type of spam? Perhaps I was going to be lured to an obscure location and sold into the slave trade. Or kidnapped. Or even worse. My imagination started getting the better of me, but as abduction scenes from *Homeland* flooded through my mind, a niggling thought crept in. Maybe, just maybe, this was for real and it was the lifeline I had subconsciously been waiting for. I could move to the Middle East and learn Arabic, or continue studying Spanish in the depths of Bolivia, Argentina or even Cuba. I might fall in love with a hunky Italian teacher in Sicily and live happily ever after on a diet of olive oil, pizza and wine. Ha. That would show these boring people here in rainy London, trudging along their conventional life paths.

Yep, that's it. It's a sign. I'd never believed in destiny before, but this seemed like an excellent time to start. On the brink of thirty, I had no job or boyfriend to keep me in London, so why the hell not?

"So Evie, Charlie's just been telling me you're looking for a man. No luck on the old Tinder recently?" asked D, as I re-entered the kitchen. "Pass it over and I'll swipe some nice chaps for you, hey? Love a bit of window shopping for damsels in distress – great entertainment for us old married folk."

I bristled at the idea my love life was nothing more than a game for this pillock with sod-all sensitivity for singletons.

"D, be nice, and I doubt she needs your help. I'm sure she

has plenty of admirers," interjected George kindly, shooting me an apologetic smile.

I took a deep breath and replied, "Yes, thanks but no thanks D. Your help will not be necessary."

He looked peeved, "You're not doubting my taste in fellas are you? Come on, pass it over."

"No, of course not. I'm sure you have great taste," I lied. "But, the fact is I'm about to move to Spain." Gulp. Bombshell dropped. As the words tumbled out of my mouth I was as surprised as anybody.

"Spain? What the devil are you going to do there?" he said with a look of bewilderment. "What's wrong with us English blokes?"

"Yes, Spain," I repeated, with far more confidence than I felt. "And it may surprise you to hear I'm not going there on a husband hunting mission. I've just won some Spanish lessons and I'm going to do them in Madrid."

Immediately everyone dived in with unwanted questions, advice and commentary. My initial burst of confidence dissolved as I began to drown in their chatter.

"Where exactly are you going?" piped up Genevieve, stroking her belly fondly.

"What are you going to do there? You do realise they are in an even worse financial state than the UK – you're literally hopping from one recession to another. Bad move Evie, bad move." Charlie's words cut like a knife, yet hardened my resolve.

"He's probably right Evie, you've got a good job, so I'd stick with it if I was you. You'll never get a job over there, particularly when you don't speak the language."

"Don't be so negative guys, I think it's a fab idea. Good for you Evie, we'll be booking a visit as soon as you're settled!" said Rosie.

"Why Spain?" added Genevieve. "I can't bear the sleazy Spanish men and they'll be all over you with your blonde hair and white skin. Urgh. Makes me shudder."

"Ha, maybe that's what she wants!" piped up D.

"But why? What's wrong with Fulham?" asked Charlie, stricken at the idea of ever leaving SW6.

"Evie, what about your new job? Didn't you only start it a few months ago?"

I took yet another deep breath, "Well, I didn't exactly plan it, but, um, well, errrrrrrrr. I quit my job yesterday."

A blush crept up my cheeks and a wave of shame engulfed me. It all came back to that single moment of madness. If I hadn't quit I wouldn't be in this position, stubbornly defending a decision I'd rashly made two minutes ago in the loo.

"So," I continued, "it's not like I've got any reason to stay. I'm about to be thirty and I feel like I haven't really achieved much with my life. I need an adventure, so I'm going to Spain. I'm off to Spain..." I repeated, weakly.

I nervously looked up from the Divertimenti plate in front of me to a sea of stunned faces.

"Who knows," I mumbled, fiddling with my napkin, "maybe I'll become a professional flamenco dancer..." My weak laughter met with silence.

Desperate to divert attention from my whimsical decision and prevent more questions as to the yet-to-be-decided details, I turned to Antonia.

"You got married in Spain. Tell me all about it, wasn't it Granada?" She happily launched into a monologue.

"Seville. It was in Seville. My parents have a house outside the city surrounded by almond trees and it was just perfect..."

I tuned out as she continued her descriptions of a magical

sounding wedding and drifted off into my own little world. Spain. Sunshine, *cervezas* and *tapas* here I come.

Charlie leant across the table and said, bringing me back from my daydreams, "Evie, do you realise something like a third of young people in Spain are unemployed at the moment? What on earth will you do? Nobody is going to employ you."

"Well, I'll never know if I don't try I suppose," I replied, sheepishly, "and anyway, maybe I'll just do the lessons and then come home and find a new job at Christmas."

"Don't you think it would be better to ask your boss if you can get your job back? I'm sure he'd understand," chipped in Emilia.

"Don't be silly Emilia, she hated the place. It's good riddance. I admire you Evie," Rosie said warmly, "don't listen to them. I think you'll have an amazing time and I can't wait to visit.

"Who's ready for pudding?" she asked, collecting up the plates.

"But Rosie, seriously," Emilia continued, "you can't really believe it's a good idea."

I felt a lump in my throat, when all of a sudden a ball of pent-up frustration exploded.

I scraped my chair back and leapt up. "That's it. I've had it. I've HAD IT!" I shouted. "Do you guys have any idea how you make me feel with your self-satisfied chat and how much it hurts putting up with your pity over my spinster status? You should listen to your warblings on about weddings, children and mortgages – it doesn't make for the most exciting of conversations I can tell you. Why are you so negative about this? It's the only plan that's excited me for months. OK fine, I may have only concocted it half an hour ago, but I've had it with being treated like a silly child. I'VE

HAD IT AND I'M MOVING TO SPAIN!"

I smoothed my hands over my hips in an attempt to look calm, "George, thanks so much for supper, it was delish as always, and I'm sorry for leaving so early but I need to start making some plans for Spain."

A dramatic exit would have been the perfect end to this outburst, but all I managed was a frustrating shuffle and squeeze behind the chairs, followed by an agonising hunt for my handbag. After what felt like an hour I finally made it into the comforting blanket of silence outside and let out a deep sigh. Sod them all, I muttered as I stumbled down the street. ALL of them. The whole smugger-than-smug set. *Adiós* my so-called-amigos, Madrid here I come.

"Evie, Evie, wait up!" I turned to see Rosie racing towards me.

"I'm sorry they are such bores, some of George's friends are so unimaginative," she exclaimed, throwing her arms around me in a tight hug. "Just ignore them – you'll have the time of your life!"

2

I woke with a dry mouth and a heavy metal concert in full swing in my head, when all of a sudden I had a flashback to my mad announcement that I was on the brink of emigrating to Spain. As if. Pah. The very idea made me laugh, although laughing was a painful error with this stonking hangover. I'd always been a home bird. Despite years away at boarding school and university, there was nothing I loved more than curling up with Marmite the family terrier on the sofa in Mum's kitchen. I'd never done much travelling, and as much as I loved going on holiday I'd always loved returning home even more. I was terrified by the very idea of leaving my friends, family and cosy flat to head off to the unknown. The unknown where, despite more lessons than I would care to disclose, I could barely speak a word of the language. What's more, I hated to admit it, but I suppose Charlie was right. What would I do there? Last night's visions of an adventurous European crusade suddenly seemed totally ridiculous. In a deep state of denial and dying for someone to give me a hug and tell me exactly what I should be doing to get my life back on track, I crawled back under the duvet, shut my eyes and let sleep envelop me.

To give you a bit of background on my working life, I should start at the beginning with my first job post university. It was an art conservation charity that was wonderfully chaotic and shambolic yet somewhat miraculously managed to restore endless beautiful works of art around the world. Sadly, the crisis put a dampener on the fundraising and nearly all of us were made redundant. Cue a massive crisis of self-confidence and several years of temping and research jobs in art galleries, museums and the like. I'd always been envious of those with a clear vocational calling, as my many interests had made it hard for me to focus my attentions on a particular career path. I'd later fallen into a great in-house PR role at an international art gallery where I'd happily spent the last two years. An element of boredom had recently crept in, hence the disastrous decision to take the agency job which led me to this current state of crisis.

Back to the present. When I finally emerged from my duvet sanctuary, the following days passed in a blur. I alternated between moments of high-adrenaline panic, sending my CV out to anyone and everyone in London, and hours of peaceful tranquillity staring into the bottom of a coffee mug in a café dreaming of *tapas* and flamenco, while Ben Harper crooned away in the background. I was lost in one of these indulgent, hypnotic states when my phone quacked in my bag, the duck ring tone bringing a smile to my face.

I hesitated when I saw it was my mother, but, reluctantly acknowledging I couldn't let the number of missed calls from her reach triple figures, I apprehensively pressed *connect*. I was immediately deafened by a verbal typhoon of questions, delivered with an increasing sense of urgency, "Darling, what's all this I hear about you going to Spain? I just bumped into your charming friend George on High Street Ken, and he told me you're moving there? What on earth is this about? Why would you want to do that? You've just started a new job – I've been telling everyone how great the company is, and how are you ever going to find a husband over there. You simply must give up this Spanish nonsense."

Gulp. I could either break down and admit the truth, or I could pretend this was a wonderfully exciting adventure I'd been secretly planning for months. Being a wimp I chose the latter, of course.

I took a deep breath and broke into the motherly monologue, "Mum, I'm sorry I've been avoiding your calls recently but George is right. I've quit my job and I'm moving to Spain."

Attempting to remain calm, I continued, "I've been trying to pretend all's well at the agency but frankly every bone in my body hated the place. I didn't want to admit it, but it just wasn't for me and I left last week."

"But, what…um, huh." She was gulping like a goldfish.

"It's fine Mum, don't worry. I'm not going forever. I'm going to do some Spanish lessons for four weeks and then we'll see what happens."

"But…what, but…but," the gulping continued. "But you're not really the living abroad type are you darling? Won't you miss home?"

"I know I've never been the most brave or intrepid person, but it's time I manned up and tried to be a little more independent. And just think, you'll be able to come and visit and you've always wanted to see the Prado. So sorry – I have to run now, but don't worry – it's all for the best. Honestly. I'll call you later. Love you lots."

There was no way I could get out of going to Spain now – within minutes the entire population of the South of England would know my plans.

***

14

I was walking down Bond Street when a hand gripped my elbow, "Kiddo! I thought that was you. How are you?" John, my old boss from the gallery, was grinning at me from underneath an old-school trilby. "How's life with the dragon at the agency?" he asked as he fell into step alongside.

"Hmm. I'm not sure actually – I haven't seen her for a little while." I cleared my throat. "In fact, um, rather a lot has happened since we last spoke."

"Really? Pray tell. All good news I hope? Do you have time for a coffee?"

"I'd love to but I'm in a bit of a rush," I lied, unwilling to face more detailed questioning on my undetailed plans. "Um. I'm not too sure how to say this really, but in a nut-shell, I quit last week." The words came tumbling out of my mouth as fast as a wave of embarrassment swelled up inside me. I looked at the pavement and continued.

"I'd had it with Corinna. She was incredibly frustrating and I'm just not cut out to work in a PR agency."

His chin dropped and it was the first time I'd ever seen him lost for words.

I sheepishly continued, "You wouldn't believe some of the clients she had me working on. Mainly awful property developers but also a guy called Hubert Ponsonby – have you ever come across him?"

"Can't say I have. Great name though. What does he do?"

"Painting, sculpture, design, a bit of everything I suppose. He refers to himself as a modern day Leonardo da Vinci, although nobody else would use that term. I've never met anyone so arrogant and his stuff was horrible. He's particularly proud of his marble monstrosities, but he's currently trying to flog a phallic lump of perspex as a £30,000 loo roll holder."

John let out a warm guffaw. "I can see that's not really up your street. So, I suppose the big question is what next?"

I resisted the urge to beg him to take me back to the comfort of my old job. It still felt alien telling people my plans. But rather than show any sign of weakness I brazened through with a grin, "I'm moving to Madrid at the end of next week. I've always thought about living abroad at some point, and I suppose now is as good a time as any."

"Wow, it sounds wonderful. Think of all the tasty *tapas!* And I imagine you'll be dating a *torero* in no time. Your mother will love that – make sure you send me a photo as soon as you find him." Typical John, always focusing on food and romance.

"Ha, I will do."

"Do you know anybody over there?"

"Nope. I've never been there, but I'm going to book myself into a hostel until I find somewhere to live and I've been given some random introductions to follow up on, so I'm sure I'll be fine."

"You *must* get in touch with Ramón. Do you have his details?" John started to reach for his phone, but I hurriedly patted his arm, "Don't worry, I still have his email, so he's on my list to contact when I get out there." In truth Ramón was on my list. My C list. He was an Andalusian artist and old friend of John's who used to pop into the gallery when he stayed in town. To be perfectly honest I'd always found him alarmingly direct and more than a little odd, so I had planned to save his details for desperate moments of loneliness, rather than contacting him immediately upon arrival. John, however, with his terrible matchmaking tendencies, clearly had other ideas and less than ten minutes after bidding him farewell, I strode down the stairs at Green Park station reading an email he'd already written to Ramón, cc'ing me.

Dear Ramón,

I've just met with Evie who is moving to Madrid to improve her Spanish and she's asked me to spread the word so she might find some work, a flat and some friends. She doesn't speak the language and she understands this is probably one of the worst times to go with the hope of finding a job, but is going anyway. What an adventurer! Any doors you could open or connections you could make for her would be a great personal favour to me. She did an absolutely outstanding job here in the gallery for two and a half years and she'd greatly appreciate your help.

I trust you are well.

Kind regards, John

To give Ramón credit he kindly insisted on coming to pick me up from the airport so I forgave John his meddling, forwarded my flight details and turned my attention to organising a leaving party.

3

Wide-eyed and overwhelmed I headed for arrivals, struggling to control a heavy trolley with four independently minded wheels. Self-conscious in the face of crowds waiting for friends, family and lovers I kept my eyes on the ground and began to panic. What the hell was I doing here? I don't speak the language, I don't know anyone and I don't have any plan other than these ruddy Spanish lessons. Why was I even studying Spanish anyway? What was the point? I stopped in my tracks as I abruptly realised that I didn't have a clue. A disturbance to the left and I turned to see Ramón barrelling through the crowds. He breathlessly embraced me in a bear hug, comforting and awkward in equal measure, and whisked the trolley from my hands. A wave of heat engulfed us as we left the building and the sun's rays tickled my bare arms. No wonder the whole landscape had looked so dry and barren as we'd flown in. The complete absence of greenery induced a pang of longing for England. Terror and excitement jostled for control, but I pushed them to the side and focused on Ramón. He was more attractive than I remembered, but there was definitely something odd about him. Swarthy, with an impressively thick and luscious beard covering most of his face, he walked with a distinctive small man bounce. His bulging biceps were bursting from his immaculately ironed shirt and his dapper appearance worlds apart from the scruffy teenage Brit I'd been nervously jabbering away to on the plane.

We zoomed along the highways, swerving in and out of the traffic and it wasn't until we approached the jams in the city centre that I relaxed my grip on the seatbelt. Ramón huffed as we sped down one-way streets and did numerous three-point turns. Finally he dropped me near Puerta del Sol and roared away to a meeting, while I pottered the rest of the way on foot.

I lugged my oversized bags up a creaky flight of stairs when I finally located my hostel, sweating profusely in the heat, and fretting about trying to speak Spanish to the reception-ist. Another twenty minutes and I was back on the street, mission accomplished; my bags settled in the depressingly dungeon-like room, room key in my pocket and Spanish conversation *número uno* under my belt. Ok, well, conver-sation is a slight exaggeration, and Spanish is a bit of a lie, but I had at least greeted the receptionist with a hearty *hola* before my brain froze and I switched into English. Maybe first interaction with a Spaniard would be a more accurate description. Anyway, no need to be pernickety.

Looking like a muppet tourist stopping at every corner to study my huge laminated map, I set off on a wander back towards the Puerta del Sol. Sol has a little plaque on the ground outside the *ayuntamiento*, the marker from which all distances in Spain are measured – making it effectively the centre of the country and an appropriate place to start my Spanish adventures. From here I strolled up to Gran Vía, built about a hundred years ago as the major east–west artery of the city. Lined with shops and bars in grand Art Deco buildings, it reminded me of Broadway. The smell of the warm, humid air, the burning sun on my skin and the gentle purr and putter of the battalions of scooters; it all put a spring in my step. Breathing it in like a drug, I looped west towards Plaza de España before heading to Los Austrias – the oldest *barrio* in the city and home to the Plaza Mayor, where I settled at a table outside a café and ordered some *desayuno* after a slimy waiter informed me this means breakfast – who knew?! I couldn't stop smiling like a maniac. Was it possible to be drunk on happiness and freedom? I giggled at the builder shouting *hola guapa*, at the Spanish men sauntering past with their slightly-too-short trousers and shiny shoes and the unpredictability of the erratic traffic lights (where one direction changes colour thirty seconds earlier than the other, leaving people stranded in the middle of a rush of traffic). The details were endlessly intriguing, and a million miles away from the familiarity of Fulham. Could I really have been there only five hours ago?

"*Leche templado o caliente?*" asked the waiter as he brought my coffee and croissant. He waved a jug of milk towards the table as I blankly returned his stare.

"You want the milk hot, cold or not so hot?" he muttered wearily.

"Oh, hot please," I replied, wondering why anyone would want anything else. I sat back in my chair, cradled the cup and surveyed the scene. Against a backdrop of terracotta buildings, groups of tourists walked under the colonnades admiring the equestrian statue in the centre while Hello Kittys and a sparkly tasselled "goat" man conned tourists out of money. Watching endless lovey-dovey couples strolling around hand in hand I felt a sudden stab of loneliness, but refusing to let my glass-half-empty-self take over, I forced myself to focus on the positives, starting with the delectable almond croissant full of custardy cream on the table in front of me, and my first relaxing cup of *café con leche*. Better than a Pret breakfast at my desk any day, and half the price to boot. Not to mention the sun. Despite the sweltering heat it was impossible not to smile with this expansive aquamarine sky and bright sunshine. The EasyJet magazine had informed me there is a local expression, *de Madrid al cielo,* which implies only heaven is better than Madrid. Others say it's because Madrid has the best skies. Nothing stands between the city and the great wide expanse of beauty, giving a contagious feeling of boundless possibility and opportunity. Yep, today was going to be a good day. Pushing all negative thoughts to the back of my mind, I paid the bill and set off, feeling like Christopher Columbus on a mission to scour the city for hot men and adventure.

I sauntered towards the Palacio Real and Cathedral to tick off some of the must-see tourist sights, but the queues were long and the blistering sun not conducive to waiting, so I continued my meanderings, heading round the western edge of the city, soaking up the details of Spanish life and trying to make out snippets of conversation from passers-by. On the rare occasion I recognised a Spanish word I felt like jumping for joy. I rounded a corner and removed my shades in surprise – did my eyes deceive me or could I see an Egyptian temple?

Closer inspection confirmed it. There really was a bona fide Egyptian temple in the Spanish capital. The Egyptians had dismantled it stone for stone, packed it up, shipped it over and rebuilt it as a gift to the government, and now the hieroglyphs, pools of water and expansive views made it a top tourist spot. I felt inordinately proud of myself for having stumbled by chance across something interesting and rewarded myself with a large ice-cream as a teenager strummed a Bryan Adams track on his guitar.

After many more hours of exploring the sprawling city

my tummy was rumbling, my feet ached and I was as pink as a prawn, despite regular and liberal applications of sun cream. I staggered into a traditional-looking *taberna* near Sol and exhaled a sigh of contentment as a cool wall of air-conditioning washed over me. A rotund, moustached and smiley waiter beckoned me over to a seat and a barrel in the corner and handed me a menu. I glanced through the offerings, giggling at the dodgy English translations. Beautiful with peppers (*bonito con pimientos*), fried guts (*tripas*) and soap of the day (*sopa del día*) didn't really appeal. I waved to the kind waiter and let him recommend some dishes in his heavily-accented and incomprehensible English. Too weak to answer in my native tongue, let alone attempt any Spanish, I nodded feebly to everything he suggested and knocked back two glasses of water and a *vino tinto* (or red whine as the menu read). I ordered another *vino* and tucked into the simply delicious plates the instant he clattered them down in front of me. *Chorizo* in cider, *tortilla de patatas*, slithers of delectable *jamón ibérico* and *pimientos de padrón* were soon happily settled in my belly while Manuel Carrasco blared out his passionate love songs on the radio. Bliss.

***

What have I done? Why on earth am I here? After starting off so purposely this morning, I'm now back in my grim hostel room, lying in bed and listening to an argument pouring out of the windows across the courtyard. I had no idea what they were saying, but Spanish people sure do speak loudly and there was no way I was ever going to get to sleep. I studied the decidedly dirty dark green pebble-dashed walls and sighed. Am I bipolar? How could I have been ecstatic earlier and yet so miserable right now? To be brutally honest, I felt distinctly underwhelmed by Madrid. As much as I hated to admit it, a few uncomfortable truths had occurred to me during my explorations. It appeared I had been more than a little naïve with my idyllic visions of a picturesque old city with Moorish-influenced buildings, rambling flowers everywhere and a sense of history seeping up from every paving stone. More than a cursory flick through a guidebook would have taught me that in reality Madrid was a relatively modern city with none of the Andalusian-style beauty I had ignorantly been imagining dominant across the country. To my uneducated eye it seemed like any European capital and the whole city failed to make a lasting impact. What on earth had the architect of the Palacio de Cibeles been thinking when he designed the monstrosity? And as for the Cathedral and the Palacio Real, if they were girls, they wouldn't exactly be finalists in the Miss World beauty pageant. Even the Prado, a living textbook of all the paintings I had ever studied as an art student, had felt overwhelming and exhausting.

The second major disappointment had to be the men. Throughout the entire day I hadn't laid eyes on one single specimen who caught my attention. Not one. In the main they were one of two extremes – prissy, overly-groomed, generic Euro-types or seriously grungy and grubby hipsters – neither of which was entirely up my street. Finding a boyfriend ranked high on my to-do list, so this was a serious setback. But guttingly, the biggest let-down of all was undoubtedly my Spanish. For the last couple of weeks I'd been breezily telling everyone and anyone I would be absolutely fine on that front. I already had enough to get by *easily*, I assured them. But, no. Every time anyone spoke to me in Spanish I clammed up completely. Every word I knew deserted me and I was left dumbstruck and blushing like a beetroot, depressed and isolated by this inability to communicate.

So, the city, the men and the language were a disappointment. And on top of that my pasty white skin was not designed for these soaring temperatures. My thoughts drifted back to the dinner party a few weeks ago when I had made the impetuous decision to come. Maybe my friends had been right with their concern and I had been too stubborn to see it. I turned over for the hundredth time, sweaty, lonely and praying for sleep to come and for tomorrow to be a better day.

***

The voice in my head shouted at me as I lay in bed the next morning, exhausted after having managed only a few hours' sleep due to the noise and airlessness as much as the whirring worries of my mind. *"Time to get proactive. NO MORE TEARS ALLOWED. GET OUT OF BED."* I knew I'd feel better with some sun on my face. Out of the hostel I filled my lungs with fresh air and started walking. I put the map firmly in my pocket, determined not to look like a tourist, before instantly realising I had absolutely no clue where to go, despite all my extensive ramblings yesterday. A deep rumble echoed up from my stomach so breakfast was a priority. I headed east of the hostel this time and pottered around Huertas, smiling as my eyes constantly fell on small details. The wonky, smaller, square stones of the pavements, the high-pitched beep of the pedestrian crossings, the plant pots overflowing on tiny balconies surrounded by decorative iron railings. The old wooden shutters, mostly still closed at 10am. And the smell. In spite of my larger than average olfactory centre I couldn't pin it down. Maybe the particular scent didn't even matter, but it was different, warm and foreign and I loved it.

Huertas had been the literary neighbourhood back in the day, home to Cervantes, Lope de Vega and the like, and its charm evidently still drew in the arty types. Quirky cafés with mismatched vintage furniture and windows lined with homemade carrot cake populated the streets, indie music drifting through their doors. The tables were crammed full of people tapping away into their Macs, media glasses perched on the ends of their noses, and a cup of *café con leche* close at hand. In my semi-conscious state, incapable of deciding where to go, I gormlessly wandered along past the cafés, *cervecerías*, *alimentarios* and chino shops.

Through the crowds I spotted a dwarf walking towards me. "*Perdón, pero hablas español?*" he asked. I stopped in my tracks and greeted him with a blank stare. The truth was that I understood him, not that *do you speak Spanish?* is a difficult question, but I UNDERSTOOD! Understanding a Spaniard in an unrehearsed situation felt like a *major* break-through and I couldn't help but grin like a maniac. Unwilling to enter into a conversation, yet too weighed down by English politeness simply to stride on by, I remained glued to the spot.

"Or you speak English? Can I speak English with you?"

"Yes, I am English, but I am in a bit of a hurry I'm afraid – I'm late for work," I lied, looking down at my watch to emphasise my rush.

"Ok, I be quick. I only ask you one thing. You are a foreign woman. I mean you are beautiful foreign woman. Can I ask, do you think my body is good? I mean do I have good body? I don't mean attractive, I mean good." He paused.

"Umm. Well, what do you mean? Good in what sense?" His pervy stare unnerved me, but I was intrigued nonetheless.

He shifted his weight onto his other foot, shuffled his rucksack around and ogled up at me,

"I mean is it good for you or is I too short?"

"Umm." He literally came up to my waist. I looked at my watch again in bewilderment, patted his arm, and muttered, "It's, umm, it's great." Before he could answer I put my head down and walked swiftly down the *calle*.

I rounded the corner and found myself in Plaza Angel, right back where I started (turns out I'm not so hot at directions without a map). My hunger had reached dangerous levels so I decided to take a pew under some umbrellas in the centre of the square, right bang opposite my hostel.

I ordered a *café con leche* and croissant and pondered my next plan while looking through the list of introductions I had been given. Priority number one this morning was undoubtedly to organise some proper human interaction – too much time by myself yesterday had proved bad for my sanity. It's quite depressing really – if I can't cope with too much time in my own company, how on earth can I expect some guy to want to go out with me? Was this what people meant when they said you have to love yourself before anyone would love you? And if so how on earth do you go about doing that? Anyway, back to the Find a Friend Project – definitely not a good idea to continue down the lack-of-boyfriend train of thought too long. I scanned the list wondering who would be the most fun to hang out with? Alvaro, the older man who my friend Isabel put me in touch with? She hadn't seen him for ten years, but strongly believed he would turn out to be the love of my life. Or maybe Belinda who used to work with my old flatmate? But then again I should probably start with Spaniards if I'm ever going to practise the language. Then there is always Johanna, the eighty-year-old sister of my Belgian uncle, who has lived here for years and sounds wonderfully intriguing and eccentric. Despite these, and many other options I had been given, I remained in a state of gormless indecision and inactivity, sipping my *café con leche* with my eyes closed and my face turned towards the sun. I had definitely been a cat in a former life – this was heaven and I could have stayed there soaking up the rays all day long. As I finished my coffee a message beeped up on my phone: "*Hola* Evie – you must have arrived by now so *bienvenido* a Madrid ☺ How about some *cañas* and *tapas* tonight? Belinda xx." We must be telepathic! Minutes later we'd made plans for the evening. YAY! Friend number one in the bag.

Feeling productive and determined to keep up momentum I pootled off to the internet café and turned my focus to flat-hunting. The websites listed thousands of ads which I trawled through, pinging off a flurry of emails to any vaguely nice-looking ones, asking if I could come and have a look. Boom. This living abroad malarkey wasn't so hard after all – why doesn't everyone do it?

I looked at the map again and decided today was the day to explore the park. Everyone talked about the beautiful Retiro, so I hopped on the metro and set off to see for myself. It was only 10.30am but it was already fairly hot and the idea of snoozing under the shade of a tree was pretty appealing.

The park had originally been the private gardens of the Royal family and I wandered down the manicured paths, past row after row of immaculate flower beds. I stumbled across a shell house nestled in the shade of large trees and a crystal palace decorated with contemporary art, before buying a *bocadillo* and settling on the bank of the lake near two Spanish grannies idly waving intricately decorated lace and ivory fans. A group of little girls dressed in floral smocked frocks, little bows tied in their hair, white frilly

socks and patent, buckled shoes were giggling as an enter-
tainer blew bubbles. Tourists rowed around the lake in little
blue boats and their chatter carried over the water, mixing
with gentle flamenco guitar music playing nearby. I dozed
happily for quite a while, before sitting up and deciding it
was time to move. Getting to my feet I heard a man call
"*guapísima!*" to me from the other side of the hedge. It was
the third time I'd been called beautiful that morning and it
put a spring in my step.

Exhausted by the heat, I headed back to the hostel to
indulge in an afternoon siesta and then set off towards *barrio*
Salamanca for a bit of an explore en route to meeting Belinda.
Described in my guide book as the Mayfair-style area of the
city, it felt far more modern and organised than some other
parts. The streets were grid-like, wide and smart unlike the
rest of the *barrios*, the shops designer and the locals a different breed entirely. It was home to the Spanish Sloane aka the
pijo, and said *pijos* possessed a swish and a swagger like no
others. The average man strolling the streets here was decked
out in blue, slightly-too-short jeans, topped with a gleaming white shirt and a leather, silver-buckled belt tightened
around his waist. He sported a glistening bald patch atop his
head, surrounded by slicked back dark hair flecked with grey
strands, with slightly-too-long, loose curls nestling around
the nape of his neck – often looking suspiciously blow-dried.
Loose and jowly, but not saggy, facial features were the result
of years of Mediterranean sun and good living, accompanied
by lots of crinkly laughter lines around the eyes. His brogues
were highly polished and adorned with tassels, and not a
sock in sight. *Pijo*-ness personified.

As I continued my stroll, I noted how the women strived
for similar perfection, predominantly clad in patterned, slim-
fit trousers with loose flowing silk blouses, and bedecked in

golden jewellery. Their glossy chestnut manes, straightened to precision, swished in the breeze with not a single hair out of place. Finished off with perfectly manicured deep red nails, they could be straight out of a Zara advert, or *Thara* to use the Spanish pronunciation. The entire area exuded an impressive gloss and sheen.

As I rounded the corner onto the Calle Velázquez a hand gripped my wrist, startling me out of my thoughts on Spanish fashion.

"Evie, you must be Evie – you weren't lying when you said you'd be the most English-looking girl around! It's so good to meet you," the small, pretty girl in front of me babbled away, wrapping her arms around me in a huge hug. "Come with me, I'm dying for a drink." Linking her arm through mine she directed me across the road and I happily fell into step alongside her.

We settled on a table outside Lateral, perfectly positioned to soak up the early evening sun. Belinda could have passed as Spanish with her dark curls and a stylish orange dress showing off her deep tan.

"Right, first things first, let's get some drinks. Two *cañas*?" she asked with a grin.

"I have no idea what that is, but sounds great!"

"Ha, it's a beer, but in a small glass – much better than a huge pint, as you drink it before it has a chance to get warm."

"Sounds good."

Our drinks swiftly arrived and we began to chat away like old friends. Belinda had been working in Hollywood for an actors' agency but had been made redundant. She'd been reluctant to return to London and having always loved Spain she set her sights on Madrid. After starting with some English teaching she landed a job with a chaotic-sounding

Spanish film company. Through her work she had met her girlfriend Gabriella who starred in one of their films, and they had now been together for nearly six months. Midway through regaling me with tales of some of their prima donna Spanish actors, she leapt to her feet, waving at two glamorous *guapas* coming up the street towards us.

"Hey guys, how are you? Come, come, sit down and join us. This is my friend Evie. She's just arrived from England."

A kerfuffle of kisses and hellos and *holas* followed and Inés and Regina drew up chairs to join us.

"*Hola* Eebee, how are you enjoying Spain?" asked Regina, a sultry sex bomb straight out of a perfume advert, in perfect, clipped English.

I was learning quickly that Spaniards seriously struggled with the pronunciation of my name – v's were mangled into b's in their mouths, making me sound like an alien.

I supressed a giggle and replied, "I'm loving it so far."

"Oh I love your accent – you are so British. Is perfect! You must give me lessons – I want to speak English like you!" gushed Inés, warmly.

"That's so sweet, but I haven't taught much before."

"No, but you must," she pleaded. "I help you with your Spanish too."

"Oh yes, well that definitely needs a lot of help."

"So what are your plans while you are here?"

"Um, I don't have many to be honest. I've got some Spanish lessons lined up for the next few weeks and ideally I'd like to stay until Christmas, so I'll need to find some work."

"Teaching work is super easy to find and I can give you some contacts in agencies if you like," added Belinda.

"You must teach English. With your accent you'll be very popular. You find students without problem," Inés continued to gush.

"I did a TEFL course years ago but I never got around to using it. I'd seriously need to brush up on my grammar."

"The beauty of this place is the best paid work is business classes. You turn up at banks or insurance companies and give 1-2-1s to the senior executives. Most of them can't be bothered to get down to the nitty gritty of the grammar."

"And most people have a level of English very good so all they want is to practise conversation and be correct when make mistakes," added Inés.

"Do many companies do this?" I asked.

"*Siiiiiiii*," they chorused, and Inés continued earnestly, "it's so important for all the companies and employees to have good English in these days, with the crisis. It's essential for much business and all people think they will have better opportunities abroad so are really enthusiastic to learn."

"Interesting. Definitely something to think about."

"It is so lovely to meet you Eebee and you must promise me we be in contact for the English classes," said Inés solemnly, pressing her business card into my hands. "I give you my details. Please send me your number and we speak."

"Don't you think it better to find teacher with proper qualifications Inés?" asked Regina haughtily as she lazily exhaled a cloud of cigarette smoke and took another drag. "Eebee tell you she no have experience."

"Don't be rude Regina, I like Eebee and am positive she is good teacher."

"Well, if you're sure," I ventured, "I'll be in touch," I said meekly, slipping her card into my bag. "It's my thirtieth birthday coming up too. I have no idea what I'm going to do, but I'll try and organise something and I'd love you guys to come."

"OoOOoOHHhhh," they all cooed in unison, "definitely count us in. We never miss an excuse for a party!"

After quite a few more *cañas* accompanied by *croquetas*, *albondigas* and delicious roasted artichokes topped with *jamón*, Belinda suggested we hit the dancefloor.

"Come on guys," she pleaded, "I haven't been to the RRR for yonks. We need to introduce Evie to the delights of Madrid nightlife!"

"Uff," shuddered Regina. "I never go that sweat place. I go home."

With exaggerated sigh of resignation, Inés agreed to the plan and the three of us hopped in a taxi.

The Rock 'n' Roll Radio Club (RRR) throbbed and thrummed when we arrived, and within seconds a swarm of horny Spaniards surrounded us. The men were all a very particular type: wearing black t-shirts and jeans, with four days of stubble covering the lower part of their faces. And supremely confident, bordering on arrogant – well, no, in fact they generally crossed the line well into the land of arrogance. One of said men approached me, invading my personal space in a manner I was learning to be typically Spanish. His boozy breath clouded over my face, but warm bodies tightly surrounded me and it was impossible to back away. We had exchanged a couple of banal sentences in Spanish when he barked,

"Your Spanish is shit. My English is amazing," with a huge grin. I turned and tried to edge my way back through the throng to the bar, but he firmly grasped my arm and whispered,

"But why you go? No go, no go. I say you, you are so creepy. You are the more creepy girl here."

"Sorry, what?" I retorted, intrigued and irritated in equal measure.

"You are soooo creeeeepy," he shouted again over the music, beaming as he gazed into my eyes.

"Creeeeeeeeeeeeeepy," he repeated, his hand reaching out to stroke my hair and tuck it behind my ear. I shuddered, but it was impossible to take even one step away.

"Don't leave me creepy girl," he pleaded.

"Stop calling me creepy!" I shouted over the music. Rage had overtaken intrigue.

"Why you not like? Is good. You is creepy, like beautiful."

"What?"

"Creepy, *sabes, como bella, hermosa*, beautiful."

Ah HA. Realisation slowly dawned.

"Listen here *amigo*, the word is PRETTY, and there's a big difference between PRETTY and CREEPY. You're the one with crap language skills."

I shoved him away and ignoring his pleas jostled my way to safety. Once reunited with my *amigas* we decided this was an apt moment to head home to bed-fordshire.

"Thank you so much for tonight, it's been so great hanging out with you guys," I gushed to Belinda as we wobbled up Fuencarral. "I've been all over the shop wondering what I'm doing here, but you've really cheered me up." I gulped, suddenly feeling emotional. Or maybe that should read drunk.

"Ooh, I know the feeling. I felt miserable when I first arrived. It takes time to find your feet, but you've done such an amazing, incredible and brave thing by moving here. We're going to have lots of Spanish adventures together and I promise you won't regret your decision!

"You'll fall head over heels with this place, I promise," she continued earnestly, giving me a big hug and adding with a giggle, "You'll be happy as a partridge in no time!"

"What?!" I laughed.

"My favourite phrase – it's the Spanish equivalent of happy as Larry, but I'd far rather be a partridge than a random bloke called Larry any day!"

4

For the first time in my life I felt like the protagonist in the story that is my life, no longer a bystander drifting along without direction and lurching from one dull job to another. I'd felt boring and bored of being English in London – here I wore my nationality as a badge of honour. Britishness was so in vogue I felt like a celebrity and tongue-in-cheek was on the verge of offering autographs. Hell, their biggest department store is even called El Corte Ingles, meaning English style. They can't get enough of us.

The Spanish lessons gave me a great sense of purpose, but the big excitement was I had FINALLY found a flat and it was a mega relief to know I wouldn't wake up on my thirtieth birthday in the grotty hostel. After looking round so many horrible places I had begun to lose heart. From the serious bachelor pad overlooking Calle Pez in Malasaña with a mountain of condoms in the bathroom and a heavy stench of weed lingering over the whole place, to the damp, dungeon-like drug den off Calle Eloy Gonzalo, it transpired a lot of people out there were demanding a huge amount of dosh for a complete dive. I let out a sigh of relief when I finally stumbled across Calle Melendez Valdes in Argüelles. The primary attraction of the flat was the sitting room where light poured in from the large, rickety windows. The place was old and pretty shabby with a pervading musty smell, but the Andalusian tiles in the hallway and the bathroom, the creaky wooden floorboards and the original wonky door-frames appealed to my romantic side. Like so many of these places the interior walls were covered with a sort of rough harling, which didn't exactly scream cosy, but hey, I couldn't be too fussy and I'd learn to adapt to Spanish ways. My new flatmate, Carolina, a Spanish architect with a wonderful face split in two by a huge smile and a mad mop of curly dark hair framing her features, was by far the most normal of all those I'd met on my flat search, and luckily the contract was only until Christmas. I suspected I'd be ready to head home by then and begin the dreaded job hunting again…

***

After the crazy whirlwind of ups and downs and last-minute decisions of the last few months, everything settled into a more regular rhythm. I began getting to grips with the archaic appliances littering *piso* 2 *derecha*, 64 Calle Melendez Valdes – not least the ancient washing machine that gave regular electric shocks – becoming familiar with the neighbour-hood and feeling settled. Argüelles wasn't the most exciting of *barrios*, and utterly impossible for me to pronounce in a way that was understandable to any Spaniard, but authentic and untouristy it burst with old fashioned *tabernas*, cafés and bars full of old men putting the world to rights. It ran alongside a huge park, and the random Egyptian temple and funkier areas of Malasaña and Chueca were only a short stroll away. Best of all it felt like home already.

My morning routine involves struggling to wash my hair with a shower head – which, to digress, translates directly from the Spanish as *shower artichoke* – that had no holder on the wall. I attempt to hold the shampoo in one hand, the artichoke in the other or between my knees, and scrub shampoo into my hair, all at the same time. Particularly tricky considering I only function at half power before my daily injection of caffeine. Mission accomplished, I then bid farewell to Carolina and bound down the street towards Plaza Olavide where I order a *tostada con tomate* and *café con leche*, feeling chuffed when I deliver my well-rehearsed lines in the local lingo, and feeling native in my food choices. No croissants or English tea cross the lips of this newly converted *madrileña* – of course croissants aren't exactly English, but you know what I mean.

With hunger appeased I mosey on down Calle de Santa Engracia for class at 9.30, reminding myself daily not to daydream too much and stumble into one of the holes the trees on the pavement sit in – a health and safety hazard I learnt about the hard way. The mornings pass by in a blur of activities, games and grammar. Like the pieces of a puzzle falling into place, the learning process satisfies my desire for logic. On the other hand, every time one simple thing sinks in I become aware of how much more there is to learn. In these moments, or when other little incidents make me feel out of my depth, unable to communicate or lonely, I wonder what on earth I am doing in Spain. The intensity of all these feelings surprises me, as does the frequency with which I swing between them.

***

So the big three-zero finally arrived. *Feliz cumpleaños* to me. I snuggled under the duvet, keeping my eyes firmly closed in a vain attempt to evade impending old age. Maybe if I kept them shut I could stay twenty-nine forever. Something about thirty seemed too grown up and I couldn't bear to think about it when I felt so young at heart. Back in the day when I was an actual teenager, thirty-year-olds looked far too confident, accomplished and sorted. Their lives were perfect, or so they appeared to naïve little ol' me. Even though I now appreciated this wasn't an entirely accurate view of older age, it was hard to shake the idea I should have achieved more by this milestone birthday, how I should have felt different, been more sorted than astray in the world inhabited by grown-ups.

When I finally manned up, wriggled out of my cosy cocoon and embraced my fourth decade I realised I had a lot to be thankful for, starting with my flatmate Carolina. We headed out to Harina for a delicious birthday breakfast of pancakes, freshly squeezed orange and the obligatory *café con leche,* and I trundled off to class.

***

The lights on the cinema glittered at Callao as I waited by the metro for Belinda. As soon as the pocket rocket arrived she gave me a hug and we strode off north towards Malasaña.

"Just you wait Evie, I'm dying for a drink and this bar is like a temple devoted to the God of Gin. You're gonna love it! I've been wanting to go back for ages, so this is a perfect excuse. *Feliz cumple* by the way!"

We turned the corner onto Calle Pez and started to walk up the hill. The street was *fenomenal,* to use my new favourite Spanish word. In the early evening warmth people were already bursting out of the bars and an excited chatter hung in the air. My smile weakened as an old man crouched on the pavement reached out to me as we passed, woefully asking for *un ayudo.* I fumbled in my pocket for some loose change, ashamed not to have more to give. He continued limping down the street, his pleas falling uncomfortably on my ears as we turned into a bar.

Despite the odd name, Adam & Van Eekelen didn't disappoint. A small colonial drawing room, painted Georgian green, it centred round an old-fashioned carved wooden bar cluttered with cocktail-making paraphernalia. Various portraits lined the walls, showing bearded, patriarchal figures staring sternly and disapprovingly out at the drinkers, while faded red velvet cushions were littered on seats round mahogany tables. We sank down into some wonderfully bruised and battered Chesterfield chairs by the window and I marvelled at the shelves behind the bar where I counted twenty-seven different brands of gin. The menu also listed endless types of tonic and added extras, from thyme to cardamom pods and jasmine flowers to pineapple or peppercorns.

"This place is incredible!" I remarked, flicking through the menu. "Who knew you could be so creative with a plain old G&T."

"It's weird, isn't it? The Spaniards are totally obsessed with the stuff. They say it was *invented by the British, but perfected by the Spanish.* Ha," she laughed. "So, what do you like the look of?"

After much umm-ing and ahh-ing I ordered an elderflower and cucumber version, while Belinda opted for grapefruit and tarragon. The barman placed them on the table with a flourish and looked on proudly, like an artist watching the public admire his latest commission. They were quite simply works of art. And the best thing about them? They were the size of *bowls* with twice the amount of gin as a standard London G&T and only half the price to boot. Maybe turning thirty wasn't so bad after all.

We walked out to the street, passing the poor homeless

man again and were barely over the threshold of La Mucca when Ramón bounded over through the crowd and kissed me, leaving specks of slobber on both my cheeks. With his hair neatly combed to the side, a grey t-shirt clinging to his, admittedly impressive, muscles and a jumper loosely tied over his shoulders he scrubbed up well, although I got the impression he would probably be far more at home in his usual attire of a designer navy blazer with shiny gold buttons. Following in his wake were the immaculately dressed Inés and Regina, my new *compi* Carolina, her boyfriend Antonio and Chloe, an English friend of Belinda's.

We settled round a large table at the back and chat turned to my life in Madrid.

"So Evie, how go your plans?" asked Regina.

"I haven't got very far to be honest. I've become slightly averse to the idea of plans."

"I ask if you will stay many months. I no like to make friends with people here for short time only."

"Why?" I ventured timidly.

"Is waste of my time," she explained matter-of-factly.

"Oh, I see," I found myself agreeing, despite feeling a little peeved I might not be worth making an effort with. "Do you have many foreign friends in Madrid?"

"No, is hard. I find more in common with espanish people. English people is very different to us," she stated in a serious tone.

"And you Chloe, how long you here?" she asked. I slunk back in my chair as she leant across me.

"This is my second year now, but I think I'll be moving back to London soon. I work for a law firm and they are closing their Madrid office at some point over the next year," she said, taking a large swig of prosecco from her glass.

On hearing this Regina sauntered over to the door and lit

up a cigarette. I watched as the homeless man asked her for change and she swatted him away like a fly.

"Just ignore her, some Spaniards are so snooty, but they're not all that bad," said Chloe, patting my arm. "Belinda tells me you're looking for teaching jobs?"

"Yep, my Spanish course ends this week, so I sent my CV out to some agencies and academies this afternoon."

"Oh that's brilliant, I'm sure you'll find work no problem."

"I hope so. I'm racing through my savings quicker than I'd hoped and I desperately need to start earning some dosh."

"Yes, like I told you Eebee, is difficult time in Spain right now," interjected Ramón, gravely.

We left La Mucca around midnight and headed back to Calle Pez where we settled in Passenger. The bar resembled a dark brown panelled old-school train and with screens next to all the tables playing videos of "passing scenery" as if out of the window. We squeezed into a booth and ordered some pisco sours.

"Eebee, I give you present now," said Ramón, solemnly pushing a bag across the table, with a wrapped gift peeking out of the top.

"You're so sweet, you didn't need to get me a present," I giggled, embarrassed.

"Go, open it," he added, encouragingly. I squeezed the soft, flat package and pulled back the paper to reveal a lilac and black t-shirt covered in an abstract pattern of gold studs.

Chloe sniggered loudly, hurriedly burying her face in her drink.

"Um, thank you so much. It's, err…it's lovely," I stuttered, unconvincingly, as he watched my face expectantly.

"I thought the colour look good for you," he said eagerly, taking the top and holding it up to my face. "Yes, I right. It looks beautiful with you," he continued, his chest swelling with pride. The others stifled their laughter and focused intently on their drinks.

As he handed it back to me I noticed the label sticking out of the top with *large* written across it in navy lettering. Large? That was plain offensive to my size ten self – how could he think I was a large? Chloe caught my eye and dissolved into giggles once more.

"Very brave of you to buy clothes for a girl, Ramón," she commented when she'd regained her composure.

"Well, what can I say? People they always tell me I have good style," he replied. My straight face began to crumble as I thanked him profusely and he left, kissing me warmly and insisting we must meet again the following week.

Hours and several pisco sours later I looked at my watch and despite the blurred vision made out the time – 4.32am.

"Woahh," I exclaimed, "it's 4.30 guys, it's 4.30 in the morning!" I slurred, triumphantly. "I can't remember the last time I stayed up this late!"

"Ha, what you say? 4.30 is early by Spanish standards!" replied Carolina, horribly perky and wide-eyed.

"Early? You can't be serious. I'm so tired I'm struggling to stand up!"

"I think perhaps that's more because of the alcohol than the time," said Chloe, wisely, wobbling on her feet.

"Ok, looks like it's home time," she continued, beginning to round up the troops.

"Is always difficult for the *guiris* at first," Regina informed me, in a patronising manner. "You will learn our Spanish hours one day."

Urgh, yet another dig at the *guiris* – not only did they label us foreigners with this ugly word, but they revelled in poking fun at our national habits and shortcomings.

"Hemingway said *nobody goes to bed in Madrid until they*

have killed the night. This night is not dead yet, but we will make an exception as you are a newbie," said Chloe.

"Beware," interjected Belinda drunkenly, wagging her finger aggressively in my face. "We *madrileñas* won't be so generous next time!"

After saying our goodbyes Carolina and I dragged our tired feet over the cobbles. "I always get melancholy and pensive on my birthday," I muttered apologetically as we meandered homewards. "Do you?"

Without waiting for a response, I continued, "I mean, I can't believe I'm in my thirty-first year now – when you're young you think thirty is SO old. I imagined I'd feel different by now – confident, capable and married with at least one gurgling, giggly child on my hip..." My words trailed off as I realised how far from this vision my life actually was.

"Instead, I have welcomed in my fourth decade in a random restaurant in Madrid with a bunch of people I either met last week, or had never met, in a country where I don't speak the language, don't have a job and most definitely don't have a husband, let alone a chubby child." The words came spilling out. Damn alcohol.

Carolina stopped in her tracks, took my arm and peered sternly into my eyes. I gulped. "Listen, you must adopt change. It is a positive thing, and it makes you a better person. I think it's super beautiful you manage to organise a party with so many people, when you have only live here few weeks. You may not have a husband or child, but you have *mucho*. You are a person especial and you have so many opportunities in Spain. Be positive."

***

The next day I dragged myself out of bed mid-afternoon and pottered off to explore more of the Huertas area where an art and design festival was taking place. Hundreds of higgledy-piggledy stalls lined the streets with velvet armchairs, feathered lampshades, glossy ceramics and all sorts of vintage furniture spilling out onto the pavement. Like a bewildered child in Narnia I drifted under origami shapes strung between balconies and dangling over the cobbled streets, stared at oversized decorated egg "seats" dotted here and there, and marvelled at the abundance of bunting fluttering prettily against the electric blue sky. To use a cliché it was *achingly* hip. Just the kind of vibe *madrileños* get spot on. Designers sat on stools of rolled-up magazines bunched together and secured with a worn leather belt. A huge whale sculpted from crushed plastic bottles swayed in the breeze over a street dancing with visitors. Retro bicycles were propped up on corners and adorned with bunches of flowers, a pug dog in the basket, or looped and laced with antique jewellery. A smell of fresh coffee hung in the air and I stumbled across a string quartet playing a Bach number. A few blocks further on a dude in braces and a bowler hat belted out some Beatles. Pretty. Darn. Cool.

I rounded the corner onto Calle de León to be blinded by the sun glinting off a huge lizard created from hundreds of CDs strung together, so big it covered almost an entire building. Lost in thought gazing at this reflective reptile, I heard shrieking.

"Evie! Evie! Over here!"

Belinda signalled enthusiastically from outside La Pirola, just up the street. Could I love this city any more? There was nothing like bumping into friends to make you feel native rather than a tourist. The bunting fluttering and flickering above cast shadows over us as she introduced her friends.

"This is Molly," she said, gesturing at the girl behind her, "and that's Ethan," she added, pointing down the street to a guy staring up in marvel at a huge construction of coat hangers dangling off a building. "They're my friends from Vancouver – I think I told you about them? I meant to tell you about this festival too – it's cool, isn't it? I love all the creativity."

"Hey Evie, great to meet you. Sounds like you had a fun birthday last night," said Molly. Tall and striking with a huge bun of golden locks piled on top of her head and massive purple shades wrapped round her eyes, she exuded warmth and fun. As did Ethan, her equally tall and smiley husband, when he finally dragged himself away from the metal and wooden sculpture. I liked them immediately.

"So good to meet you too, and yep I had a great night, although I'm definitely suffering today," I admitted, letting out a slight groan.

"You know what? I'm dying for a coffee and I'm sure it would help your hangover. How about we head off to Carmencita?" asked Molly.

"Coffee sounds like a great plan," I replied.

"Carmencita is a super cute bar, well restaurant really, run by my friend Miriam. She has *the* best carrot cake. Her mum makes it every week and it's totally out of this world."

We fell into step and strolled off through Malasaña.

"So, how long have you guys been here?" I asked.

"We moved last November, so coming up for a year now. Ethan works for an internet company and they have their European headquarters here."

"Sounds cool. Are you going to stay for long?"

"No clue. It all depends on his job really. He loves it, but I'm keen to get home. My Spanish is brutal and I'm not cut out for this place. It's so dirty, the Spaniards are so freakin' rude and it's such a disorganised place. I miss Van."

"What's it like there?"

"You've never been? You must come visit one day – it's fabulous. Totally fabulous. I mean it's so healthy and green and clean. It always tops charts as the best place to live for quality of life. There's skiing super close too. I wanna be back there before next season."

"Oh," I muttered quietly.

We came to Carmencita on a side road off San Bernardo, and Molly elbowed me in the ribs and ushered me in. A small place, it was cosy and warm and we pulled stools up to the bar. Miriam, the owner, rushed around serving everyone, her long, dark hair swinging around her face as she animatedly chatted away. We started with coffee and carrot cake before moving on to *cañas* and then as dusk finally arrived, the obligatory gin and tonics. Hair of the dog and all that.

"Have you got a boyfriend Evie?" asked Molly.

"God, no. I'm useless with men. I haven't had a boyfriend for a while and I found the apps so useless I've given up. I'm hoping I'll have better luck with Spaniards."

"You can't be serious about wanting a Spanish boyfriend," she said, "they're such wet noodles. I could never date someone who still lived at home in his thirties. Period. Spanish men are spoilt and lazy."

"They're not all that bad are they? My life is so bleurgh and PG at the moment, I need some excitement."

"Well I've met plenty who conform to the stereotype I can tell you."

"To be honest, it's been so long since I had a boyfriend, I'd happily date anyone right now," I joked. "And as everyone keeps telling me, a Spanish boyfriend is the best way to improve my Spanish."

"That's true," Molly agreed. "Ok, well if you can put up

with them for the sake of your Spanish, good luck girl."

My romantic history didn't exactly read like a gripping bestseller. After a long-term relationship with a guy from uni which ended badly several years later, I'd been on an endless stream of dates and had flings, but hadn't managed to settle back into a relationship. At times I had relished this carefree independence, while at others I craved the comfort of a loving boyfriend, and I now found myself envying the close affection between Molly and Ethan.

"And how about you guys? How did you meet?" I asked, curious.

"I was snowboarding in Whistler with my sisters a few years back. It was a gorgeous day and out of nowhere this guy came bombing down the slope, totally out of control, and flew straight into me, breaking my leg in the process."

"No way!" I exclaimed.

"Yes way. The next day he came to the hospital with flowers, we started chatting and boom. We were married six months later and it'll be our third wedding anniversary in the fall."

"Amazing. Maybe I need to take up skiing!"

"You never know when it's going to happen Evie. You never know."

5

"Nicky is about to do a trial class and as my colleague called in sick today I'm afraid I need to observe it," Elizabeth whispered conspiratorially, as I introduced myself and took a pew at the back of the room. A nervous-looking girl shuffled papers by the whiteboard, and I shot her an encouraging smile as eight adults filtered in and took their seats.

"I thought it might be interesting for you to see?" she added. "And then we can grab a coffee and talk about the opportunities here." A friend of Belinda, Elizabeth ran a language academy and had offered to fill me in on the trials and tribulations of TEFL teaching in Madrid.

"Great," I replied, nodding. "It's been a while since I've even given a passing thought to English grammar, so this'll be very useful. Thank you."

As I sat there, attempting to blend into the garish patterned wallpaper, a divine-looking guy called Manu arrived for class, lugging a vast suitcase behind him.

"*Qué es eso*? Why you need bag so big?" asked David, the burly guy by the window.

"I go at the house of my parents this weekend. I go my *pueblo*."

"*Sí*, like always, like every weekend, but why you need bag sooooo big?"

"I think is his washing. I think his mother wash his clothes every weekend," said Cristina, flicking her long hair over her shoulder and leaning forward confrontationally.

"Ok everyone, good morning. My name is Nicky and today we're going to be looking at some prepositions," the poor girl by the board mumbled.

Manu ignored her and feverishly denied Cristina's claim: "I wash my clothes. I do it, not my mother," he asserted as he snatched the bag away from David's suspicious scrutiny.

"No, is your clothes. Come on. You say it," continued Cristina.

"Is not clothes," Manu protested, more anxious and agitated by the second.

"Come on guys, let's concentrate. We're going to start with the prepositions, but I thought first we could play a quick game to warm up." Nicky tried to interject when David's arm shot out and in one swift movement he dragged the bag towards him, simultaneously yanking on the zip. Out fell not only a bundle of dirty washing but also a heap of tupperware boxes. Silence hung in the air and poor Manu stared determinedly at the desk in front of him.

"Sorry, but your mother give to you food every weekend? *En serio? No puedo creerlo! Tu pobre madre!*" exclaimed Cristina.

"*Joder!* You are thirty-five years old. Your mother still cooks for you? I can't believe it. Is wrong. Is *totalmente* wrong," she continued, vehemently. "I hate these boys *mimados*, how do you say *mimados*? Spoilt, yes. I hate spoilt boys."

My heart bled for Manu as he stubbornly tried to defend himself, "but she like it. She insist in cooking for me. I try say no but always is the same she insist."

"Tsk, men. I no believe how bad you are. How did you survive when you lived in Boston? Did she send you bags of food over there?"

"No, I tell you again. I can cook, and I did cook in Boston. But here, my mother like to cook, and I like her to be happy. It make her happy. *Y hasta. Empezamos la clase ahora por favor.*"

Poor Nicky shook like a leaf and struggled to regain control for the rest of the lesson.

***

The suitcase incident lingered in my mind as I pottered off to have a late lunch with Belinda and Molly at Juicy Avenue near Alonso Martínez. We weren't exactly embracing Spanish culture by going to an American sandwich bar for lunch, but the smoked salmon bagel and salad made a welcome change from *tortilla* and *tapas*.

With my eyes closed and only half listening to Molly's holiday plans, I adopted my favourite cat-like pose, turned my face to the sun and almost purred with happiness.

An email from Ramón woke me from this heavenly state:

Hi Evie, These days are going so quickly! Hopefully and as discussed, will we have a day to meet up? Best, Ramón

This message summed him up completely. Friendly and formal in equal measure. I thought we had got through most possible conversation at my birthday the other night, but felt it would be rude not to meet up after all his kindness, so for lack of any other ideas I replied instantly.

Hola. I can't believe this week has gone so quickly either! I don't have any plans for tonight if you're free? Otherwise let me know when would be good for you, Evie

He responded immediately.

Evie, give me your number, I can't believe not to have your mobile number by now! Would be great to see you tonight. We can have a few wines and mushrooms in a place with lots of character I know, in the old part of Madrid, then we can go to a gin and tonic place I know, a few friends might join us later there?

"What's going on with all this messaging?! Are you talking to a guy?!" Belinda asked, grinning.

"Ha ha, Ramón has asked me for a drink tonight," I admitted.

"Ramón – the one who gave you the dodgy t-shirt?" she asked, sniggering.

"The one and only!"

"Do you like him?"

"Not in that way, no, but he's very kind to me and I have to admit I enjoy the attention."

"Well he definitely likes you – sounds like a date to me!" she joked, teasingly.

"It's not a date," I said emphatically. "And besides, it's a free meal and I can't turn my nose up at that when my bank account is in such dire straits.

"Anyway, I haven't told you my big news, have I?" I asked, keen to change the subject. "Belinda, your friend Elizabeth gave me some great advice this morning and I've decided to sign up for the Native English Teaching Assistant programme."

"What's that?"

"It's run by the government to get more native English speakers into local schools. They give you a great salary and all you have to do is help out in someone else's class for sixteen hours a week. After seeing Nicky's experience this morning, I definitely don't want to be responsible for a class on my own!"

"Sounds ideal," she agreed.

"I mean it may be a little dull, but it will be great to have some dosh coming in every month and a distraction from the slooooow progress of my Spanish."

"Brutal, my Spanish is totally brutal," sighed Molly. "It would be so much easier if everyone just spoke English."

"Is it primary or secondary?" asked Belinda.

"Either, but I'm opting for secondary – I've had enough of the little ones with all the sibsprings."

"What the hell is a sibspring?" asked Molly, incredulous.

I grinned. "I'm really proud of this. I talk about my nephews and nieces so much it frustrates me there is no collective noun for them, so I've decided to call them…sibsprings! Siblings' offspring, geddit?!"

They chuckled, "It sounds like some kind of monster."

"If you're desperate for money you should find some business classes too," added Belinda.

"That's the plan. And I'll meet lots of hot, eligible men doing business classes, right? A win-win situation!"

"Old, married men more like," Belinda laughed, "but I like your optimism."

"My luck with men has to change soon. Maybe one of my students will turn out to be the love of my life."

"Urgh," shuddered Molly, "I still can't think why you'd want to go near a sleazy Spanish man. A charming English guy would be far better in my book."

"I don't know about that. In my experience English men aren't all they're cracked up to be."

***

I skipped off to the Ministry of Education on Gran Vía and announced I had come to sign up for the Native English Teaching Assistant scheme.

Alba, the coordinator, rose from behind a mountain of papers and beckoned me over to her desk. She wore a pastel pink jacket over a silk blouse with a loose bow tied at the front that struggled to cover her large chest. She monotonously repeated information about the programme as if in a trance, having completely lost the ability to sound even remotely enthusiastic.

"You will be a cultural representative for your country and your language. It's very important to speak English at all times, not just in the classrooms, regardless of how good your Spanish may be."

"OK. My Spanish is terrible," I assured her, "so I can promise you that will be no problem at all." Ha. As if I could really speak anything else – this sounded like a great excuse to be lazy and stick to my native tongue.

In a voice perfect for train announcements she continued, "When you receive the address of your allocated school you may think it's too far for you to travel, but you must check online for travel options as the buses and trains in this city are very good and there may be fast alternatives.

"We will be in touch as soon as we have processed your application," she droned on. "Thank you for coming in today."

Before I reached the metro my phone beeped with a message, "Thank you Evie for your interest in our programme. We will send you your confirmation email with the address of your school and start date within the next twenty-four hours. Please contact the office if you don't hear from us and good luck with the placement."

Boom. Easiest interview ever and my first proper job in

Spain. I headed home on a high. I can't believe how much I'm enjoying being away from the confines of my London life. Everything is simpler here and I'm amazed how quickly I've adapted to somewhere new. It's proving easier to listen to my own intuition, make my own decisions on things like flats and jobs, and simply follow my own path away from the multitude of unsolicited advice, opinions and suggestions of friends and family, however well-meant they are. Life's sunnier, happier and more straightforward away from the rigidity and complexity of London and, without the distractions and obligations of normal everyday life, ex-pats are much freer to concentrate on themselves. It's ironic many people have recently told me how brave I was to come out to Spain when it feels like one of the easiest and best things I've ever done.

***

It was 9pm, the rain was pouring down and I had no idea where exactly in Plaza Mayor Ramón and I were going to meet. I buried my chin in the fur collar of my coat as I aimlessly wandered around under the colonnade, enjoying the dark and fresh smell of the rain. My tummy gurgled. It had been six hours since my last meal and I was really struggling to adapt to these Spanish hours. And what's more, I did not appreciate this weather. I'd been cruelly misled by the idea it was always sunny in Spain. The equestrian statue of King Felipe III in the middle of the plaza was vaguely illuminated by lanterns, their warm light reflected in the puddles and raindrops. It could have been a film set. I tried to imagine the music playing right now in a scene from the film of my life. Perhaps it would be Adele's *Set Fire to the Rain*, to suit the weather, or maybe a Mumford & Sons number. No, scrap that, some cheesy Spanish ballad would be much better.

Awaking from my daydream (well, evening-dream, to be specific) as to who would play me in this Hollywood blockbuster, I rounded a corner to see Ramón furiously tapping away into his phone. His hair was slicked across in a wide side parting with a liberal application of gel, not a single strand out of place. A crisp white shirt peeked out from beneath an expensive-looking black jacket with a large Nehru collar. I buried my chin into my scarf and strode over to kiss him hello.

"Eebee, how are you?" he asked, a huge grin spreading over his face. He appeared genuinely thrilled to see me as he held me at arm's length and gazed into my eyes.

"You look beautiful. Really beautiful," he added with intensity. I simpered like a puppy.

"I'm great thanks. I got a job today!"

"*Enhorabuena*! Is great news we must celebrate," he exclaimed. Linking his arm through mine, he pulled me close and we marched across the square sheltering under an umbrella. He expertly navigated the way down some labyrinthine streets, while my boots wrestled with the cobbled stones and my feet became steadily soggier from the puddles. We turned into a narrow doorway and down some wooden stairs to be greeted by a smart green-waistcoat-clad waiter who gave Ramón an enthusiastic hug with much backslapping. He was evidently a regular. The waiter whisked us past a metal counter overflowing with large platters of food to a table in the centre of a large cave-like room with rough stone walls. A jowly man, with an impressive chest rug poking out from the top of his black nylon shirt, was playing the Wet, Wet, Wet classic *Love is All Around* on a keyboard and I struggled to contain a snigger – Wet, Wet, Wet took me back to some seriously cringeworthy teenage discos.

"Are you OK Eebee? Is everything all right?" It appeared the snigger hadn't been confined to my mind and Ramón cocked his head to one side, looking concerned, as I attempted to fold my knees under a low table next to the piano man. Most definitely easier said than done when I was significantly taller than your average Spaniard.

"I'm fine, yes," I replied as I knocked over the menu and spilled pepper everywhere. My blush intensified and I looked down to avoid eye contact, running my hand through my hair to try and lessen the frizz brought on by the rain. A few wriggles later and I fitted myself onto the stool, tidied up the pepper and breathed a sigh of relief.

Ramón ordered a bottle of wine and we chatted away about my job as the pianist smoothly flitted on from *Candle in the Wind* to *Careless Whisper* and other such delights. The menu listed endless indecipherable options, so I happily left the ordering to him while I lapped up the stream of retro tunes, their English lyrics adding a surreal angle to the evening.

With a flourish Señor Waistcoat reappeared and clattered a humungous plate of mushrooms down in front of us.

"I am so hangry," exclaimed Ramón, loudly, rubbing his stomach.

"Why, what's wrong?" I asked.

"Nothing is wrong – I am ready for the mushrooms," he replied, perplexed.

"So why are you angry then?" I asked, equally puzzled.

"I'm not angry – I said hangry!" he clarified, gazing at me as though I was a retard.

"Ahhhh, HUNGRY! Sorry, sorry, I thought you said angry. If I can't understand English I don't know how I'm ever going to get on with Spanish!" I tittered.

He leant over and took my hand, "Don't worry Eebee, I will help you."

"But first you must try a mushroom. The mushrooms I tell you about. Here, take one," he said, pushing the plate in my direction.

The infamous mushrooms did indeed look delicious piled high and oozing with garlic and herby melted butter. Crammed on the side was a little pot of cocktail sticks. Having been genetically blessed with a small mouth and a generous dollop of clumsiness, this sort of eating had never been my forte, so I nervously picked a stick and stabbed it hard into the centre of a mushroom, lifting it to my mouth and hoping against hope I wouldn't spill butter everywhere. Or drop the damn thing. Ramón continued to clasp my other hand in his clammy paw, so I'd have no chance of catching it if it did fall. With impeccable timing he chose the moment I was struggling to keep my mouth closed and chew the, admittedly mouth-watering, mushroom, to pronounce sternly.

"So, I think we must speak in espanish now. You need to practise your espanish Eebee."

He studied my face attentively, waiting for a response as I munched and crunched self-consciously.

"*Sí, por supuesto!*" I eventually replied with fake enthusiasm, the wine beginning to take effect. He'd had the privilege of hearing me utter a few words in Spanish before, so how he thought a conversation was possible I had no idea. The wine must have been clouding his mind too. "*Pero es difícil – no puedo decir mucho!*"

"*No te preocupes, poco a poco*, you will get there. We must practise."

Here we go again – *poco a* flipping *poco*.

In the last few weeks I'd heard the expression a million times. Spaniards used it in relation to everything, but in particular to learning their language, and for some inexplicable reason I found it immensely irritating, not to mention patronising. "*Oh yes, you will learn espanish soon, poco a poco...*"

"Ok, so teach me something in Spanish. Otherwise I'll have to stick to my limited vocabulary and ask you where you live and how old you are!"

"OK. Repeat this after me, *tres tristes tigres comen triga en un trigal.*"

"What on earth are you on about?" I asked, baffled.

"Come on, repeat it – *tres tristes tigres comen triga en un trigal,*" he said, gravely.

I attempted to repeat the tongue twister, but failed miserably and dissolved into a fit of giggles, as the pianist moved on to a passionate rendition of *Eternal Flame*.

"What does that even mean?"

Leaning over the table and grasping my hand yet again, he whispered,

"It means three sad tigers eat wheat in a field of wheat."

Bewildered, I dissolved into yet more laughter and extracted myself from his firm grasp to reach for my wine glass.

"Not *exactly* the most useful phrase is it?" I joked.

He sighed.

"Ok, so we speak in English if you prefer Eebee. Tell me about your day, other than the new job. How have been your Spanish lessons?"

"*Muy bien gracias*, but to be honest they are totally exhausting and I don't really feel like I am improving much."

"If you no practise, you will not improve," he responded, sternly.

"I know, I know. But I like to talk and I find it so frustrating not knowing enough to have proper conversations."

"OK. Well, when you want we practise."

"Thank you," I mumbled, fiddling with a cocktail stick.

"And the people in the classes, they is nice? Do you make friends?"

"They were all very nice, but quite young. I'm pretty geriatric in comparison." I swigged another big gulp of wine. "But the weirdest thing has been hanging out with so many Americans – I hadn't realised quite how different they are. Their sense of humour, their language, everything feels alien to me."

"You don't like the Americans?" He pushed the mushrooms towards me. "Go on, have more."

Reluctantly I stabbed another one and whisked it into my mouth, dribbling butter down my chin and onto my top.

Trying to inconspicuously wipe it off with a napkin, I continued, "It's not that I don't like them, I'm just surprised by the differences in our cultures. It was quite funny in our break on Monday, I had a coffee with an English girl, Alison, and Justin, a lanky, preppy guy from California. She wanted to know if it was his first visit to Europe and he told her he'd only ever been to Amsterdam. She said what, to smoke weed and shag prostitutes? Hilarious, right?"

A stony silence greeted my giggles.

"Well I fell about laughing at this while he launched into a passionate monologue about how he would never, ever pay for sex, the very idea was abhorrent, marijuana should be legal for medicinal purposes and blah, blah, blah. I mean he took it SO seriously – he was properly offended and made the poor girl feel terrible…" I trailed off, realising Ramón was still looking solemn.

"You English love your sarcasm but I think there are many nationalities who don't find that funny," he responded with the expression of an angry headmaster.

"Seriously?" I asked, incredulous that my attempt to

lighten the mood had disappointed him even further.

"Yes," he replied.

Luckily the mushroom mountain was nearly demolished, so after subtly stuffing in the final few while he went to the loo, away from his watchful stare, I sat back and turned my attention to the pianist. The impressive one-man version of Magic FM crooned Lionel Richie's *Say You, Say Me*, and winked when he noticed me watching.

On Ramón's return, the swarthy man finished his song, scraped back his chair and loudly proclaimed.

"*La próxima canción es por la pareja enamorada aquí*," and waved in our direction with a flourish. The next song is for the couple in love? Oh god, this was mortifying.

Ramón and I studiously examined every crack and scratch on the table, as our fellow diners burst into applause.

*Ohhhhhhhh, my love, myyy darling…I've huuuungered for your touch…*I sank low into my chair as he passionately crooned and some of our neighbours raised their glasses in our direction. After two verses I couldn't bear it any longer.

"*Vamos*? Shall we head off to the bar you mentioned?"

"Yes, good plan," he gushed, eagerly jumping to his feet. "Is in the Salamanca area of Madrid and it is owned by my friend Federico. It is very nice."

We swiftly headed for the door, nodding and smiling as we squeezed through the tables.

Grateful to be in the darkness and away from the attention, I relaxed into the back seat of the taxi. The streets whizzed past as we rushed through the centre of the city and I smiled. I realised I was falling in love with the randomness and hilarity of this place as we screeched to a halt in front of La Paloma d'Oro, and Ramón took my hand and led me through a swanky entrance. The shimmering wall next to the stairs was covered in twinkly lights dangling from the ceiling while the whole place felt cleaner, glossier and a hell of a lot smarter than the Malasaña bars I'd been frequenting recently, and the clientele pretty different to boot. Lots of dyed blonde manes were tossed over shoulders, bowl-sized gin and tonics were aplenty (not a *caña* to be seen) and Enrique Iglesias' *Bailando* blared in place of an unknown indie band. The dancefloor writhed with wealthy Eurotrash dripping in bling jewels, sufficiently surreal to fit perfectly into the clichéd film this night had become.

"You like it here? Is nice, no?" he asked, pulling back my hair and whispering into my ear, "Federico, my friend, has many businesses. He has a gym too, very popular, and this is his third bar." His chest swelled with pride, clearly honoured to be friends with this Alan Sugar figure.

"Come, I present you to Federico and you meet my friends," he continued, propelling me towards the bar with his left hand firmly grasping my arm and his right lingering on my lower back.

"*Hombre!*" exclaimed a tall, attractive chap, "*cuanto tiempo! Cómo estás?*" He walked towards Ramón and embraced him in a huge hug, followed by two kisses and much back-slapping on both sides.

"*Tío!*" replied Ramón, "good to see you!" And turning to me he added, "This is Eebee. She is from England!" Federico winked at him and planted two warm kisses on my cheeks.

"Ramón, good work. She is *guapísima*," he said approvingly, his intense stare making me uncomfortable as he reached out to stroke my hair. "What handsome, golden hair."

He put his arm around my shoulders and led me away from Ramón to the bar.

"Eebee, it is pleasure to meet you. What can I get you to drink?" His American drawl oozed confidence, as much as his appearance screamed wealth.

I trembled as his breath brushed my cheek while a fleeting image of them selling me into the white slave trade flashed into my mind.

He leant in towards me, slipping his hand around my waist, and asked, "So Eebee, tell me about yourself. What brings you to Madrid?"

"Well, I won a competition of lessons…" I trailed off, feeling insecure and took a big gulp of the G&T that had appeared in front of me. Before I could continue, Ramón swooped to my side.

"Enough of you dominating her Federico, we dance." He grabbed my drink, placed it on the bar, and pulled me towards the dancefloor. We wriggled through a throng of people, my heart pounding.

He turned towards me and holding my hands started to gyrate to the music. His eyes bored down into mine and I found it hard not to cringe at his attempts to dance. A sweaty man in a tight t-shirt jostled into me and I stepped forward onto Ramón's foot.

"Oops, sorry," I giggled. The pair of us massively lacked rhythm, but nothing shook his stare as his hands moved lower and pulled my hips to his groin. Enough was enough and with a deep breath I wrenched myself out of his limpet-like grip, turned and headed towards the bathroom. I had barely made it halfway across the dancefloor when his hand grabbed my elbow and I turned.

"Eebee, what is wrong? Are you ok?" he asked, concerned.

"*Sí, sí,*" I reassured him, "I just need the bathroom, and then I think it's probably time to go home," I muttered, twisting out of his grip again.

"Before you go, I need to say, umm. I want to say you…I no know how to say…" His words drifted off as he restlessly shifted his weight from one foot to the other.

"Don't worry – I'll be back in two minutes," I trilled quickly, failing to escape his clutches. Glamorous folk swayed around the dancefloor to the Latin beats and a wave of drunken exhaustion suddenly overwhelmed me.

"Wait, Eebee, what I want to say is…" he took my head in his hands, lowered his face and clamped his soft, wet lips on mine. Surprised beyond measure I froze on the spot. Too tired to think, let alone protest, I stood motionless as his tongue explored my mouth and his hands groped my body.

"Ramón, I'm sorry, you're so kind," I said, placing my hands on his chest and pushing him away, "but I'm going to go home now."

"I no understand," he mumbled, crestfallen.

"*Sí*, yes, thank you for a lovely evening but I need to leave now!" I shouted over the music, fleeing the club. I gratefully gulped in the fresh air outside and flagged down a taxi, flopping into bed fifteen minutes later.

***

I turned over, groaning, and my eyes slowly focused on the clock. 12.00. Wow what a long sleep. Pulling myself out of bed I gingerly padded into the corridor to find a lycra-clad Carolina standing on one leg, holding her other foot out behind her.

"Oh god, you've been doing exercise again, haven't you?" I asked, wearily shaking my head. "How do you have the energy?"

"I need to keep training for the marathon so I have been running to Retiro," she replied.

"I wish I was sporty like you," I said enviously, as I slumped against the wall. "I don't have the discipline – as soon as I start running I end up walking."

"One day you come with me. I no let you walk," she replied, fiercely. "Anyway, is a super beautiful day, Evie. If you no have plans we go and have lunch in the sunshine?"

"Sounds good. Let me have a quick shower and I'll be ready." I stumbled to the bathroom, shouting back over my shoulder, "and I LOVE how you pronounce my name properly – have I told you that yet?!"

Half an hour later we pulled into the metro station at La Latina.

"This is the place where all the people in Madrid comes on Sunday," she told me, knowingly, as we barged through the throng, up the stairs and onto the heaving street. Crowds spread in every direction, laughing, chatting and strolling in the sunshine.

"Come," Carolina said, taking my arm and leading me down the street. "We go to El Rastro. Is biggest flea market in Europe and is here since hundreds of years." Rounding the corner, we found endless stalls stuffed to bursting with flamenco dancers and bullfighter magnets, ink sketches of *madrileño* tourist sights, brown pottery jugs and handmade jewellery. The shops on the narrow, cobbled side streets brimmed with curiosities, vintage clothes, black and white photographs, antique lamps, furniture and paintings and I was unconsciously swept along in the sea, tourists and Spaniards alike, lapping up the buzzing ambiance as wafts of *jamón*, *tortilla* and *cervezas* floated through the air.

We passed under a huge pair of inflatable legs topped with shiny red high heels hanging over the balcony and stumbled on to a group of performers acting out a scene from *Don Quixote*. Popping into a bar on a side street in an attempt to avoid the chaos, we were confronted by yet more madness. Men and women cheerfully shouted across the room to each other, over the heads of many more. *Cañas*, glasses of vermouth and *vino* flowed at an alarming rate while plates of food clattered down on the bar and an air of joviality hung in the air. We tucked into *sobresada* and olives while I relayed the events of the night before.

"I mean, it's not a big deal – just dinner and drinks with a guy, but my life here feels so entertaining and surreal. Every moment, even if it's awkward or downright weird like last night, adds a spring to my step and a smile to my face."

Several *copas* of vermouth had revived my spirits and I couldn't stop gushing about my new sense of adventure.

"I feel so positive and liberated. I know it's cheesy, but I feel AWAKE for the first time in years. Everything is so exciting here. I mean I bought some painkillers from the chemist yesterday, and I paced up and down outside for ten minutes beforehand, rehearsing my lines and psyching myself up to go in. The high when I came out with the pills was unreal – you would have thought I'd achieved world peace or something, but it left me in a good mood for hours."

"I think the Spanish people is positive and friendly so I am not surprised you are having fun," she commented as she ordered another round of vermouths.

"But tell me, back to Ramón. What do you think of him in truth?"

"He's been so kind to me but we really don't have much in common and he's so serious at times it makes me nervous."

"I don't think he is right for you, but it's all an experience."

"Exactly, and maybe once I start working next week life will begin to feel more normal and less like a comedy film.

"Enough about me though, how is everything going with your building project?" I asked. Carolina was in the midst of designing a wonderfully modern, light and white home in Chamberi for a demanding Spanish couple.

"Is ok," she sighed, "but the clients, they is too much

sometimes. As always the project is *retrasado,* is delayed and they no understand. It will hopefully finish soon and then I need holidays." She laughed, picked the olive out of her glass of vermouth and popped it into her mouth.

"Antonio and me, we want to go to Tuscany for to relax and enjoy Italian food."

"Ooh, how romantic," I exclaimed, "Tuscany is amazing."

A little while later the bars were deserted, the piles of scrunched-up, greasy napkins, cocktail sticks and stains covering the floor the only clues to the chaotic festivities that had taken place hours earlier.

We strolled back in the afternoon sunshine, through Malasaña towards Alonso Martínez.

"Oh Evie, we are near my favourite place. Have you been yet in the Museo Sorolla?"

"Not yet, no," I replied.

"*Perfecto!*" she exclaimed gleefully, "we go now."

We sauntered down the wide streets lined with trees casting long shadows on the tiny terracotta coloured tiles of the pavements.

"This is the area where there are many political offices and official buildings. Most of the embassies are in this neighbourhood," Carolina informed me as she directed me through an arch in the brick wall and we emerged into a magical garden. Trickling water provided background music, coloured tiles lined the path, the walls and fountains and a wave of fresh coolness and tranquillity enveloped us. Rambling vines covered the pergolas and sheltered marble sculptures which ushered us towards the museum entrance. The building burst at the seams with huge frames of sunny beach scenes and intimate family portraits and we spent a blissful few hours nattering away and enjoying their radiating warmth.

6

Sprinting from pillow to door in a matter of minutes, I cursed myself for having slept through my alarm, today of all days. After a mad dash to the metro, I found myself racing around a *glorieta* in Getafe, desperately searching for the B37 bus. I rubbed sleep from my eyes as I waved a crumpled pink post-it note with the bus stop details under the nose of a friendly-looking woman. With a disdainful glare and a torrent of barely distinguishable words, she directed me off down the street.

I sat myself down at the bus stop and shivered in the cold as I pulled up the fur collar of my coat and tuned into the rain falling from the roof of the shelter, drippety drop, droppety drip. After all my chat about the constant sunshine and bright light in Spain, this truly grey and miserable day was having a seriously dampening effect on my mood.

The bus duly arrived and on I hopped. Thawing under the heaters, I glanced around at the other passengers wondering whether any of them were going to the school too. No one returned my nervous smile, so I listened to Cat Stevens to calm the growing nerves. This is what my Spanish adventure is all about, I told myself, new challenges. No need to be nervous, and the best part was that if it proved horrendous I could always quit, run back to Duvet Kingdom and no one would be any the wiser. Maybe that was the reason everything was such a joy here, with no obligations, everything felt new and fun rather than a chore, and no one back home had any idea what I was up to.

Peeking at my map to check the directions I realised we were almost there. Out of the window my eyes fell on a series of vast, almost-windowless bunkers next to a busy roundabout and a second check of the map confirmed that was my school. My knees shook slightly as I stepped off the bus and noticed a large expanse of wasteland behind the buildings, surrounded by a high fence topped with barbed wire. This can't be right. This isn't the nice secondary school in a leafy suburb I'd been expecting – it didn't even remotely resemble a school, much less a place where I'd like to spend my days. The rain had stopped but heavy clouds ominously lingered above me and the building.

Rooted to the spot I continued to survey the scene. Between the bus stop and the entrance to the school stretched about 200 metres, yet in my path stood about thirty or so lads loitering by the gates smoking, chatting and passing around a football. Feeling like a twelve-year-old child as I approached the crowd, I kept my eyes firmly on the ground and tugged my green mini-skirt towards my knees. Silver hoops dangled from my ears, in contrast to the huge plastic rings punched through many of their earlobes. Their chattering turned to silence as I came near, the football stopped moving and they stared sullenly as if I was an alien. I quickened my pace and stumbled as I passed a guy with filthy dreadlocks dangling down to his waist, but failing to conceal the hairy butt cheeks poking out of his jeans. I glimpsed the words *never back down* tattooed on another's forearm but still I blindly plunged forward.

At the reception desk, sweating profusely, I whispered

in my best Spanish that I had come to meet the Director, Fernando.

What was this place, I wondered as I looked around the waiting room. The walls were clinically bare, the only colour in the room coming from a selection of motoring and aviation magazines scattered over the table. I rapidly typed the name of the school into Google on my phone, trying to establish what was going on and what had happened to my cosy secondary school. There must have been a mistake. The page was still loading when an earnest pint-sized man with thick dark curls and Harry Potter glasses on the end of his nose bustled into the room. He bounded over to greet me with two wet kisses, his navy overalls splattered with stains and stinking of oil.

"Welcome Eebee, welcome to our Instituto. I am Fernando. I is director, and we is *muy* happy to having English teacher here *por fin*. I am sorry I no have much time now, but the first class is waiting in classroom. You have one class only today. *Vale?* Is class of two hours. *Vale?*"

Without pausing for me to respond the words kept tumbling out of his mouth,

"Later today I send to you email with timetable of classes for all the weeks. *Vale?* You have fourteen hours with the boys and two hours to teaching English to teachers. *Vale?*"

At this point I had to interject, "But, I'm sorry, what is this place? It doesn't seem like a normal school?"

"No, no," he chortled, "we is not school. We is *instituto* for aero-mechanics and car mechanics. We are five hundred and thirty boys here – no girls. All boys!" he announced, proudly, leaving me lost for words.

"Is *muy importante* for the boys to have good English. *Inglés técnico*. Technical English. They need English for to understand manuals of planes and cars. We had English teacher last year, but she go to home and no return. She no like being only woman in the building and no want to continue. I hope you like boys? They have seventeen to forty years and are good boys really. You be estrict and all ok. Any problems you tell me. *Vale?*"

Gazing at the floor, I shifted my weight from one foot to another, totally at a loss as to what to say.

"Come, come, we is late," he said, glancing at his watch, "*Vamos.*"

He bustled out of the room and I floated down the corridor after him. Blind panic set in en route as my brain whizzed and whirred leaving me powerless to speak, let alone to think remotely clearly. What was going on? This couldn't be reality – I was totally unprepared and had absolutely no materials with me for a start.

Looking back over his shoulder as he waddled along he shouted, "So, you start with fifteen-minute writing test to learn level of boys, yes?"

"Great idea, yep, great idea," I nodding, incapable of any other response. Make that at least a half-hour writing test, I thought to myself. We made it to the classroom, he opened the door and steered me inside. My eyes widened and my heart stopped. Literally, stopped. In front of me sat thirty of the most menacing-looking guys I'd ever seen. Every single one of them wore a hostile expression that turned my knees to jelly. I wiped my clammy hands on my skirt, smiled nervously and desperately resisted the urge to bolt.

"Is Eebee. Your new teacher of English. She is of London," said Fernando, adding sternly, "and you must give respect for her. Or we have problems."

A series of grunts and surly stares was his only response.

My blushing face reached new extremes of rouge, not restricted to my cheeks. The stain had crept up behind my ears before swooping down to cover my neck and dipping lower onto my chest. In fact, if I took off all my clothes I strongly suspected my whole body would resemble a beet-root. The door closed as Fernando left the room, the noise levels rose and chaos brewed.

"Um, so, ok. Um, hello everyone," I stuttered, sheepishly, to absolutely no effect.

I cleared my throat and raising my voice a little, continued, "So, um, I need to find out what you already know in English. So can everyone write me a letter please telling me about your Christmas holidays, your family, your interests etc. Include as much information as you can – I want to see exactly what you have learnt already."

Uttering those few sentences felt like my second marathon of the day. My mouth felt as dry and furry as a blanket and my body was shaking so much my words slurred. Tears started welling – not little elegant drips, but mahoosive tears, determined to make a break for freedom and flow down my cheeks.

Clutching at the desk for support I sank into the comfort of the chair and concentrated all my efforts on calming the blind panic taking hold of my mind. My inner monologue sped into overdrive: *pull yourself together you moron! Don't be such a wimp!* it shouted, while a gentle voice in my head simultaneously urged, *run, run for your life! Get out of this hellhole while you still can!* While this inner argument continued at full throttle I realised that the boys had miraculously started to write.

Wiping a bead of sweat from my scarlet face, I noticed a terrible smell of BO, followed by the more terrible real-isation it must be me. I was sweating like a pig. I pulled one sleeve out of my jumper and then paused. Oh shit, was that my pyjama top? Damn it – I'd been in such a rush getting dressed I was still wearing the Magic Roundabout t-shirt I slept in and even worse I had forgotten to put on a bra. There was no way I could take my jumper off now, so pushing thoughts of sweat away I wondered what on earth I could do when they finished their letters? My brain flitted from one useless idea to the next as the minutes continued to tick by. Suddenly, an idea popped into my head – a classic TEFL exercise I heard about years ago. I had no idea if it was remotely appropriate for these guys, but it would just have to do. The students were put into groups and told their country has discovered a new island of which they have been put in charge. They needed to choose a name, a currency, design a flag, select ten celebrities to take with them, and answer multiple other questions like whether or not it will have a prison or the internet etc. At the end of the lessons they all do a mini presentation, take questions from the class and we vote as to which island we would choose to live on.

My hands shook as I scribbled a list of barely legible topics and questions for them to cover on the board, grateful for the opportunity to turn my back on their unsettling gazes. Then I nervously collected their papers and set them off on this task.

As I returned to my desk my phone beeped. A quick glance at the screen revealed a text from Ramón. *"Estoy cansado hoy y necesito un poco de energía. Me das un beso? No hemos hablado desde la noche en el bar – nos vemos esta semana? Besitos."* *

He wants a bloody kiss? Weirdo. He'll be lucky to see me again as the odds didn't look good that I'd survive this afternoon. I pushed him to the back of my thoughts and focused on the boys.

---

*I'm tired today and I need a little energy. Will you give me a kiss? We haven't seen each other since the night at the bar – shall we meet up this week? Kisses.

The group at the front had begun to act a little suspiciously, jostling each other and whispering.

"Ask titcher, go on, ask titcher," mumbled Juan, scratching his balls.

"No. You," replied Paolo.

"No, you ask titcher, *coño!*" Juan petulantly spat back.

"Ok, enough. What do you want?" I interrupted, determined to try and assert at least an ounce of authority.

Mohawked Rafa, with his glinting diamante earrings, cockily interrupted the sniggers.

"Ok, ok, I ask. So you know when people are fucking at same time and you doing lots of people together at same time. What is called?"

"Hmm, what?" was all I could manage to say.

"You know, when you make sex with lots of girls, beautiful girls all together. Party, sex, girls. Is good times, good sex," replied Juan salaciously, looking up at me expectantly.

"Ok, ok, I get the picture," I mumbled. A long silence passed and I was aware for the first time since I'd arrived they were totally quiet and all sixty or so eyes were trained on my burning face.

Perplexed and terrified in equal measure I took a deep breath and whispered, "Umm, I think you're talking about an orgy, but why?"

"Orgy going to be national sport on island," Rafa stated, gleefully. He leant back in his chair and his shirt fell open, revealing a t-shirt reading *your hole is my goal.*

"All the Sundays is orgy day," added Luis.

The menacing clouds outside loomed closer as I walked, trance-like, back to my desk, resisting the urge to burst into tears and dash out of the building without looking back.

A timid knock on the door interrupted my thoughts and a man with luscious brown hair and a tanned, puffy face etched with deep furrows, entered the room and shuffled towards me.

"Um, hello titcher. My name is Winston. I wait in wrong room for hour, but now I know my mistake and I find class. Is ok?"

"Of course Winston, take a seat," I replied, returning his smile and waving at a free desk towards the back of the room.

"Thank you. Sorry I is late."

"No problem – I like the name Winston. It is very English."

"Yes, my parents they like England very much so give me name English."

He was so sweet and polite I could have hugged the gentle giant, yet I managed to restrain myself and gave him instructions for writing a letter, before announcing it was time for the presentations to begin.

Ander took the board marker from my desk and started to draw a very detailed picture on the board. "Is our flag," he told me earnestly.

"Err, what is that?" I asked when he finally finished, craning my neck to see better.

"Duh," he replied rudely, "it's an elephant and a lighter, *obvio*."

I swallowed nervously.

"So why have you chosen them for your flag?"

"Because burning elephants is our national sport. We do it every day," and the whole class erupted into hearty laughter.

"Ok, whatever," I said, letting out an exasperated sigh. "So what is your island called?"

"Is Eebee's Crazy Island. All the people who live there are crazy. Is a home for crazy people. You are president if you like." He smiled as he said this, leaving me unsure as to whether it was a joke or pure insolence.

After more mindless witter their presentation came to an end, and we moved on to Rafa's group.

I resorted to flicking through my phone while they drew their flag on the board, and saw I had several more messages from Ramón – "Evie, I see you read my message. You ok? Why you no reply? I call you too and you no pick up? We ok? We talk later?" Gimme a break. I shoved the phone back in my bag as Rafa announced.

"We is finished titcher."

My eyes widened when I looked up to the whiteboard.

"Um," I stuttered, hesitantly. "Is that what I think it is?"

"Tits and napples," replied Rafa, grinning defiantly. "Is tits and napples." And it sure was. Their flag took up almost the entire board and consisted of two massive boobs with lengthy nipples, enclosed within an anarchy symbol.

"Why?" I whispered, my hands starting to shake again.

"Is easy. We love tits and napples. Is called Freedom Island and have girls with tits and napples everywhere. No clothes are *permitido*."

"Yes, tits and napples is my religion. Is religion on my island," piped up Angel.

While guffaws raged around the room I tried to regain control.

"If it is your religion then you at least need to say it properly. It's NIPPLES, not napples."

"No, they is napples teacher, they is napples," corrected Angel, smugly, as his index fingers lazily circled his nipples.

"What's your name again? Angel? Listen. English is my language and these," I responded firmly, pointing to my own, "are nipples." Yeah, I thought nervously, I'll show you who's boss.

They chortled away, when over the noise Daniel shouted.

"Titcher, show us yours!"

Daniel was one of the more terrifying guys. One of the ones I would quite frankly not want to be left alone with. Slumped morosely at a desk to the back of the room, everything about him screamed seedy, from the long, greasy hair plastered around his spotty face to the deadened eyes gazing directly at my chest.

"Yes," they chorused aggressively, "Show us your napples."

"Nap-ples! Nap-ples! Nap-ples!" they began to shout, slamming their hands on the desks in time with the chant.

Gulp. Help! Call the fire engine to calm the fire on my face! I turned to face the blackboard, unsure as to whether to cry, laugh, scream or flee or all of the above. For a fleeting instant the idea of pulling up my sweater and flashing my boobs at them seemed like a plan. What did I have to lose?

My hands lingered on the bottom of my sweater when the bell rang and common sense got the better of me. The boys began to bound out of the classroom, still chortling to the max but my knees felt too weak and wobbly to hold my weight as I quietly sank into my chair. As I despondently tried to summon up the strength to move and pack up my stuff I noticed Winston approaching my desk.

"Titcher, sorry they is rude," he said gently, his kindness bringing me close to tears, *again*.

"Thank you, Winston, but don't worry. It's not your fault."

With a deeply furrowed brow he continued earnestly, "If you have time, you can read my letter now? Is important for me improve my English and I would like to knowing my mistakes."

"Of course, no problem," I replied, taking his paper and starting to read.

"...My name is Winston. I have thirty years old and I am from Uruguay. My family live in village near of Montevideo and I have two sisters and two brother. I went to school in

Montevideo and I make job as mechanic. But life is difficult there and I move to Spain for more *oportunidades*. Here I want to study and obtain good job in mechanic studio and better life quality. I like to reading and walking in the park and I use weekends and holidays to walk and see my friends. I work much and study much because I need good notes in my exams, so I don't make parties."

"It's good Winston, well done," I said, marking the corrections as I read.

I turned the page and continued to scan his scrawl.

"And have I yet found the one? No, I have not. But you is nice person teacher and I think you are very pritty. Maybe we can start a relation by writing to us both and then later go to cinema or restaurant? I look for a nice girl like you. I no have body of Brad Pitt but I is good boyfriend and care for you…"

His eyes were burning holes in the top of my head as I read this, while I focused firmly on the paper, speechless. A sideways glance to the door revealed all the others had left the room. Eek. Pretending to labour over correcting his minor mistakes I racked my brains for inspiration. Failing miserably, I replaced the pen lid and pushed the paper towards him, saying hurriedly, in a single unintelligible string, "Very-good. You-have-a-good-level-of-English-Winston. I'm-afraid-I-have-to-rush-now-or-I-will-miss-the-bus-see-you-next-week."

I literally fled the classroom, ignoring him as he shouted, "What you think of my idea?" and sprinted down the thankfully deserted corridor, flinging open the door, gulping in the fresh air and running for the bus as if my life depended on it.

***

"I don't understand it. I just don't understand at all. How the hell did I end up there without realising it wasn't a normal school? Why didn't anyone tell me? I've never felt so unprepared and stupid and out of place in my whole life," I rambled on incoherently while the others stared on open-mouthed.

"I think I'm in a state of shock."

"Give the girl more wine, come on Ethan, more wine. Stop hogging the bottle and pass it here." Belinda took charge, refilled my glass and I knocked it back in one fell swoop before she instantly topped it up again.

Ethan, Chloe, Belinda and I were huddled around a wobbly wooden table in La Musa. I'd called them on the bus back to Argüelles, desperate for some friendly company and relative normality. I don't think I'd ever craved a simple hug so badly.

"But surely they told you you'd been allocated a CIFP rather than a *colegio?*" asked Chloe, the English lawyer who was immensely practical in all things and whose presence was deeply comforting.

"Nope. Nothing. She just sent me the address."

I wilted further in my chair, despondently, "I suppose it's my own fault for not doing an ounce of research into the place."

Belinda leant over the table, "I met an American girl who does the same programme but she plays with cute children at a primary school. It's totally bizarre how you've been placed at the mercy of these sex-pests instead."

"What do I do now?" I pleaded, "I can't tell you how creepy some of them are. I really don't think I can go back there."

"Hey, I think you're looking at this all wrong. Look on the bright side – five hundred and thirty men for you to potentially date. It can't be that bad can it? I bet one of them will ignite your spark plugs, or no hang on, they'll be putting a spanner in your works in no time!" I loved Ethan's attempt to perk me up, but I retched at the very idea. Physically retched and wailed in protest.

"But you don't get it, they are terrifying. I know I'm prone to exaggeration but they really are something else. I don't know how I could get up in front of them again. The way some of them looked at me was so gross…" I trailed off as the tears burst through their barrier once more.

My friends swarmed around like buzzing bees, alternatively attempting to comfort and distract me, and I felt overwhelmed with gratitude for their kindness. I let their positive words wash over me as my shoulders drooped lower and lower.

"Remember – you don't *have* to go back. It's not as if you have a contract or anything and from the sounds of it I don't think anyone would blame you for quitting. You did brilliantly to simply survive today!"

Belinda was right, but the idea of giving up on another job seemed even more abhorrent than the idea of actually getting on a bus back there.

"Every bone in my body wants to quit, but I can't quit again after walking out of my job so recently. I hate the idea of quitting every time I feel uncomfortable." I paused, noisily blowing my nose. "Yet I genuinely worry I won't survive in there."

"Do you have class tomorrow?"

"Yep, one in the afternoon. But as soon as I start thinking about what to do with them I get into a panic and I can't even begin to think clearly. I think I'm going a bit psychotic…" I whispered, my insides churning as waves of terror ebbed and flowed. I pushed away my *bomba,* the scrumptious deep-fried meat and potato *tapa* that was one of my favourite discoveries in Madrid, untouched, and gazed blankly at the multi-coloured light bulbs hanging from the ceiling.

"It's funny, when you describe it, it sounds like a film. All you need to do is end up having a passionate affair with one of them, falling in love and living happily ever after here in Spain. Then when someone makes the film we will all be paid a fortune to act in it. Boom. Success for everyone!" Belinda's perky attitude usually cheered me up no end, but after the best part of a bottle of wine I think there was little chance of my seeing the silver lining tonight.

"Talking about lurve," giggled Chloe, "how's my friend Ramón?!"

"Oh god, he's been messaging me endlessly today but I never replied."

I peered down at my phone on the table.

"On the one hand he's super charming and I can't deny I like the attention. I don't know a million people here so of course I'm going to say yes when he invites me to things. But," I hesitated, "on the other hand I feel I'm some sort of project for him and I'm a constant disappointment coming out with silly comments and not speaking fluent Spanish."

I sighed, "I mean, you've met him. He's a little weird, right? And he's acting pretty desperate right now."

She laughed, "He's definitely a nutter, but a sweet nutter to be fair. What have you got to lose?

"It gives you funny stories to relate to us, if nothing else and it's always good to have a distraction," she added, chuckling as she took another sip of her *vino*.

"True, but anyway, he's the least of my worries for now," I said as I put my phone away again, "I'll reply to his messages another time."

Breaking from deep thought, Ethan chortled, "Believe me Eebee, one of them will flood your motor within a week!"

"Come on Ethan, you can do better than that!" Molly admonished, punching him playfully on the shoulder.

"Make her engine purr?! Blow her fuse?! Rev her up?!"

We collapsed into giggles and by the end of the evening the panic had subsided slightly and we had come up with a plan of action. I would finish the week before I made any decisions. Belinda was going to send me some of her old lesson plans to use for the next few days, taking off the pressure of preparation and giving me some leeway to get my head around the whole extraordinary situation.

7

I dragged my weary body into the kitchen to make some coffee, to find Carolina sitting at the table, her mad, dark curls a manic mess atop her head, *El Mundo* spread out and a large cafetière already prepared.

"Morning Evie, I have not seen you for days. How is the *instituto?*" she asked, as I slumped into a chair and helped myself to her coffee.

"I'm surviving, just," I replied, putting my head in my hands and gazing into the steaming mug of molten adrenaline. "I can't believe I've made it through two whole weeks. It's so exhausting every bone in my body is dying to quit."

"You mean teaching?"

"Yes, I really don't think I'm cut out to be a teacher. I'm in a constant state of panic," I replied as the floodgates opened. "I feel stressed about running out of materials, but then I rush through everything I've prepared way too quickly."

"No, no. I'm sure you are a great teacher," she assured me with a smile. "You always explain things good to me."

Her kind words did little to improve my worries and after topping up my coffee cup I continued. "At the beginning of every class I feel like a child at the top of a ski slope with no idea how to get down. It feels like the time goes SO slowly and then it's such a relief every time class finishes and

I realise I've survived."

"*Poco a poco*, you will learn how to control them."

Staring at the blue, yellow and white tiles on the walls I continued glumly, "I'm just throwing out every game I can think of to fill the two hours. I get so flustered and they just sit scratching their balls and petulantly chewing gum, creeping me out with their seedy stares."

"And how are the other teachers?" she asked.

"They are the only redeeming feature of the place to be honest. Some of them are really priceless caricatures. It's only a handful – most are greasy mechanics who look at me like I'm a complete retard and talk about cars so there's absolutely no way I can understand them. I feel like such a muppet in the *cafetería* at break time. My face hurts from smiling as I pretend I know what they're on about. On the odd occasion when they address me directly I freeze and they all go silent and stare. Why am I such a bloody WIMP? But on the bright side I suppose it gives me added motivation to learn Spanish. Particularly when I know they are talking about me."

"Well," she laughed, "is good if it inspires you to learn!"

"I know, but then there is one teacher who speaks English relatively well. He's called Manuel, a gentle soul who teaches bodywork. I clung to him last week, but he's now beginning to annoy me. His favourite line is 'My English is not good. I am forty-three years old. Can you believe it? Forty-three years old. You have only been learning English for thirty years but you speak it fluently. *Es injusto!* I want my English to be better. I want my English to be like you English. You speak so well English. Can you believe it? I cannot believe it. How do you say *injusto?* Yes, is unfair.' It's so irritating. David, the small, energetic Erasmus coordinator keeps implying Manuel needs a girlfriend and I would be perfect, but there are only so many times I can grin and pretend I find this funny. Maybe I should save myself a whole lot of hassle and quit."

"No, remember we made a deal. You must do one month before you can quit. And I am sure things improve anyways. *Seguro*."

I nodded, glumly. We'd made a pact to extend my week to a month when I'd got home on day one and she'd caught me off guard.

"Ok, yes, I remember the deal. But a month feels like a very long time."

"You will be fine, and anyway, more importantly, Alba tell me you are to go on date with her grandson?" she grinned. Alba was a lovely old lady who lived in the flat above us. Small, rotund and smiley, she wore floral dresses and large open-toed sandals and spent all her time lingering at the entrance to the building, ambushing anyone who passed and diverting them with long-winded gossip. Getting up to our flat without having a conversation of at least ten minutes was a rare achievement. She was totally unfazed at the realisation I only understood about 20 percent of her enthusiastic warblings and gestures, but despite their one-sidedness, I enjoyed our meetings.

"She's hilarious. She cornered me on the stairs the other day and told me I had to meet him. Apparently he's dying to practise his English and when she demanded my number I couldn't say no!"

"I no know him, but maybe he will be your orange half!"

"My what?!" I laughed, bemused.

"Your orange half, *tu media naranja*. Is how we say in Spanish your true love," she explained with a wink.

"Actually I should probably run or I'm going to be late." I drained my coffee and got to my feet.

"Have fun," she shouted as I headed to the bathroom. "And tell me everything tonight!"

A little while later I twiddled a sachet of sugar in my fingers, savouring the smell of coffee, as I sat in a café on Calle Valverde, waiting for the infamous Andrés. He was already fifteen minutes late. Or maybe he was having second thoughts about his grandmother's matchmaking attempts.

"*Hola, eres* Eebee?" I looked up and was taken aback by the velvety brown eyes of a serious hulk of flesh. Tall, with colossal shoulders, biceps bursting out of his t-shirt and surprisingly skinny hips, he was an inverted pyramid topped with a thick mane of dark hair and nothing like the nerd I had been imagining.

"*Sí*, yes, um, *sí, soy* Evie. Andrés?" I gulped.

"*Ah, qué bueno. Encantado,*" he said. I half got up as he moved in to give me the obligatory *dos besos*, and knocked the table in the process, having to lean heavily on him to regain my balance. Not the best of starts.

Flustered, I returned to my seat as he shuffled into the chair opposite, his knee brushing against mine in the process. The familiar flames of a blush were ablaze in my cheeks before I'd had time to blink.

We ordered *dos cafés con leche* and I tried to pull myself together and act normal.

"So, what do you do Andrés?" I asked.

"*Mi abuela* no has told you nothing? *Jaja*. She tell me lots about you. She tell me you *guapísima* and she right."

I cleared my throat and giggled nervously, as his eyes burnt the clothes off my body.

"So what is it you do for work?"

"I work in airline complaints centre. I love airplanes." His chest swelled with pride as he proudly pronounced, "I have an engine for a heart and petrol in my veins."

"Oh, great," I sighed.

"You see *Top Gun*? Tom Cruise like airplanes too – I am like Tom Cruise, no?" he asked, flexing his biceps and giving me a wink.

"Um, yes, identical. You look exactly the same as him," I agreed, unable to suppress my laughter at his childlike enthusiasm.

"I also study *tiempo parcial* to be mechanic," he continued.

"Ahh, do you enjoy that?" I replied, my heart sinking. Was I destined to be with bloody mechanics every day in this city?

"No, no, study no is funny. But yesterday at work very funny. A man is trying to, *cómo se dice demandar?*"

"I have no idea, hang on." I fiddled about on my Word Reference app. "Ah, to sue."

"Ok, he try to sue the company. He and his wife went on holidays to Italy last year and their *maletas*, their swuitcases, were lost for three days. His wife made pregnant and he sue company because the contraception is in swuitcase and he no want child. Crazy guy," he laughed, shaking his head.

"That's hilarious!"

"What mean hilarious?"

"Very funny."

"Ok, *gracias*. You is good t-shirt."

"Sorry?"

"You is good t-shirt!"

"Haha, you mean teacher!"

"*Sí*, is what I say, t-shirt!"

"Well, I hope so. It's my job!"

"*Sí, mi abuela* tell me. Where you work?"

"I teach in an Institute for mechanics and I'm starting some business classes next week too."

"NOO," he shouted, banging the table with his hand, "I

no believe it. You teach at the *instituto* en Getafe?"

I nodded, surprised at his glee.

"*Qué casualidad!*" he exclaimed. "*Mi hermano, mi* brother Rafa study there and yesterday he tell me about his new t-shirt. Is you!! *Qué injusto.* Is unfair. I no get marks enough to study there – otherwise you would be my t-shirt too!"

"Rafa? Rafa with hair like this?" I asked, placing my wrist on top of my head with my fingers in the air.

"*Sí, sí.* Is my brother!"

"I don't believe it!" I exclaimed.

"*Sí, el mundo es un pañuelo,*" he cried, banging his hand down on the table with a guffaw.

"What? The world is a handkerchief?" I asked, perplexed.

"It means world is small place. All persons know all persons."

"*Sí, sí.* It's true," I agreed.

"So is Rafa good student?"

"Um, yes," I responded cautiously. "He's enthusiastic for sure. To be honest I have only just started there and I'm finding it a bit difficult, but we will see."

Desperate to avoid the subject of the Institute I asked, "So where are you from, Andrés?"

"I live outside Madrid, but my family is from Canary Islands. You know Canary Islands?"

I shook my head, "No, I've never been there, but I'd like to at some point."

"You must visit one day with me. I like see you on bitch in bikini."

I choked on a sip of coffee and spat it over the table as he continued.

"You have good body, *guapa*, like Rafa say me." He sat back in his chair, kissed his fingers and waved them in the air, continuing to lecherously scan my body.

"*Gracias*," I mumbled, blushing, and wiping the dribbles of coffee from the table with a napkin. Despite his sleaziness I couldn't help but smile at his exuberant charm.

"And you have skin beautiful. So white," he commented, reaching out to stroke my arm and sending shivers down my spine.

"You must be Viking?" He chortled loudly.

"What?" I asked, affronted. "A *Viking*? A big, ugly man?"

"Nooo, Vikings are Real Madrid fans – they colour is white. They wear white.

"Is *broma!*" he assured me. "I is joking!"

"Oh ok, I get it! Sorry, I know nothing about football," I admitted, and a shadow of disappointment came over his face.

A silence hung in the air and unsure of what to say next I asked, "Um, so where do you live Andrés?"

"I live with my family. With my mother and sister and brother. The women care us well. Is good."

He leant forward on the table and asked intently, "So, is this good for you? Is good for me. Is good for you? We meet more times?"

"Um, ok," I stuttered, unsure. "But listen, I'm going to have to run now as I'm meeting some friends."

"English friends?"

"Yes, but…"

"I come with you and practise more?" he interjected, eagerly.

"Err, sorry, not this time. But let's speak next week, ok?" I said as I got to my feet.

"*Sí, sí, vamos hablando, guapa*," he replied. Reaching out to take my hand he pulled me in and brushed his mouth dangerously close to my lips, followed by a squeeze on the bottom.

"Oi!" I exclaimed, surprised and unable to suppress a grin.

With another wink he sauntered out of the café, leaving me giggling like a schoolgirl.

***

At least fifty pairs of eyes followed me as I made my way towards the classroom, lugging a rucksack overflowing with half-finished lesson plans and worksheets. Wolf whistles greeted my arrival and my clammy hands began to slip on my books, when I spotted Rafa's familiar face pushing through the crowd.

"Titcher, you date with my brother? *Es verdad?*" he shrieked. "You kiss him? He say you kiss him good."

"He said what?" I hissed, shifting my rucksack to the other shoulder. "No! We did not kiss."

"But you went on a date?"

"We met for coffee," I whispered, adding emphatically, "Your grandmother organised it, but it was NOT a date."

"He is *gilipollas!* I know he no say me truth," said Rafa, triumphantly. "Who you love more titcher, me or Andrés?"

"See you later Rafa." I strode defiantly past the boys to the classroom. Taking a deep breath, I pushed on the door, but fell against it when it didn't move, much to the amusement of the sniggering lads. I took another deep breath, *pulled* the door and entered the room. Putting my bag down I surveyed the scene and even maintained eye contact with a few – a definite improvement on last week. My baggy jumper and jeans excessively protected my body from the most lecherous stares, yet despite the chilly temperatures outside, the classroom was already steamy from the sun pouring through the large windows.

The second conditional was admittedly an ambitious

topic, but I had prepared some fun exercises and had high hopes they'd enjoy it. Sadly, the weedy remnants of my confidence chose to vanish and my hands started to shake as we revised the structure and examples on the board. Their concentration fading and noise levels rising, I whipped out some coloured flashcards.

"Right, in your groups, pick a card and complete the sentence using the second conditional, like we've practised. I know you're all experts with the second conditional now. For example, if you could meet a famous person from history, who would you choose?"

I looked up expectantly, only to be greeted by a wall of silence.

"Come on boys, who would you choose? Anyone? Sergio, who would you like to meet?" I couldn't help picking on him. The greasy little twerp lounged at his desk, smugly twiddling his pen and flicking through his phone.

"I'd like to meet Freddie Mercury," he muttered nonchalantly. "But I'd be scared, I am *guapo* so I'd keep my back to the wall…"

"I'd choose Scarlett Johansson and make sex with her all the day," piped up Rafa.

Do not rise. Do not rise. Do not rise. I took a deep breath.

"Ok, moving on. Adrian, if you were married…?"

"Easy, I would divorce," he retorted without a second's hesitation.

"Excellent," I replied with a grin as the boys dissolved in a sea of sniggers. I suppose I should be proud, at least their answers were grammatically correct.

Sebo piped up, "Teacher, if I was married I would bored, but my mother happy."

"Okey dokey Sebo, very good, but it's *I would BE bored.* And Marcos, if you were a girl?"

As the words came out of my mouth I felt bad. Despite the dirty dreadlocks hanging down his back, and baggy jeans hanging even lower, Marcos was a gentle giant and I didn't want to embarrass him in front of the class. I smiled encouraging and he spat back.

"If I were a girl, I'd touch my pussy."

Obviously I needn't have worried about sparing his feelings.

My palms felt sweaty, my armpits prickled and positivity deserted me. How was I supposed to respond?

The howls of laughter continued as Sebo and Angel whispered conspiratorially in the second row.

"What? What did you say?" I asked.

"Noooo, noo, not woman. Not for woman."

"Tell me," I repeated, stamping my foot in frustration.

"No for woman, no woman," Sebo repeated. Looking very chuffed with himself, he suddenly pushed back his chair, stood up and broke into song, "No woman, no cry," he crooned while Angel accompanied him, tapping his hands on his desk. Seconds later he leapt on to his chair and the whole class loudly joined in. "*No woman, no cry...*"

I had to hand it to these boys, they never failed to surprise me.

Daniel, the creepy dude sitting sullenly at the back of the class suddenly spoke up.

"Titcher, is possible you help me here?" he asked, beckoning me over to his desk with a blank expression. My nose curled at the stench of his stale sweat and all vestige of colour drained from my cheeks as he pointed to the paper on his desk. Scribbled in a messy scrawl I read the words, *you make sex with me now.* I shuddered and gave him my best filthy stare before lifting his pen, putting a line through *make* and writing *have* above it, dismayed he'd burst my bubble and I felt hopeless once more.

***

My head buzzed the following evening as I walked towards Los Jerónimos, trying to process the recent turns my life had taken. I had barely slept thanks to noisy neighbours and I yawned widely as I pressed the buzzer outside a very grand building behind the Prado. My uncle's wonderfully eccentric-sounding sister Johanna had asked me to supper to meet two of her sisters who were visiting. I heard the unmistakable clip-clop of high heels clacking on a wooden floor and glancing down at my jeans, nice-ish-but-slightly-creased-and-in-need-of-an-iron-blouse and decidedly old and grubby ballet shoes, I wondered belatedly if I should have put on something a bit smarter. When the door opened I was warmly enveloped in a cloud of pearls, diamonds and perfume by three very glamorous Belgian women, and I realised yes, I most definitely was very under-dressed. Oops. From the looks of the silver platters and champagne flutes this was a rather upmarket affair, and I could hear a loud buzz of chatter wafting out of the drawing room.

Lovely jubbly, there were obviously far more than the four of us. I snuck off to the loo and stared at my distinctly scruffy self in the mirror wondering helplessly how I could smarten up. The short answer was I couldn't. I didn't even have a hairbrush in my bag. Hey ho. I headed back to the drawing room, instantly overwhelmed by the arrival of more figures sporting Chanel suits, designer dresses and dripping with glittering jewels.

Delightful Johanna took my arm and whisked me round introducing me to everyone, predominantly in Spanish, and insisting on giving me the lowdown on the background, Ambassadorial post or foreign aristocratic title of each guest. The Marquesa of Toledo, a Principessa from Sicily, the Ambassador of Sweden and his stunning, bird-like wife ...speaks six languages, don't you know? The list went on, in one ear and out the other. Several men kissed my hand, and I stared out through the large windows over the botanical gardens in the evening light, feeling distinctly out of place and lost as to how I should address these people. Suddenly I longed for the crassness of the mechanics.

Like a contented, smiling butterfly Johanna fluttered around the room offering silver salvers of canapés to her guests and endlessly refilling their glasses. Entertaining obviously came naturally to her and by the sound of it she thrived on social events. Her adorably childlike giggle rang through the halls as I inspected her eclectic possessions. Wonderful etchings and engravings adorned the walls while ceramic figurines and a stunning silver samovar took centre stage on the buffet table.

A large Picasso-style painting dominated the main wall of the drawing room, and it transpired it was one of Johanna's early works from her youth. Was there anything this lady couldn't do? She spoke several languages, was immensely knowledgeable and well-read about international affairs both past and present, and on top of that possessed bound-less creative talents. Humbled, I limited my conversation as far as possible and settled into a gentle rhythm of smiling and nodding. "Oh how fascinating," "What an interesting life you've had," and "Isn't Johanna marvellous to organise such a wonderful party" were the sum total of my insightful comments and the limits of my Spanish.

A circle of Spanish matriarchs drew me into their midst and asked how I occupied myself in Madrid. I took a large gulp of wine.

"Well," I started, launching into the tale of my classes in

stuttering Spanish. The wine definitely loosened my tongue and I regaled them with anecdotes of the mechanics' explicit outbursts with increasing confidence, before a particularly glamorous lady cut in.

"I'm afraid I don't think this is appropriate conversation. What would your parents say? I would *never* allow a daughter of mine to be in such a situation.

"Come, Carmen," she said firmly, "I want you to meet Francisco." She took the arm of another lady and directed her over to a bearded man by the window. My shoulders slumped as the others followed suit, when the largest of the matriarchs leant over, gave me a wink and muttered in perfect English,

"Don't worry dear, I'm sure it's doing you the world of good. The British have never been great at talking about sex in public. It sounds like this experience will stand you in good stead for the rest of your life."

***

I giggled silently to myself as I surveyed the café and noticed a man daintily eating a doughnut with a knife and fork, before my eyes settled on the blindingly white church on the other side of the road. I was marvelling at the brightness, and its contrast with the perfectly turquoise sky, when a kerfuffle at the door distracted me. A homeless man with a filthy wool hat covering half his face, a baggy grey overcoat loosely hanging off his shoulders and sandals five sizes too big, had stumbled through the door and started to push his grubby paper cup towards people. "*Por favor, un ayudo, por favor*," he kept pleading, with an air of such intense desperation I immediately fumbled for some coins in my pocket. Yet around me, everybody ignored him completely and carried on with their conversations oblivious. How could they not be moved by this man? I dropped my change in his cup and returned to my coffee and doughnut feeling uncomfortable. No one else even acknowledged him, and his begging became more heartfelt and anxious. Seconds later he fell, sobbing, to his knees, his voice cracking with emotion as one of the cashiers, armed with a broom, aggressively moved to push him out of the door. When the poor man resisted and implored for help, he was literally swept out onto the street. I felt uncomfortable prickles in my eyes. Why was I staring wide-eyed and immobile? Why didn't I do something to help?

Still affected by the general reaction to the beggar, my hand shook as I pressed the buzzer outside Inés' flat. Regina opened the door in a Japanese silk dressing gown.

"Inés, *es tu profe,*" she shouted over her shoulder as she retreated to her room without giving me a second glance.

I nervously crossed and uncrossed my arms as Inés sashayed towards me like a model on a catwalk, her greeting warm in contrast to her sister's reserve. A well-tailored navy suit clung to her enviable figure and heavy gold jewellery jangled at her ears, neck and wrist as she swept me into an impeccable flat straight out of a World of Interiors spread.

"Eebee, wonderful to see you. Would like a drink?" she asked politely as she directed me into their sitting room.

"I'd love some water please," I replied, sinking into a deeply luxurious sofa and admiring the lavish display of lilies in a vase on the table. Moments later she returned with a silver tray topped with two crystal tumblers of iced water and napkins.

"So, how are you?" I asked.

"I am well thank you Eebee, although tired. I have a long week with work."

"What do you do for work?"

"I work for a bank and I work in the marketing department."

"Ahh, yes. I remember. You must keep very busy. So anyway, what do you want to do today? Would you rather practise grammar, or conversation, or what?"

"Well, I have classes every week at work, all grammar. What I would like is conversation. I need to be more fluent. So I propose we speak and talk gossips," she giggled, "and you correct me when I do mistakes. It is OK for you?"

I breathed a sigh of relief. "Of course. I am an expert when it comes to gossip!"

"So, we begin. Do you have a boyfriend Eebee?" she asked, earnestly, articulating every word slowly and clearly in an exemplary accent.

"No, I don't. Do you?" *Right back at ya missy.*

"No, I no have boyfriend," she replied, distracted, as her phone beeped with a text message and she fished it out of her handbag.

"I *don't* have a boyfriend," I corrected, "but do you like anyone? Is there…"

"Oh nooooo," she broke in as a stricken look crossed her face. "Is from him!"

"Who is he?" I asked, confused.

"Is a long history, but is an espanish called Juan. We have been friends for a long time. I think I told you about him when we met."

"Oh yes, the very handsome guy you showed me a photo of?"

"*Sí*, yes, he is *guapísimo!*" she exclaimed.

"What happened?"

"We work together, and we started to date. He work abroad often, so is complicate, but we had a very good relation."

"*Relationship*," I interrupted. "So what happened?"

"He moved to London *hace tres meses*, three months ago unfortunately. We have been flitting, sorry, flirting all the time and I think all is good. But just now, he sent me a message saying 'Good Morning sweetpea.' SWEETPEA!" she shrieked in despair, "He thinks I'm a *guisante dulce? Joder!* I no understand!" She sighed despondently. "Clearly he doesn't like me if he is calling me a vegetable."

"He's not comparing you to a round, green vegetable," I laughed, patting her arm as I explained. "A sweetpea is a flower. A very pretty flower and totally different to a vegetable pea! He gave you a compliment. Look, I will show you a picture on my phone," I said as I typed it into Google.

"So I am not a vegetable?" she repeated, timidly.

"No!" And we both dissolved in giggles.

"Thanks god. You English, you have strange way to say compliments!"

"And you don't?" I laughed. "Someone told me the other day *estar como un queso* is to be fit, or good-looking. I would never take it as a compliment if someone told me I looked like a cheese!"

"Is true, and we also say *el esta como un tren.* If a man is like a train he is like a studmuffin," she said, articulating the word like an illness.

"Studmuffin?" I laughed, choking on my water, as she continued.

"I looked it up on Word Reference, but I no not understand if studmuffin is a good thing? Is some sort of cake?"

"It's not a common expression, but yes, it's a good thing!" I assured her, still chuckling.

8

BEEP! BEEP! I leapt onto the pavement to escape being flattened by a van – I still hadn't adapted to the damn traffic lights in this place. "*La chica más guapa de Madrid!*" shouted the driver as he passed, blowing me a kiss out of the window and making me simper like a child.

I poked my head round the door and tiptoed in like a guilty trespasser, the silence broken by my shoes squeaking on the clean lino. A huge bar ran along one side of the room and suddenly the penny dropped and I knew why the name Antonio Valdes had sounded familiar – it's a massive international alcohol company, like Diageo. How stupid of me not to have realised earlier. I surveyed the impressive array of alcohol: diamante-encrusted vodka bottles, whisky, tequila, rum and more. Meetings at this place must be fun. Rounding the corner I stumbled into the chest of a mighty fine specimen of a man and my stomach lurched as I raised my eyes to his face. Maybe in his mid-thirties, with thick glossy hair and the perfect amount of stubble surrounding a mouthful of glistening white teeth, a battered leather jacket hung from his shoulders and a motorcycle helmet dangled from his hand. This whole teaching malarkey was definitely looking up.

"Titcher, you must be the new titcher," he purred, planting

two scratchy kisses on my burning cheeks. His winning smile made my knees weak and barely holding it together, I mumbled, "*Hola* Jorge. My name is Evie and I'm from London," resembling a muppet introducing myself on *Blind Date.*

"George, call me George. We is in England now," he said as a deep guffaw rose from the depths of his stomach and he threw his books down on the desk.

"Or my friends, they call me Jor," he grinned, knowingly.

"Seriously?" I laughed, incredulous.

"Yes, and it was many years before I know what means it," he laughed. "Jorge is difficult for English persons to say so if you want, I is George."

"I love the name George, but let's stick to Jorge," I replied, stubbornly, articulating the word with an excessively throaty rasp.

"So, you is English," he continued, "where you live? In Londres?" His rich, confident voice sent my heart racing as he sized me up with a typically powerful Spanish stare.

"Yes, I live in London. In a place called Fulham," I replied, nervously, unable to look him in the eye.

"Flam? *No es* a real place," he said, laughing.

"No, F.U.L.H.A.M." I corrected, spelling it out on a piece of paper. "It's in the west of the city."

"*Qué dices* – Fulham, *lleno de jamón?* Is place full of ham? *Jamón por todos lados?*" he asked, dubiously.

I couldn't control my grin.

"Ha, no, I have never seen a lot of ham in Fulham, but it's a good point!"

More of his warm guffaws filled the room as I continued, "Have you been to London?"

"Yes, I been in London," he replied, still fixing his intense gaze directly on my blazing face.

I took a deep breath and continued, "What did you see?"

"I visit the Tower of London."

"And…"

"Aunt? *Tía?* Why you talk about my aunt?"

"No, I said and. A.N.D. not aunt. Can you hear the difference?"

"You mean ant, like *hormiga?* The insect?"

Genuine mistakes, or was he taking the piss?

Through uncontrollable giggles I corrected, "*Tía* is aunt, *hormiga* is ant and *y* is and. Ok?"

When our laughter finally subsided, he pushed his chair back, stretched out his legs and said.

"So, gimme the fucks teacher. What we study this term?"

"Sorry?" I asked, wide-eyed.

"Gimme the fucks," he repeated innocently, flashing his devastating smile.

I'd happily give this guy anything he asked for right now, but I restrained myself from leaping over the desk into his arms, and tried to keep a straight face as I corrected him.

"Facts, it is F.A.C.T.S. So, I'm going to start by asking you some questions to see what you know and what you'd like to learn this year."

We giggled our way through the level test and then moved on to the laborious list of questions on the needs analysis form. I asked about his previous lessons to get an idea of what sort of style he liked and when it got to the last question, "Describe the best teacher you've ever had," he replied as quick as a flash with a wink, "But you are my best teacher. You are the best teacher *en el mundo*."

Be still my beating heart: Jorge sure was a charmer.

***

A few hours later Chloe and I joined Belinda for drinks on the rooftop terrace of Mercado San Anton in Chueca. Gin and tonics were the order of the day, after we'd gorged ourselves silly on the *pulpo*, *foie* and *huevos rotos* from the stalls downstairs. Now happily ensconced on the sofas and wrapped in blankets under twinkling fairy lights, Belinda entertained us with tales of her struggles to grasp the Spanish language.

"I mean this morning I tried to recharge my mobile in a *locutorio*. When they asked me what network I had, I said Vodafone in my *best* Spanish accent, and they cracked up. *Boda fone* they said, like wedding phone?! You call for husband?"

"Haha, that's hilarious!"

"Funny now, but after ten minutes of miscommunication and laughter I had to resort to writing it down for them. Am I ever going to be able to speak this bloody language?!" she asked, theatrically.

"Pronunciation isn't their strong point either – my friend Katherine came to stay the other day and they insisted on saying her name as if she was a catering company!" chuckled Chloe.

"If only there was a helpline we could call to find us husbands," I pondered, gazing dreamily into my G&T. "That would be awesome."

Belinda stood up, waving her hands in the air. "I'm sure husbands are overrated, although speaking of men, how's it going with Dave, Chloe?"

"Rubbish. He's been in New York for six months now and we've seen each other twice. This whole long-distance thing is crap, and to make it worse, it's now looking like his project is going to be extended for another year."

"You're off to see him soon aren't you?" I asked.

"Yep, I'm going on Saturday and it's gonna be make or break for sure."

"Well, don't worry about it for now and I'll get us some more drinks," said Belinda, heading to the bar.

"*Gracias*," we chorused.

"God, this is paradise isn't it?" I sighed, gazing out over the rooftops.

"Sure is. And thank god this week is over. I couldn't take a minute more of Antonio." Chloe, an intelligent and highly capable solicitor, worked in a law firm and struggled with the chilled Spanish way of doing things. She had lost all patience with her new boss when he had arrived four months ago, and now looked forward to returning to London when the office closed down at some as-yet-undecided point in the near future. "He is a total imbecile and he's not telling us anything about what's happening with the company or when I will be sent home. All he *can* tell me is there's no chance of a secondment to the New York office."

She drained her drink and sighed, "But enough about me. How's your work going?"

"You poor thing. Don't worry, I'm sure you'll sort things out with Dave when you see him. As for my work, I actually feel much more relaxed about it now. I'm still not sure I want to stick it out at the Institute till the end of the year, but until I can figure out what else to do I desperately need the money."

"Didn't I tell you it would get easier?" chuckled Belinda, returning with yet more drinks.

"Haha, yes, thank you for pushing me. I wouldn't go as far as to say I'm enjoying it just yet, but it has its moments and I think I've actually taught them a few things recently! Some of the boys have gone off on their Erasmus now too so the classes are smaller which is great."

"Before you know it you'll be left with just Winston!"

"Oh god, please no. He's so keen I can't take it!"

"I think you should go for a drink with him – you never know…"

"NO! I absolutely do know. And anyway, I have a new distraction who is much more exciting. I started classes with THE most gorgeous new business student today."

"What about poor Ramón? I'm on Team Rameebee!" giggled Chloe. "Incidentally, why haven't we seen you in that fetching t-shirt yet?!"

"You and I both know how I feel about Ramón and *that* t-shirt! He's taking me to El Escorial tomorrow though as he thinks I need to see more of his country."

"*En serio?* How romantic," she giggled.

"Hmm, not sure about that. But I'll keep you posted."

"Every young girl simply must spend some time in Italy or Spain as the male attention does wonders for her confidence!" Chloe interjected in a warbling high-pitched voice, making us all laugh. "That's what my aunt used to say."

"More importantly though, back to the hot guy," cooed Belinda enthusiastically, finishing off her G&T and snuggling under the blanket, "You know you have to hook up with at least one of your students while you're here. Is it going to be him?"

"I hope so! He is totally gorgeous and so funny. It's such a nice change to have an utterly charming student after the mechanics."

"How's his English?"

"It's not great but his mistakes are so endearing they make him even more attractive. Earlier we did an exercise on personality adjectives. He looked totally perplexed when we came across the word *selfish* and with the most earnest expression he asked, "*What is selfish person? Is person who sells fish for job?!*" I mean it's totally logical but would you ever have thought of that?"

***

Cool, calm and collected was not an accurate description of my state when persistent phone buzzing woke me the following morning. Trying to ignore the thunderstorm raging in my head, I fumbled around and located it under my pillow.

"*Buenas días* Eebee!" chirped Ramón down the line. "How are you today?"

"Um, goooood. Good, thanks," I managed to mumble. "And you?"

"*Muy bien, gracias.* I say you I am leaving now so I arrive for you in fifteen minutes. Ok? We meet on corner by the *supermercado*. Ok? *Vale? Hasta pronto.*"

He hung up before I could say another word.

Oh god, I groaned, and dragged myself out of bed. At this sudden movement the headache unleashed its full force.

I waddled to the bathroom and started to brush my teeth when Carolina bounced in, looking fresh-faced and perky.

"Are you OK Evie? You no look good. Is a super-beautiful morning. You have plans?"

"Umm," I stuttered, licking my horribly dry lips and leaning on the basin for support, "Ramón is picking me up in fifteen minutes to go to El Escorial. But I'm not sure I'm going to survive – I only got home two hours ago."

"Ooohhh, another date with Ramón hey?!" she teased.

"I'm going to cancel. I can't face it." I replied, perching on the bath and ignoring her question.

Stern-faced she said firmly, "No, you no cancel. Take a shower and you feel better. I make a coffee for you."

With a gleeful expression, she pushed me towards the shower and her lycra-clad body bounded off down the corridor towards the kitchen.

My deeply instilled English politeness prevented me from calling and postponing, and luckily post-shower I did feel significantly better, although still far from normal. On top of the hangover I felt confused about seeing Ramón again. We'd had limited contact since our kiss as I'd taken ages to respond to his messages when I was overstressed with the Institute, and then he'd been travelling round the country with his latest exhibition. I hoped he'd found another girl to lavish his attention on in the meantime and it would all just be water under the bridge.

Five minutes later with a large amount of caffeine whizzing through my veins I leant on the wall outside the supermarket, barely capable of holding my own weight. My sunglasses were firmly wrapped round my eyes and all my attention concentrated on staying upright when I heard the indecently loud roar of an engine tearing up the street. The deep noise resonated painfully in my head and I looked on in horror as it screeched to a halt in front of me. As my blurry eyes focused I saw Ramón's face peering out of the window.

Leaping out of the car he exclaimed, "Eebee, good morning! You like my new car? Is great, no?" and I reluctantly shifted my bodyweight away from the delightfully supportive wall as he enveloped me in a tight bear hug. Thankfully he didn't try and kiss me. Small blessings.

"Isn't it *perfecto?* My new baby," he crooned, lovingly stroking the gleaming bonnet as if it were the soft head of a new-born child. "I always want Porsche and then my friend Miguel he tell me he want to sell his Porsche and I say I buy! *Es estupendo*, no? You like it? I hope you like it."

"*Sí, sí*, um, it's great," I replied, unconvincingly.

"So, *vamos*, we go now!"

We flew off through the arch of Moncloa towards the mountains and the monastery of El Escorial.

"Um, you like to drive fast don't you?" My body stiffened and my grip tightened on the seatbelt.

"You want go faster? I am the master of faster!" he cackled gleefully, the engine letting out another roar and drowning my pleas to slow down.

The landscape turned greener and greener and I felt a rush of liberation as we left the city far behind and sped out into the countryside.

"I haven't been in a car for weeks!" I said loudly, over the noise of the car.

"But I always use car. You no use public transport do you?" he asked, screwing up his face in disgust and gazing across at me.

"I find the buses a bit confusing, but yes, I use the metro all the time. Why wouldn't I?"

"No, no," he said, gravely, "you must use taxis Eebee. I always use my motorbike, my car or taxis."

"But the metro is one of the best things about this city – I love it."

"Pah!" he exclaimed, "Is horrible and I never use it."

"Why not? There are never delays, the air-conditioning is amazing and you have great phone reception. It's fantastic!"

"But is dirty and crowded. Is horrible."

"You should try the tube in London. Far more sweaty armpits and there are always problems with the lines."

As I said this we caught our first glimpse of the town, nestled into the side of the snow-capped mountains. The breathtaking view made me come over all poetic. Cows dotted the hills, the Mediterranean sun was burning through the hazy veil of clouds and rays of light fell on the small town of El Escorial, bouncing off the turrets of the monumental monasterial complex in its centre. The turquoise blues of the sky and the burnt orange and brown colours of the leaves in the surrounding forests hung together with the warm hues of the stone buildings to create a perfect postcard view, and it was glaringly obvious why Phillip II had chosen to build his palace in this beautiful spot.

"Is designed in shape of a *parilla,* a grill, for the death of San Lorenzo," he informed me as we wound our way through the streets, the deafening engine shattering the tranquillity of the place. As we got closer I realised the beauty of the countryside had softened the impact of the monastery: close up it really was just a whopping hulk of granite. Sombre, austere and downright imposing.

We headed through the entrance and began to walk around the vast compound. As dour as it was on the outside, the interior told a different story. Brimming with art, mainly from Spain's Golden Age, it rambled on and on in a never-ending cultural labyrinth.

"Ahh, Eebee, look at this. Is not the most beautiful picture?" asked Ramón, gesticulating at a Dutch still life of flowers, fruit and a butterfly.

"Um, yes, it's nice," I lied, always having found that sort of art quite artificial and soulless, "but this portrait is gorgeous," I added, pointing to a large, intense painting of Saint Jerome with a wonderfully thick, curly beard, executed in a much more expressive style.

"Oh no, this still life is so precise, so detailed. *Es mucho mejor.* I am inspired by this work when I create my own paintings," he replied passionately.

"But look at Jerome's face!" I enthused, "there's so much emotion in so few brushstrokes, you can almost put your fingers right into his beard.

"It's got so much more expression," I added.

"But can't you see the beauty in the butterfly wings here?" he asked, pulling me back towards his favourite work. "So delicate and detailed."

"Yes, it's lovely," I conceded, "but it's just not my style. By the way, you must show me some of your paintings one day."

"Of course. My exhibition comes to Madrid soon. I send you invitation. I cannot believe I no show you before," he replied as he grudgingly tore himself away from the artwork and followed me towards the Royal Pantheon. At the bottom of the stairs we entered a circular room lined with elaborate black and gold coffins, separated by marble and gold pilasters.

"Here are the bodies of nearly all of my country's kings and queens from the last five centuries," Ramón announced proudly, gazing around in reverence.

"It's a bit creepy isn't it?" I asked, hairs standing on the back of my neck. And horribly opulent and ornate I added to myself.

"Why you not like these things Eebee?" he asked, imploringly. "This is the heart of my country. Is the soul."

My stomach growled, the room began to blur and exhaustion was taking hold in a major way.

"It just feels a little bit macabre, but you're right, it is impressive. Anyway, shall we head for some lunch now?" I suggested meekly.

"You English people, you eat so early. *Es ridículo. Pero* ok, we go."

My audible sigh of relief coincided with his exaggerated sigh of frustration as he took my hand in his clammy paw and pulled me towards the exit. We strolled over the cobbles and paused to lean on a wall and admire the pond, the immaculately pruned gardens and the expansive view of the mountains beyond. My eyes began to glaze over as I drank in the scene, but I was abruptly brought back to reality by Ramón cupping my face in his hand and jerkily pulling me towards him. Woooaaahhhh! Before I could articulate a word, his lips found mine and I didn't have time to *hacerme la cobra* (a wonderful Spanish phrase meaning to make like a cobra and duck out of the way of a kiss). His arms clamped around me, his mouth and body so rigid I couldn't stand it any longer. Pulling away, I stepped back, reaching out to pat him on the arm and ask.

"Did you hear my tummy rumble? Definitely time for lunch! Come on!" I turned to make my way up the hill, but he pulled on my arm and pleaded.

"But Eebee, why you go? I want to say you is very *guapa* and I like you very much."

"Thank you Ramón – you're very sweet," I said, puzzled. "Come on though, let's have lunch or I'm going to pass out!" Weak, bemused and desperately in need of food, I turned and marched up the hill.

We soon settled at a table in a small, pretty colonnaded piazza with a view down towards the monastery. I closed my eyes and soaked up the golden autumnal sunlight as the waiter brought us *cañas, jamón, albondigas, boquerones* and other such delights. After a few moments Ramón's phone rang loudly.

"I'm sorry, I must answer. Is my mother," he said, flustered, as he walked off down the hill jabbering animatedly into the phone.

I basked in the warm sunshine and wondered what was going through his mind.

"T-shirt! T-shirt!" I suddenly heard loudly behind me. "Is

you, t-shirt?! What you do here?!" I lifted my sunglasses from my face and my eyes fell on Andrés. Tall and buff, muscle outweighed brainpower in this guy, and his huge bodyweight zoomed into focus as he swooped in to kiss me hello.

"*Hola* Andrés, what a surprise. How are you?" I asked, trying to be nonchalant. What was he doing here? Had I inadvertently signed up to a bizarre version of *The Truman Show?*

"Good. I is good. Welcome my home town. You like my town?" he asked animatedly, taking a pew in Ramón's vacant chair and helping himself to some *jamón*.

"Yes, it's lovely, but I didn't realise you lived here."

"*Sí, sí*, I tell you. You no listen to me t-shirt?" he chortled. "I live here with my brother and the women. If you want I show you best things of El Escorial later…in my bedroom," he continued, with a lewd wink.

Out of the corner of my eye I spotted Ramón bustling back through the square. He stopped next to the table in surprise, looking down on the grease monkey in his seat, and I smiled as they exchanged mutual looks of disgust. Ramón's eyes nearly fell out of his head when he spied the tattoo *Fuck authority* scrawled on Andrés' muscular forearm.

"Sorry, I am so rude. Andrés, let me introduce my friend Ramón. And Ramón, this is Andrés – we met a few weeks ago. His grandmother lives in my building and his brother Rafa studies at the Institute where I teach."

Ramón made no response as he raked his eyes over all the details of Andrés' appearance, from the metallic spikes piercing his earlobes to the dirty jeans miraculously clinging to the bottom of his butt and the shiny jacket sparkling in the sunshine.

"*Sí*, she is my t-shirt of English, *jaja*. She is good t-shirt. You is her boyfriend?"

Ramón's mouth opened and closed, at a loss for words. Ignoring the question and keeping my eyes firmly on my shoes, I finally broke the silence.

"So, Andrés, how is work going? Any more crazy complaints?"

"No be shy, you is on date together?" he probed, giving Ramón a knowing wink.

Still mute, Ramón gave an involuntary shudder and I leapt to my feet.

"We are friends Andrés, just friends. And actually we're leaving now. We need to get back to Madrid, but good to see you and enjoy the rest of the weekend," I laughed. Ramón paid the bill and we walked over to the Porsche.

"I call you t-shirt. We meet again soon babe!" Andrés called out behind us, adding, "Hey, nice Porsche. You give me ride one day?"

Ramón continued to ignore him as he rapidly got into the car and slammed the door shut. "Is he the type of person you is teaching?" he fumed. "No wonder is difficult. You must search new job, with good people. I help you when we return to Madrid."

"Don't be such a snob and you didn't have to be so rude to him. He was trying to be nice!" I exclaimed.

"He is a bad person – I can see just looking to him he is not good person," he repeated loudly.

"You're so judgemental! He's harmless and the mechanics aren't so bad either. In fact some of them are really quite sweet."

"Sweet? SWEET?" he screeched so loudly I had to resist the urge to put my fingers in my ears. "You is too nice Eebee. Is dangerous for girl like you."

"No, honestly, they freaked me out at first, but we've been having more fun recently," I replied, defensively. "Last week they serenaded me for the second time! Rafa, Andrés' brother, apparently loves Marc Anthony," I giggled.

"Marc Anthony?" he asked.

"I know, right?! Anyway, when I said I didn't know any Marc Anthony songs he leapt onto the desk and belted out *Valió la pena.* I have to admit he was pretty damn good!"

"Pah, just because he sings good no mean he is good person," he spat out. "I explain you…"

"You explain me what?" I interrupted angrily.

"I explain you the boys," he started to say again.

"I will explain TO you," I shrieked, irrationally frustrated by his missing preposition. My rage had turned me into a grammar Nazi.

"The boys are harmless and I like them."

So there I nearly added petulantly as I crossed my arms. My blood boiled as we zoomed back to the city under corrugated pink skies, both fuming in the silence.

9

With her legs splayed and framing a beautiful bunch of flowers emerging from her, um, lady garden, the woman on the front of the card 'invited me into her world'. *Sexual, yet refined*, was how Ramón had described the invitations to his latest exhibition, and I laughed as I glanced at it again to check the address of the gallery. Pulling on some heels, I sprayed scent on my wrists and neck and trotted off to the show, intrigued to finally see his bizarre artwork in the flesh.

A contented sigh left my lips as I pulled open the door and stepped into my comfort zone. Art galleries were my cosy blanket, my spiritual home, and back in London I'd attended private views at least once a week for work. It felt blissful to be in a familiar environment without a single mechanic in sight.

The large gallery on Calle Jorge Juan shone white, light and bright and oozed wealth. My heels clacked on the gleaming marble floor and I spotted the image from the invitation hanging in pride of place at the end of the gallery. The side walls held further rough, sketchy paintings of women draped around intricate depictions of flowers and fruit clearly inspired by the Dutch still life paintings he had so loved at El Escorial. They reflected the contrasting elements of his personality and I smiled at their comical combination.

A willowy waitress sauntered past and, swiping a glass of champagne from her tray, I scanned the room for Ramón. We hadn't seen each other in the two weeks since our tripette to El Escorial, and in hindsight I felt embarrassed for acting like a rude, ungrateful child. I hoped to make it up to him, in a platonic way, obviously, by enthusing about his art.

Gesticulating wildly and deep in conversation with two glamorous women, he broke off and waved when he spotted me clip-clopping towards him.

"Eebee, I am so happy you come tonight! You like my art?" he asked, puffing out his chest as he surveyed the room.

"It's impressive Ramón, congratulations. And this is a fabulous gallery. You must be doing very well to have a show here."

"Weeellllll, I have much luck, you see my friend Fernando he own this place," he admitted. "He like my work very much and is my patron, like the Lorenzo de' Medici in the Renaissance of Florence."

"How lucky to have such a good friend," I remarked, spotting two delicately painted peaches over his shoulder, which formed the ample bottom of a lady. I took a large sip of champagne to hide my giggles.

"*Sí, sí,*" he nodded enthusiastically, "but now I tell you about my art. Picasso, he say, the purpose of art is wash dust of life from our souls and this is what I do with my paintings. They are clean and *puro* and they lift your soul, no?"

I smiled as he continued, "I like say that in my paintings I show my respect *profundo* for the Dutch masters of still life, but in combination with the expressive work of El Greco and Goya, the Spanish passion and feeling. The detail of the Dutch with the passion and sex of the Spanish. You understand Eebee? What you think?"

"Your style is very unique," I remarked, choosing my words carefully. Tilting my head to one side to avoid his stare, I feigned focus on the peachy bum in front of me when a petite girl in tight leather trousers rushed over and saved me from having to profess further opinions.

"Come, Eebee, let me present you to my friend Sofía," he said, taking my arm firmly and turning me to her.

"Sofía this is Eebee, she is from England, and Eebee, Sofía is old friend from my village. She just say me she want lessons of English. Maybe you teach her?"

"Eebee? Eebee the titcher of Jorge? I recognise you from my office. You teach English to Jorge, no?"

"At Antonio Valdes? Yes, yes, I do," I smiled as she nodded enthusiastically. "I thought you looked vaguely familiar."

"He tell me you the best teacher of English *en el mundo*, and I need improve my English too. Can you titch me? I want to speak like Kate Middleton!" she proclaimed, dissolving into infectious giggles. "I love her."

"Of course I can teach you!" I gushed, "I'd really like that. Although I'm not sure I can make you speak exactly like her."

I was chuffed to discover Jorge didn't see me as a completely useless teacher swooning at his every word and Sofía and I made plans to start classes when she returned from her holidays.

"So where are you going on your trip?" I asked.

"We go to Greece, we visit some islands."

"That'll be wonderful," I cooed. "Have you been before?"

"No, never, but always I want. I am very looking forward. Sun, sea, bitches... We Spanish, we all love to go to bitch."

I smirked at my favourite Spanish pronunciation mistake.

"You have plans for to go holidays?" she asked.

"I'm so tired at the moment with all my classes, I'd love

to go on holiday," I sighed, "but I have no plans other than going home for Christmas."

"But you must go to a place warm. Go to holiday with your boyfriend and everything will be better."

"What, my imaginary boyfriend Juan, here?" I joked, indicating to the empty space next to me.

"You no have boyfriend?" she gasped in horror. "No is problem. If you need boyfriend we can make a casting for you. I like making castings."

"Castings?" I questioned, with visions of hundreds of men queuing up for *X-Factor*-style auditions.

"Yes, yes, castings to find you boyfriend. We do one for my colleague. He needs a beautiful girl. But we do them all the time for work."

"Seriously?" I interjected, "is that how you interview people for jobs?"

She nodded enthusiastically.

"Isn't it illegal?!"

"No, at first people are overwhelmed, but soon they get used to it. I am very bad. The agencies send us photos and I say no she has big nose, or I no like her eyes. And my colleague Juan – he looks good, but he is the worst. He say me afterwards – Sofía, don't you think she has big head? And things like that."

She smiled, giggling.

"Sometimes we have castings in office and is very funny. Jorge is the worst too – often we are making casting in the big room and we turn and there is Jorge. What you are doing I say him but he only laugh and stay in room."

"It doesn't surprise me!"

"No, is fun. I have much luck with my job. And don't worry Eebee, we do casting and find you boyfriend," she laughed, giving me a knowing wink.

***

The next morning I peered into the mirror in the lift, wondering how a spot I had so carefully covered in make-up only half an hour earlier could be so visible already. Oh well, it's not as if Jorge was remotely interested anyway.

"Eebee," he said, as I approached his office, "come in. Hello! You know my colleague Juan?"

I shook my head, remembering Sofía's comments.

"Hi Juan," I said, smiling. His handsome face oozed charm and confidence. Good looks were clearly essential to the recruitment procedures of this place.

"His name is Juan Lopez but we call him Pezones," and he broke into chuckles, "*entiendes?* You understand?" His laugh echoed round the room, and I was sure everyone in the building could hear it.

"Err, *pezones*, like big fish?" I felt rather proud of myself, surprised I could understand a word in Spanish. To explain – *pez* means *fish* and the suffix *–ones* means big or great, so he must mean big fish, right? Although I had no clue as to why this could be quite so funny.

"What?! Why you say fish? No fish. Is neeps," Jorge responded, pointing to his nipples. "*Pezones* is neeps. An important word for you to learn," he continued, winking at me.

"Haha, but these aren't called neeps! They're nipples," I sniggered, realising we were all pointing to our own. "So *pezones* must mean nipples then?!" I laughed. "It's an important word for you to learn in English!!" I winked back at him and started taking out my books.

"Nipples! See you later alligator!" he shouted to Juan as he sat down at his desk.

"In a while, crocodile," drifted back in response.

"Ooh, I love rhyming idioms," I said. "What others do you know?"

"See you soon, baboon. And of course, my horse. They are what we learn in school."

"How about what's cooking, good looking?" I suggested, coyly.

"Yes, I like this one. I use it in future," he grinned, his gaze igniting a fireworks display in my stomach.

"And also, I been thinking how now we are friends, we must make Facebook friends," he continued.

"Um, ok," I said, surprised, as he opened the app and typed Evie Fuller in the search box. Moments later he guffawed loudly and showed me an image of an old, wrinkly face surrounded by grey curls, staring out of the screen with a stern grimace.

"Is you! Is Eebee Fuller in morning before make up your face!"

"Don't be ridiculous. Give it here," I laughed, scrolling through the Evie Fullers to find my profile and clicking *add*. "There you go."

"Perfect. I will look at page and tell everyone the gossips about you."

"Don't forget I can do the same for you!" I giggled. "Now, let's get on with some work."

We spent the lesson doing a unit from the textbook about asking people out/making plans and how to respond to invitations etc., and towards the end we began practising future tenses to make plans. We both had a diary and we had to make a plan to go out.

Jorge started first.

"So, is this a date? We make plan to go on a date?" he asked, scanning over the textbook on the desk in front of him.

"Um, yes, if you like," I stuttered, while a voice in my head screamed YES PLEASE!

"So, are you busy on Friday night?" he asked, with yet another wink.

"I'm afraid so. I have football practice every Friday," I joked.

What was wrong with me? Where on earth had that come from?

"Ahh, of course, you play football. You have good legs," he replied with a leery grin.

The room was already sweltering. Literally. The idea of going on a date with him was too much for me to bear and I'd never been good at taking compliments. My face couldn't have gone a deeper shade of red if I had plastered on an inch-thick layer of blusher.

Next we had to "make a plan" for Sunday night.

"So, why don't you come to my flat to clean and wash for three hours and I promise I will take you out for dinner."

"Three hours of cleaning?" I replied with a laugh.

"Yes, the swimming pool is very dirty and the jacuzzi too," he joked, getting into the swing of the role-playing malarkey.

"And how much will you pay me for my cleaning services?" I demanded.

"Three euros an hour."

"Three euros? Pah. No chance. Change of plan. I'm going out with my friends instead," I laughed, sitting back in the chair.

"Nooo, you must come to my flat. And I will take you to dinner afterwards."

Adrenaline raced through my veins and I could barely control my excitement at the, albeit fictional, idea of going for dinner with him, yet my mouth seemed incapable of forming any sensible sentences.

"Where would we go? I bet you're thinking of McDonald's," I managed to articulate.

"Ha, good idea, McDonald's. Yes, we go McDonald's and I buy you cheeps and a burger."

At the end of the class we walked towards the lift and I asked, "What are you doing this weekend?"

"I am playing poker with some friends," he replied.

"Are you any good at it?"

"I never play so I think I am very bad. But don't worry, I will only take 100 euros so I will still have money to pay you on Monday, for our last class before Christmas!"

"You are ridiculous! But it sounds good – I don't want you losing all your money and having to stop classes!"

"Oh and next week I must remember I want to give you some boobs for Christmas," he continued, collecting up his papers from the desk while I stood open-mouthed.

"Did you say boobs?!" I laughed.

"*Sí*, I give you some boobs. What you like best – vodka, gin or champagne?"

"Oh you mean booze!" I exclaimed, "Booze! Maybe just call it alcohol in future to avoid confusion – I thought you said boobs!" I fell about laughing, pointing to my breasts.

"Titcher, no. You are obsessed," he said, shaking his finger at me in a jokily disapproving manner. "I is worried about you."

Gazing out of the window on the metro a little while later, I felt almost euphoric about the fact we had become Facebook friends. Whatever happens at least I can now drool over photos of him all day long.

OH GOD! Blind hysteria took over as I suddenly remembered how my idiot friend Jamie had put up lots of skinny dipping pictures from our Irish holiday last summer. There was no way in hell I wanted Jorge to see those unflattering photos – I'd been meaning to de-tag them all week. I fumbled madly around in my bag for my phone and tried to open the Facebook app when a screenshot of my naked body flashed up, accompanied by the message, "Nice neeps teacher! See you next week, Jorge."

10

The boys started filtering into the classroom and I began to draw the outline of a man on the board, beginning with the head and working downwards. As I embarked on the first of his legs I began to wonder how this was going to turn out. I'm not exactly Picasso and the leg seemed a wee bit small, so I took the board wiper to erase it, only to discover the new board pens didn't rub out very well and the poor man ended up with an unfortunate smudge between his legs, predictably greeted with great sniggers from the boys. I replaced the pen cap, took a deep breath and cleared my throat before turning to face the class.

"What goes in middle titcher? In middle of legs?" piped up Rafa with a smirk.

I sighed. With his diamond earrings glinting in the light, Rafa leant enthusiastically across the desk and I glimpsed the words *Beware of Yourself* tattooed on his forearm in an ugly block typeface.

He continued, "Why don't you say dick teacher, it's called dick. You see dick?" He pushed back his chair to point to his own, and for a second I thought he was about to pull down his shiny tracksuit bottoms and whip it out.

Ignoring him I swallowed to clear my dry throat, "I'd like

you all to come to the board and we're going to label the parts of the body."

They trudged to the front of the class and huddled round the board bickering over the labels and debating the spelling of different words.

"Ok, just the last couple to do," I interjected, when they had nearly finished. "What's this?" I asked.

Sebo piped up, "is called uncle."

"Not quite," I smiled, "but nearly."

"Es *tío*, uncle is *tío* you idiot. It's the ankle," corrected Rafa patronisingly, looking at me smugly. "I is good at English right teacher?" he winked.

"Yes, well done. *Tío* es uncle and *tobillo* es ankle," I said, chuffed I actually knew these two words. I then pointed to my cheeks, "Marcos, can you remember the name for these? For your *mejillones?*"

"Haha titcher, you Spanish is shit," he laughed. "*Mejillones* is in sea, not face. These," he said, pointing to his cheeks, "are *mejillas.*"

The howling continued and my brief moment of Spanish glory ended as soon as it had begun. Damn it. *Mejillones* are mussels. Important one to remember. *Mejillas* are cheeks.

"Thank you everyone, but this isn't a Spanish lesson," I muttered, wishing I could vanish under an invisibility cloak.

"Ok boys, now I want you to take these," I said, passing out worksheets, "and fill them in describing yourself and your partner. For example, I have red hair and he has green eyes, etc."

As they sauntered back to their seats Rafa muttered, "José has ugly dick."

"Is more big than your dick," replied José, petulantly, as they jostled each other somewhat aggressively.

"Boys, please," I sighed.

Once they had finished trading insults, the next task on the sheet asked them to describe their perfect woman. Rafa grinned lecherously and gesticulated wildly to draw a page 3 model in the air.

"My perfect woman has fat lips and I no want a girl with chest operations." He cupped huge, imaginary boobs on Hector who had the misfortune to be sitting next to him. "How do you call them? *Falso* titties?"

"They really called titties titcher?" Hector asked shyly. Tall, gentle and softly-spoken, Hector represented the antithesis of Rafa in nearly every way, but the two were inseparable.

"Ha, well. Yes, you can call them titties. It's more common to say boobs. Or breasts I suppose. Or of course just tits."

Desperate to change the subject, my face rivalling the colour of an aubergine, I asked, "And her hair? What type of hair would your perfect woman have?"

"But wait, how you call girl with big titties?" Rafa could not let it go.

"Um, I suppose you could call her curvaceous. Or you can say she has big breasts?"

"How you spell breasts?" asked Carlos.

Sighing again, I turned and wrote boobs, breasts, tits and curvaceous on the board, before remembering it was damn near impossible to erase these new pens.

"What is the difference of boobs, breasts and tits?" Jesús, the gentle Ecuadorian, asked pensively, the first time he'd volunteered a question in class.

"A damn good question," I replied, racking my brains for an answer.

"Well, I don't know really. I suppose girls would call them boobs, but a doctor would say breasts." I paused. "Yes, and guys would say tits," I finished, triumphantly. It seemed inappropriate to be directing this to a man named Jesús, but I felt supremely satisfied to have come up with an even vaguely coherent answer.

"How you say *falso* titties? Are silicone implants?"

"Probably the best thing to say is she has had a boob job," I responded, sweating profusely, but weirdly enjoying the frankness of the conversation. I'd never seen the boys so focused.

"And how you compliment girl on her tits?" Rafa continued earnestly.

An email flashed up on my phone and diverted my attention.

Dear Evie,

We hope you are well and enjoying a good start to the year. We are busy planning a careers day for current students on 25th March and are looking for some old girls to come and talk to the current pupils about their work since leaving school. Would you be interested in attending? We would all be very keen to hear about your career progression so do let me know.

Best wishes,

Wendy

My old school headmistress flashed into my mind, standing with her hands on her tweed skirt-covered hips and a stern look of disapproval plastered across her face. Career? I somehow didn't think she would appreciate my regaling the girls with tales from the Institute. I laughed and pushed her to the back of my mind, scrabbling away in the deep recesses of my brain for something suitable to say in answer to Rafa's question.

"Um, well. You tell her she has nice tits I suppose," I replied hesitantly, unsure what else to say.

"Now I'm going to give you pictures from magazines and I want you to write personal profiles for these people. So by personal profile I mean a name, age, appearance, pets, hobbies etc." I broke off having uttered all the sentences in one breath to ensure no one could chip in with a boob-related comment. Thankfully it worked and Alejandro asked sweetly,

"What is appearance?"

"It is a description of what a person looks like," I explained. "For example, describe my appearance."

"Titcher has no chest mountains," piped up Rafa. "No titties."

"Titcher has yellow hair."

"No Rafa, titcher is beautiful," said cute, dimpled Carlos earnestly, making me blush furiously to roars of laughter.

"Thank you Carlos," I replied, turning around to write beautiful on the board in order to avoid their stares and laughter.

Alejandro laughed, saying, "Ohh teacher, it's getting hot, we *encender*, how you say *encender*, we turn on the heat?! She has red face, titcher is red face! Oohhh, it's hot here!" Everyone cracked up yet again.

"Oooh, Carlos love teacher!"

"Teacher no love Carlos," objected Winston, strongly, "no is true."

"I think titcher love my brother Andrés," said Rafa.

I took a deep breath and turned round to face them.

"Enough!" I stamped my foot. "Titcher doesn't like any of you right now. Let's have a break – go and smoke but be back here in five minutes. FIVE MINUTES ONLY, OK?" I wondered whatever had possessed me to plan a class on body parts and appearances with a bunch of hormonal boys? Hindsight would be a wonderful thing, if it could only arrive a little earlier.

Ten minutes later my calm was restored and I passed out worksheets on the safer subject of comparative and superlative adjectives as they filtered back into the classroom.

"So, Cristian, number one please," I asked when they'd had time to go through them.

"Is happy, happier, happiest," he replied with a grin. "You are happy and I is happier!"

"Perfect, but I *am* happier. And Alejandro, number two?"

"I think is tinny, tinnier, tinniest. But what is tinny?"

"It's TINY, not tinny," I corrected, "and it means very, very small." I held up my thumb and forefinger close together to illustrate.

Rafa coyly leant over his desk, saying, "Titcher, can you use tinny to describe part of body?"

"You can use *tiny* to describe anything Rafa," I sighed, knowing exactly where this was going.

"*Jajaja*, so Carlos is tinny, titcher – he is TINNY." This was greeted by guffaws from the class and poor Carlos let out an expletive-laden tirade in defence of his manhood. I rapidly moved on to the next question.

"Quiet boys, come on. Let's continue. Hector, number three?"

"Is pretty, prettier, prettiest."

"Perfect. Can you give me an example?"

"Spanish girls prettier than English girls."

I giggled but before I could respond, as quick as a flash Winston piped up, "No, no, no, Eebee is the prettiest girl in the world."

"Haha, top marks Winston, an excellent use of the superlative," I said, chuckling away, "let's put that on the board shall we?!" I turned as they wolf whistled and made kissing noises like five-year-olds.

"Winston love Eebee," they chorused and I reluctantly

smiled, accepting that control had totally escaped my clutches yet again.

***

Was it really almost Christmas? With only ten days to go and a humungous, twinkling Christmas tree plonked in the centre of Puerta del Sol, along with painful holiday tunes ringing out from shops all over the city, there was no denying it any longer. The days passed crisp and wintery, and despite the consistently falling temperatures the sky still shone clear and glittering blue – a welcome and uplifting change from grizzly, grey English winters. I wrapped up warm in my big, blanket-like Zara scarf, skipped out of my last class of the week and sauntered down Fuencarral feeling like Cameron Diaz in *The Holiday*. Fiesta Friday had arrived at last.

Carmencita was heaving by the time I arrived, festive in my most Christmassy, sparkly top. I spotted Ethan talking to a pretty girl by the bar and headed over to join them.

"Hi Ethan, how's it going?" I asked.

"Hey Evie, have you met Kitty? She's just started working here."

"Hi Kitty, congrats!" I said. "Must be a fun place to work."

"It's awesome, I mean I love this bar and everyone is super-friendly," she gushed, with a heavy American twang.

"*Cañas* girls?" asked Ethan, "My round."

"Great, thanks," I replied, turning back to Kitty. "So, how long have you been living in Madrid?"

"It's been almost a year now although it's totally flown by," she said pensively, flicking her long blonde hair over her shoulder.

"Tell me about it. Time really flies here. Do you reckon you'll stay long?"

"You know what, I'm so happy here I skip down the street every day with a smile on my face. My senses were muffled back home in the US, like underwater, but here I feel perky and alert and I'm planning on staying as long as I have that feeling."

What a great answer. It summed up so perfectly the sense of positivity, possibility and options in the city – remarkable considering the state of the economy and the country, but true nonetheless.

"So what do you do Evie?"

"Well, I've ended up working as an English teacher in an Institute for mechanics. It's bizarre really and the guys only want to talk about sex and aeroplanes – neither of which are my topics of expertise!"

"Oh you love the blokey chat Evie, I know you do," joked Ethan, rejoining us with the drinks. "Have you taken any of them for a spin yet?"

I laughed. "You know, I have to admit I've had some truly hilarious moments with them, but I feel bad I haven't taught them anything about maintenance manuals, which is what they need. The other day I made them play *Simon Says* for twenty minutes when I ran out of materials."

"Haha, bet they hated that?" remarked Kitty.

"Yep, they sure did, but I got a real power trip from bossing them around. The more irritated they became, the more I enjoyed myself!" I laughed.

"So, any romance with the grease monkeys?" asked Kitty. "Sounds like an ideal hunting ground!"

"Hell no!" I exclaimed, "although some of them are actually quite sweet."

"She won't let any of them ignite her spark plugs," teased Ethan.

"Are you every going to stop with these crap jokes?!"

Laughing, I turned to Kitty, "To be honest, I have a MEGA crush on one of my business students, so none of the mechanics get a look in."

"Jorge? Your booze guy Jorge?" asked Ethan.

"The one and only," I nodded. "I still find myself swooning every time he walks into his class and I've been desperately flirting, but he never takes the bait."

Ethan laughed. "I can't believe you haven't sealed the deal yet! I told you, just do a class on clothes, and every time he learns a new piece of vocab you take off that piece of clothing. By the end of the lesson you're both naked and you throw yourself across the desk at him. Easy. No guy would say no."

"Of course," I laughed, "why hadn't I thought of that?!"

"Anyway, cheers people," I said, raising my glass, "I've extended my contract on the flat and so I'm definitely going to be here till the summer now. Bring on the fun times!"

***

A few hours later, I merrily hopped into a taxi over to *barrio* Salamanca for party *numero dos*, and from the moment I arrived at Inés' flat it was clear this was a very different vibe from the Carmencita jamboree. A maid in a black dress with a white frilly apron took my coat, presented me with a glass of Bucks Fizz and shepherded me through to the living room. I felt like a celebrity as Inés tottered across the room in incredible high heels, greeted me warmly and whisked me around introducing me to everyone.

"You remember Eebee don't you Alfonso? I told you all about Eebee," she gushed to a tall, dashing Spaniard.

"Ahh, Eebee, *sí*, Inés talks about you all the time. Next time we go to my house by the lake you must come too."

"And Emilio, let me present you Eebee, my English friend," my lovely hostess continued.

"Ahh, Eebee, *sí*, you are the wonderful English teacher who gives lessons to Inés. It is a great pleasure to meet you at last – we have heard a lot about you."

When this introductory whirlwind came to an end I found myself talking to José from Cordoba. Frightfully polite, he was immaculately dressed in a crisp paisley shirt and green velvet jacket with impeccably polished brogues boasting shiny buckles. I had heard men from Cordoba were known for their exceptional manners and class, but they can also be supremely arrogant and snobbish. This guy fit the bill perfectly – I couldn't fault him for kindness, interest and conversation, but when he said, "Spanish society is so closed, I'm surprised you're here Eebee," I wasn't sure whether to be flattered or affronted and felt disappointed by his lack of faith in his friend's attitudes.

I flitted between what felt like two different personalities throughout the night; at times a mute child, too self-conscious to attempt to speak in Spanish in front of a group, but then strangely comfortable in my familiar territory of making self-deprecating jokes when the conversation turned to English. I held court triumphantly, basking in the attention, when the conversation turned to my looks.

"Eebee, you is so exotic, so English," remarked José, admiringly.

"Thank you, I suppose. Do you say that because I'm as white as Michael Jackson?" I replied, flippantly.

"You are too funny, so funny," guffawed José, bent double in laughter. "Josefa, Lucia, you must meet Eebee, she is the funniest person," he continued, beckoning his friends over to join us.

"No, but seriously, this is actually quite tanned for me," I added. "I'm not sure I've ever been this brown."

"See," said José, turning to Regina and guffawing to the max, "*la inglesa es muy divertida*. She is very fun. She will do well in Madrid I think." The three of them fell about laughing as Regina glided over to the group, ignoring my smile.

"You have met Eebee? I no understand why Inés invite her teacher," she sneered with a frosty stare.

"Regina!" Inés exclaimed, "Eebee, I am so sorry, my sister she no like the English. Her boyfriend quit her for English teacher like you."

"Oh, I see," I replied meekly, my confidence bubble well and truly burst by Regina's words.

Patting my arm, Inés continued, "Come and I present you to Eduardo." Dressed in tight turquoise trousers, a crisp white shirt and a designer navy blazer, Eduardo completed his look with a silk cravat and seriously over-long slicked back brown hair. He was deep into a discussion with Cristina, a trendy-looking girl in leopard-print trousers, a leather jacket and massive mop of messy dyed blonde hair, about a ball he'd recently been to in a palace in Paris. With his American twang he told us how lavish it had been, how many thousands of people had attended, and what a privilege it had been to join them. Between flicks of his hair, he then started talking about how he was off to a ball in London next month.

"How interesting," I said, struggling not to let my inner giggles escape. I couldn't resist adding, "are you a professional ball-goer by trade?"

My sarcasm fell on deaf ears as he replied earnestly, "No, I work in investments actually."

"Ahh," I joked, "so a professional ball-goer and an investment banker. Sounds like a busy life!"

Cristina reached out to clasp his forearm, "And how much

it cost you these balls?" she asked in her husky voice, puffing away on a ciggie, and sizing him up.

Ignoring her, he turned to me and earnestly said, "Eebee, I would like to take you to dinner one day. It is important to know English people. Can you give me your number and we stay in contact?"

I laughed to myself and recited the digits of my number, wondering what on earth we would talk about.

"I call you now to give you my number," he said. "And we speak next week to make a plan." Smoothing his long locks back from his face he pressed the dial button and looked at me expectantly.

"Wait, it says me this number is incorrect. You give me wrong number?" he asked moments later, offended.

"Whoopsie, silly me," I giggled, looking over at the screen, "it should be a six at the end, not seven."

Cristina shuffled her feet, impatient to get back to the subject of his international party lifestyle.

"So you go to balls in England?" she wanted to know. "Have you met Kate Middleton?"

"Sorry, but no, I've never met her," I replied.

"Oh," they sighed, united in disappointment.

"She is so wonderful. If only Letizia is like her more," replied Eduardo, turning to Cristina.

"Exactly," she agreed, "Kate is perfect and Letizia no act like queen. She is so common." She shuddered in disgust and took another drag on her cigarette.

"I see in *Hola!* magazine this week she eat popcorn on Princesa Street!" she continued, indignantly, shaking her head, "is wrong. Kate never would do this. She is beautiful, royal person."

"Anyways, tell me who else you meet at your ball Eduardo,

Eebee and me come with you next time." She continued to flirt away in pursuit of an invitation.

***

In a rare Facebook status update the following morning, I wrote a post wishing farewell to Madrid until next year, "*Adiós Madrid y gracias por cuatros meses fenomenales. Hasta el próximo ano!*" and skipped off to Café Julia for my last *tostada con tomate* and *café con leche* of the year. Slouched at the departure gate a few hours later I logged on again to be greeted by twenty-seven comments underneath my status. Oops. It appears I had typed an *n* rather than an *ñ*, so rather than saying *until next year,* I had written *until the next anus.* Damn it, how embarrassing. How could so many of my friends suddenly be experts in Spanish? My cousin Ali led the charge with, "Hey, have you actually learnt any Spanish over there, or are you just shagging lots of men?! Your Spanish obvs *ñññeeds* a lot more practice!!!" I put the phone back in my pocket and boarded the plane with a grin.

11

The smell of London was different. It was a generic urban smell I suppose, but unfamiliar and lacking the richness of fumes lingering around Madrid. It was extraordinary how something so stupid could make me feel homesick, but I couldn't deny a cloud of sadness hung over me. Perched in EAT near Moorgate station, I stared out of the window in the midst of a massive crisis of confidence, the driving rain a perfect reflection of my mood. What I couldn't figure out is what I really felt homesick for (let's ignore the fact I had referred to Spain as home, itself a disturbing development in our merry little saga). Did I miss my life in Madrid? Yes. I was longing to return to the sun, cheap drinks, gorgeous men, constant sense of adventure, random conversations and meetings, lack of obligations and general quality of life. But something else niggled away at me – what if it was more of a desire to run away from London, rather than a specific desire to return to Madrid?

The last few days had undoubtedly unsettled me – hanging in the comfortable companionship of old friends, going back to my old flat and facing the inevitable onslaught of memories. Not to mention a two-day hangover and sheer exhaustion making it almost impossible to process everything that had happened recently, let alone sort out my head and my packing. What bugged me principally was the realisation that perhaps my whole, wondrous time in Spain was simply an exercise in escapism. Escape from my ridiculously huge family. Escape from social expectations and the feeling of being a failure and disappointment by not having bagged a husband. And escape from the general lack of direction in my life. If this was true, it made me feel pretty childish. But on the other hand, what's wrong with escapism – maybe I should embrace the fact I'd managed to flee London, particularly when it led me to such blissfully sunny climes? The real dilemma had to be whether it could continue long-term...

I'd been through a cycle of emotions since coming back to the UK. Initially, a deep hatred of London took over – *the weather is better in Madrid, everything is so much cheaper in Madrid, did you know in Madrid EVERYTHING'S PERFECT* I wanted to scream at every passer-by. I banged on about Spain to anyone who would listen and every bone in my body longed to be back there. Then after a few days with friends and family I settled back in to old routines and begin to realise how great all those people were. Yes, I had friends in Madrid, but not like the golden oldies in England who knew me inside out. And lastly I entered the current "stress" stage, dithering about whether I was doing the right thing and if I should move back to London.

Gazing gormlessly out of the window, I fought back tears of exhaustion, and watched the bustle of London life whistling past. Endless black- and grey-clad figures paced along the pavement, engrossed in their blackberries and phones. A harassed-looking FedEx man rushed through the glass doors of an imposing office building clutching papers and speaking into his headset. A horde of office workers chattered away as they headed back to the office with M&S sandwiches to be eaten at desks, crumbs falling into the keyboard as they surfed the *Daily Mail* website attempting to look busy and important. All of these people were strangers and yet their type so familiar. Together they represented a rut. A rut I had floundered in for eight years and a rut to which I did not wish to return. I can't deny it was comfortable, but I felt weak that a part of me craved its easy familiarity. The blonde girl in a belted camel coat and black suede boots could have been me a few years ago. She giggled into her phone making plans for the weekend, maybe off to meet a friend in Pret, or popping into Boots. I loved it at the time. Didn't I? I'd had a purpose, on the working treadmill, following the beaten path of life like so many others before me. At the risk of sounding melodramatic, it now felt like a toss-up between a life of novelty and relative adventure in Madrid (yes, ok, so I wasn't exactly herding goats in Mongolia or off on a solo Antarctic expedition), and a Return to the Rut. That would make a good name for a film, wouldn't it? Should we constantly be challenging ourselves, or is it better to recognise your comfort zone and stick to it? WHY was the grass always greener? My generation was so unsatisfiable. I have no idea if that is even a word, but I was a particularly bad example, so seemingly obsessed with originality and unable to stick anything out for too long. Argh, I couldn't keep thinking like this or I would drive myself crazy. Time to end the analysis paralysis.

***

Twenty-four hours later I lugged my bag wearily up the stairs of Moncloa metro station and the moment I emerged into the warm rays of bright sunshine, a wave of contentedness washed over me. My shoulders opened up, I held my head higher, and I grinned like a nutter as I skipped off to the flat. I was home.

After dumping my bags I sauntered off to Retiro to revel in my return to this glorious city. I loved the little things. The late afternoon sun cast a warm light over the trees and created a magical atmosphere. It was so uplifting I felt like a carefree, liberated child. It was the combination of the clouds of weed smoke wisping through the air, mixing with the tinny notes of the bagpipes floating up through the leaves. The crazy old man cutting some serious shapes while listening to his headphones, oblivious to all those watching and laughing. The three matriarchs enveloped in thick fur coats, wildly gesticulating and gossiping round a table as they knocked back *caña* after *caña*. The glistening droplets falling like diamonds in the sunshine made the most ordinary of fountains a work of art. Endless immaculately dressed children accompanied their parents on a *paseo* through the park without a care in the world and with no sense of urgency or purpose in their path. Did people in London ever walk this slowly? I doubt it, but I noticed these things in Madrid. And I *loved* them.

As I continued to stroll, I began to wonder if there was something essentially selfish about living abroad. Ever since I arrived last year I'd been overwhelmed by an immensely liberating sense of freedom. Why on earth did I previously get so stressed about calling all my friends, remembering birthdays, writing thank-you letters etc. I'd been remarkably lax about these things recently and of course it didn't matter. Madrid had given me distance from social and familial expectations and for the very first time, at the ripe old age of thirty, I felt truly independent.

At a family dinner over Christmas the children were so loving and adorable I had suddenly felt convinced it was time to move back, until in the middle of the meal, my niece Cecily piped up with *Auntie Evie, why are you such a disappointment? We've been praying every single night for you to get married. When are you going to hurry up and find your prince?* She was only ten, and it wasn't her fault her parents are so overwhelmingly obsessed with love and romance, but an irrational sense of fury boiled up inside me at the fact I had to deal with this same question ALL the time. No doubt they meant well, but it was immensely frustrating. I felt absolutely no pressure in Madrid to be married, to have children or to be on any particular path – life was more relaxed and society less rigid. Maybe it was just expat life in general where you are one step removed from the routine of reality. Spaniards growing up in Madrid may well feel the same restraints I did back home, but I felt an unparalleled sense of freedom in the city and it seriously appealed. Thoughts of returning to England were banished from my mind.

***

Happily committed to Madrid for the time being, priority *numero uno* had to be improving my Spanish. General criticism of my linguistic skills over Christmas had hurt more than I'd care to admit, and I was dying to understand what the mechanics said about me in class. Capitalising on a wave of proactiveness I logged onto lingocambio.com and posted an advert for an *intercambio*, only just managing to confirm the post before my battery died. I had a quick shower and then pulled my phone off the charger, heading out to meet Molly and Chloe for supper in El Perejil on Cava Baja. *Como siempre*, I arrived first – I still hadn't got the hang of everyone always being late for everything in Spain – and I nursed a glass of vermouth as I waited. Glancing at my phone I gasped in astonishment – within less than an hour I had received *fifteen* emails in response to the ad. My chest swelled with pride at my popularity.

The girls arrived before I had a chance to read them, so I put my phone back in my bag and turned my attention to the conversation.

"I love this place, don't you?" said Chloe, as she made a great effort to fit her long legs under the small, wooden table. "It's so authentic." *Peinetas*, patterned fans and bullfighting prints covered the walls and shelves, along with vintage Tio Pepe posters and sepia photographs. A deep green covered the walls behind, and there was a wonderfully buzzing and chaotic ambiance.

"Urgh, I suppose so," answered Molly, begrudgingly. "But can we go somewhere less Spanish next time?" She ran her finger over the table and screwed up her nose at the dirt it accumulated.

Ignoring the general cleanliness of the place, we ordered partridge pâté, olives, *jamón, pulpo a la gallega* and caught up on all the gossip over a steady flow of vermouth.

"It's so depressing," said Chloe, "I thought I could speak Spanish – I've studied it for eight bloody years now – but I don't have a clue what those people are on about," she added, waving at the locals at the table next door. "At least now my contract's been extended I'll have more time to practise, I s'pose."

"I'm so glad you're not leaving yet, and don't worry about your Spanish, it's far better than mine," I replied, despondently. "I'm not sure I'm ever going to get the hang of it."

"Are you still having lessons?" asked Molly.

"I need to find a teacher, but I'm reluctant to spend too much money on classes, so I put up an ad for an *intercambio* this afternoon."

"In fact, check this out," I continued, pulling out my phone to show them my inbox.

"OMG," I screeched in surprise as I looked at the screen, "It's up to forty-one responses already!"

"Here, gimme a look," exclaimed Chloe, grabbing the phone from my hand and flicking through the messages. "Ooh, Santi's a hottie. No wait, hang on, Javi. I'd go for Javi. Who needs Tinder when there's Lingocambio. This is amazing!"

"Let's see," said Molly, "I'm her official dating advisor, so I get to make the final choice."

"This one sounds a bit dumb, 'Hola Evie, My name is Rafa and I'm twenty-eight. My level in English is B1 and I want to improve. I am a Spanish. In fact, I speak Spanish very well.' Well, I should hope you do speak Spanish very well Rafa, if you are Spanish!" she chuckled.

I scoffed my way through the remains of the *pulpo* and mashed potato as she scrolled through.

"How about this one. 'Hello Evie, How are you? I am fine and hope you are in the very best of your health. I am *muy* interested in the language exchange with beautiful ladies as I am keen of doing TEFL next year. Touch me by email, or you got skype or WhatsApp so we can know each others more intimately? I want touch you. All right, take care, peace out, Shah.'"

"Are there any normal ones?" I laughed.

"This one's the best!" Molly exclaimed. "You gotta listen to this.

"So," she continued, grinning and raising her voice dramatically, "Arturo."

"I love the name Arturo," I cooed.

"Well, Arturo says '*Hola Evie, soy masajista gay y preparo Advanced, sí quieres intercambiamos conversación en inglesex*

140

masaje. Cheers, Art'." She paused as the giggles took hold and her entire body shook with laughter. "He wants English AND sex – a win win situation!!"

"Lemme see," I grabbed back the phone.

Was a gay guy offering me an English sex massage?! What the hell was that?! Scrolling through the email I realised *inglesex* must be a typo and he'd probably intended to write *inglés x masaje* – he'd like an English lesson in exchange for a massage.

"Does he want me to know he was gay so I won't be worried about getting naked in front of him?!"

"Only one way to find out," urged Chloe.

On the way home I pondered the responses – the majority had sent pretty standard messages and I had no idea how to choose between them. Did I reply to Enrique who wants help for a job interview, Juan who designs furniture and sent me a photo of himself flanked by two Zulu warriors in South Africa, Valentin whose email address is ripperthe-stripper@hotmail.com or David who's definitely looking to hit on English girls, but has offered to teach me how to play padel which I've always been intrigued by? I had no idea. Oh well, I thought, maybe this isn't such a good idea after all. There must be an easier way to improve my Spanish.

***

Almost unaware of the cold in the flat the next morning, I stared in shock at the emails continuing to flood into my inbox. Reading through them I concluded they were still mostly more oddballs or boring generic responses, so I texted Belinda and arranged to meet for lunch in Malasaña. Food was a necessity right now, as was somewhere with some central heating.

I found her waiting when I arrived, and she leapt up to greet me.

"So, how was home? Tell me all about your Christmas. Did you survive all your family?"

"Just about," I replied, sinking low into a vintage armchair in the corner of Café de la Luz. I loved this place, but even its retro furniture, tasselled lampshades and delectable carrot cake were going to struggle to perk me up today. "It was fine. I shouldn't complain, but I feel in need of a holiday again already. It was all pretty chaotic."

"I don't envy you with all those kids. At least with my two nieces it's all quite civilised and they're good at going to bed relatively early."

"It just takes soooo long to do ANYTHING when children are involved. I mean, you need twenty minutes to find their clothes and get them kitted up to go outside in this weather. Then after the whole palaver, the instant you make it outside they slip on some ice, fall flat on their face, you're deafened by their wails and you all head back to the kitchen for *yet* another cup of tea."

"Rather you than me," she shuddered, "how about your parents? It must have been good to see them?"

"Yes, it was, but poor Mum was run off her feet looking after everyone so I didn't see too much of her. Dad appreciates the need for normal, child-free conversation so we played G&T-fuelled games of Scrabble hiding in his study."

"Did you catch up with many friends?" she asked, placing a large forkful of salad into her mouth.

"Yep, I saw quite a few," I hesitated, twirling my glass round and round, "and it was lovely to see them, but I got so fed up with their questions."

"Let me guess. They wanted to know if you eat *tapas* all day long?"

"Haha, yes," I agreed.

"And how many hot Spanish bullfighters are you dating?"

"Yep, and their disappointment when I admitted I haven't even met one!"

"The one that really gets on my nerves, oh, so you must be fluent in Spanish by now?"

"I mean," I agreed, "I know I'm not a natural at languages but I reckon you'd have to be superhuman to master it in three months."

"Don't worry, I've been here nearly two years and I'm no better than you."

"What's wrong with us?!"

"Nothing you idiot! But if we really want to be fluent we need to be strict, study more and not hang out with English people."

"I can't face it now, not with all the lesson prep I need to do. At the end of the day it's enough of an effort to string a sentence together in English, let alone attempt to speak in Spanish!" I exclaimed, "But I'm on the case trying to find an *intercambio*."

"Good plan. I used meet up with a Spanish guy last year and it really helped. He moved to Peru annoyingly, but I should get on the case with finding someone too."

"By the way, did I tell you a girl called Rebeca moved into our tiny box room at Christmas? The landlord finally got around to fixing the leak. She doesn't speak a word of English so hopefully that'll help me."

"Ideal," she replied. "What's her story?"

"Well, she's a flamenco dancer from the south. She's pretty glamorous and to be honest a bit intimidating. I love listening to her and Carolina witter away in Spanish though and I'm sure some of it must be sinking in. Hope so anyway. She has a great friend who starred in last year's season of

The Voice and he keeps coming over and giving impromptu concerts which is pretty cool."

"Oh by the way," she said, "speaking of concerts, the Love of Lesbian tickets for next week are all sold out. Sorry."

"Damn, I wish we'd thought about it earlier. Thanks for trying." I raised a fork of cake into my mouth, a misshapen walnut lodged in its creamy icing, and let out a groan of delight. "This is so damn good."

"It almost rivals Carmencita's cake, doesn't it? I'm still listening to *Incendios de Nieve* all the time – I love it. We'll have to get tickets next time," she said.

I continued, "Actually, I nearly forgot. This'll make you laugh. One day in the holidays everyone had gone out and I was having Madrid withdrawal symptoms, so I put some Spanish music on YouTube.

"Well, I thought nothing more of it and the next day when Mum and I were driving to the supermarket, she kept shifting around nervously in her seat. She obviously wanted to ask me something but couldn't quite bring herself to say it. After much huffing and puffing she suddenly blurted out *Darling, is there something I should know? Is there something you need to tell me?* I had absolutely no idea what she was on about. Then she exclaimed, *I mean, I found LESBIAN websites on the computer last night. Is it…are you…I mean… of course you can tell us and it would be quite alright, but I'd really rather know…* My mind went blank as she warbled on and then I realised I must have left the Love of Lesbian YouTube page open. She hadn't even looked at the site – she'd closed it down in case the kids came in and saw it – and so she'd obviously had a sleepless night about the whole thing!!"

We giggled away.

"My mother still thinks I date guys, despite having met Gabriella several times!"

"Classic," I replied, laughing, "how's it all going? I can't believe I've only met her once – are you ashamed of me?!"

"Haha, no, I'm sorry. It's crazy how much she is away at the moment and when she is here it's always so brief we end up spending time just the two of us. I promise I will sort out a proper meeting soon."

"Ace."

"Her current film should be finished in the next few weeks, so hopefully life will be a little more normal after that."

"It's so nice to be back here, gossiping away," I sighed. "It really does feel like I've come home."

"It *is* your home, silly. Now tell me what's going on with your work, and any gossip to report from the Christmas holidays?"

"*Nada,* zilch, literally nuffink. But, I'm actually going on a date tomorrow with a guy called Raul."

"Raul? Who is he?"

"I met him at one of Carolina's friends' Christmas parties. He's from a *pueblo* outside Valladolid where apparently they speak the best Spanish, so he's offered to help me practise. In fact maybe he can become my *intercambio!*"

"Ahh, interesting. Very interesting indeed. Do you like him? And what about Ramón?!" she asked with a wink.

"To be honest I barely remember Raul, and as for Ramón," I chuckled, "he's stopped harassing me with messages now so I imagine he's found some other poor soul to lavish his attention on!

"It's so frustrating. Jorge is the only guy I really like and that's evidently going nowhere. He chortles away at my jokes and we have such a good time in his classes, yet he seems oblivious to my adoration. For all I know he has some super glamorous girlfriend and I don't stand a chance," I said, glumly.

"I can't believe you still don't even know if he has a girl-friend, but you never know. It sounds like you guys get on well and men are always impossible to read."

"You're right, and anyway, speaking of men, I should go and do some prep for the mechanics. I'm a bit worried about starting there again tomorrow."

"You'll be fine, I'm sure of it," she assured me, in her end-lessly positive manner.

"I would be if I could find any vaguely technical stuff or books to help. They are losing patience with my random games and activities. One of them even had the nerve to ask me if I had a course plan back in December."

"What cheek! What did you say?"

"I blushed, for a change, and said I was working on it. He made me feel like a bleeding child."

"It's all character building!" she laughed and sauntered off down the street while I headed home.

12

Was it listening to the heartfelt tunes of Rodriguez on my iPod? Or the fact I'd just had a large glass of Ribera in a Tabernita so my cheeks were a little rosy? I loved the guilty indulgence of stopping for a glass of wine on my way home, and happily justified it by sitting at the bar and chatting to the barman – who could argue with free Spanish practice? I couldn't put my finger on why exactly, but I felt deliriously happy again after a dull, rainy grey morning.

Let's be honest, the real reason I'd perked up was Jorge had called to arrange his lesson for next week and his chat never failed to brighten my day. I'd been trying hard to forget about him over Christmas, but it pained me to admit he'd never been far from my thoughts, and I'd loved relaying his jokes to my pals back in London. Now my lessons were starting again and I was getting back into the swing of things I felt mega chuffed to be back "home". Jorge also provided a welcome distraction from the nerves building in anticipation of my imminent date.

Truth be told I wasn't entirely sure I would recognise Raul, and a quick peek at his blurry Facebook photos hadn't helped. I scanned through his first message again, "Hola Evie, I made my research looking for you, *espero que no te moleste*, the other day we were having a very nice conversation and i no know what happened, but you disappeared or maybe i was drunk and i didnt see you...or I'm thinking right now perhaps you hide from me? If that so...*Quizás no quieras tomar un café conmigo un día de estos* and chat more? *Un beso* and Merry Christmas!!"

Despite not remembering him, I found his mix of English and Spanish endearing and we'd arranged to meet up but now I was feeling a wee bit apprehensive. Approaching Bilbao metro station, I spotted him perched on the railings opposite Café Commercial, seeming equally anxious. Ridiculous. Two grown adults going for a drink and we both looked like we'd prefer to be having root canal treatment. Tall and dark with an attractive spread of stubble covering his chin and lower cheeks, the retro, wire-rimmed glasses perched on the end of his nose gave him a literary air. Wrapped up in a large navy jacket, he turned up the collar and stuffed his hands into his pockets before kissing me warmly and launching into a Spanish verbal typhoon. I clearly wasn't the only one with a dodgy memory and it appeared he thought I could speak Spanish fluently. In fact, rather disconcertingly considering the blankness of my mind, he knew all kinds of things about me and said we'd spoken for over an hour in Spanish at the party. As we pottered around for a while I set him straight on my true level of Spanish and we settled in an old-fashioned bar on a back street off Gran Vía. I leant back in a window booth, studying him as he shuffled to the bar and ordered drinks. Taking in his navy jumper, ripped jeans and faded green trainers, I concluded he was cutely scruffy. I was unconvinced by the serpent tattoo that wound around his neck and I wouldn't describe him as remotely *my type,* but he was intriguingly enigmatic and pretty attractive nonetheless.

He soon returned with *cañas, chorizo* and olives and leant across to grasp my thigh, sending my pulse racing.

"All good Eebee?"

"Indeedy. *Salud*," I smiled, raising my glass to clink with his, happily realising his hand still lingered on my leg and I was becoming accustomed to the human contact so integral a part of communication here.

"You Spaniards like to touch, don't you?" I remarked, laughing as he clocked me looking at his hand. "I feel like I'm always being pawed and patted here."

"You no like it?!" he smiled, slowly removing his hand.

"I hated it at first. We Brits love our personal space, while you Spaniards invade it at every opportunity. Conversation is like a contact sport here."

He laughed.

"But," I continued, "I love it now and kissing everyone is so much more friendly than shaking hands."

"You like kissing everyone?" he teased.

"Not like that!" I tittered.

"*Sí, sí*, you English are very cold with your shaking hands."

"Maybe," I admitted.

"So, tell me about your work. You told to me at the party that you teach *mechanicos* in an *instituto técnico*?" he said. "You like the men, huh?! You kiss them all too?!"

"Haha, definitely no kissing there," I stated emphatically. "But yes, I teach English."

"Conversation?"

"Basically, yes, although it's supposed to be technical English so they can understand maintenance manuals, but I know nothing about engines so we stick to general stuff."

"We should not get on airplanes if your students fixed them," he said, chuckling warmly.

"Yep, good plan. Avoid the Iberia ones. Although I was delving around in the library at the Institute the other day and I came across a book called *Technical English* which I hope will help me teach them something more useful. I nearly wept for joy."

"A book made you cry? You English, you is strange."

"Not literally, it's an expression! I'm not entirely sure the book is relevant for them, but for the sake of my sanity I'm going to use it all the time and hopefully it will help a bit with the plane stuff. The only problem was the CD is so badly scratched I had to record all the listening exercises with a friend, putting on different accents."

"Sounds funny."

"Our accents are terrible and we laugh all the time, but it's better than nothing I suppose."

"You must tell me how goes it and I would like to meet these mechanics one day. They are lucky to have you." Smiling, he reached across and gripped my knee once more.

"Enough about me, let's talk about you. What do you do?" I asked, popping a piece of glistening chorizo into my mouth to distract from the burning touch of his hand.

"I work for an insurance company. Is good job, but is not *muy interesante*," he laughed, gently stroking his stubbly chin.

"I prefer to talk about you Eebee Fuller. Do you like to read?" he asked, taking off his glasses and cleaning the lenses on his sweater.

"Yes, although I don't read much at the moment."

"You must read in espanish," he said earnestly. "Is the only way to improve."

"I know," I replied, nodding. "I really must, but the only thing I've managed so far is *Esio Trot* by Roald Dahl."

"I know the perfect book to make your espanish fly. I will search it at home tonight," he said keenly, "don't you worry. With my help you will be fluent in no time!"

The rest of the evening passed in a blur and I realised how

much I enjoyed male company. His gave me goose bumps every time his hand clasped my arm or leg, and I could still feel his touch as I lay in bed that night.

***

The next day, armed with my *Technical English* book, I decided to attempt Unit 1: Parts – Assembling a skateboard.

"Morning boys, do any of you like skateboarding?"

"Yes titcher, we like skateboard in break times. You must come watch."

"Alvaro is on video YouTube with skateboard."

"Is he? Right, well if we finish this in time we can watch it at the end of the class. First though we are going to start with labelling this diagram of a skateboard." God it made a difference having a book to work with. We had barely even started the lesson, but I felt so much more in control. I handed out the sheets and returned to my desk where a text message diverted my attention. "*Halagar* – your new Spanish word for the day. It means flatter. I am flattered you spend evening with me Evie Fuller. You are very special and I hope see you soon. *Besitos*." Raul's words made the hairs on my arms stand up and I couldn't stop a grin spreading over my face. Moments later I cleared my throat, looked up at the boys and began to go through the answers.

"Which bit is the axle?" I asked them.

"The axley? I think the axley is number 2," said cute Carlos with his dimpled grin.

"Yep, correct, it is number 2, but it's pronounced axle."

"Axley?" he repeated.

Never mind. Pretending not to hear him I continued, "which part is the deck?"

"Teacher, what's a dick?"

I looked up quickly, "what?" I asked.

"What's a dick?" he repeated.

I couldn't help but snigger childishly. "A DECK is the flat part of the skateboard, the bit you put your feet on."

Carlos flapped his t-shirt around, muttering, "Ufff, it's hot in classroom."

"Is because you're shitting by the radiator," replied Ricardo.

This time I really couldn't control my laughter. I corrected him to *sitting* and made a mental note to urgently work on their pronunciation.

Winston was still struggling with the skateboard deck, "Is number 3 the dick?"

"Deck," I corrected.

Rafa innocently asked, "Why the two different?"

"They just are, ok?" I sighed. "And you know it. A deck is part of a skateboard and a dick is part of a man," I explained, writing both clearly on the board.

I could see the blue B37 approaching the roundabout as I left the building an hour later, and I sprinted across the road still bewildered we'd spent a significant amount of the class talking about dicks. What was happening? I leapt on the bus and as we trundled off towards the city centre I reflected on how much my life had changed over the last few months and how much I had begun to care about the mechanics and their English progress. Despite the frustrations, the adrenaline rush I got from an entertaining class was unbeatable, and the ability of the boys to make me chuckle, both with and at them, boundless.

On my way to Jorge's class the following day, I reminded myself of my new mantra: New Year, New Attitude. The plan was to turn over a new leaf and be the very definition of professional in his classes. Note to self, stop gazing adoringly at the top of his head while he completes worksheets, and no more tittering like a schoolgirl at everything he says. I strode confidently into his office full of resolve.

"Hey, what's cooking good looking?" he asked with a wink as he swaggered over to me. My knees went weak and my face flamed as he kissed me on both cheeks. Staying business-like was proving to be harder than I thought.

"How was your Christmas?" he asked, throwing his books on the desk and lazily pushing his hair back from his face.

"Lovely thanks, although I'm super happy to be back," I replied, struggling to get the words out, my throat as dry as a bone.

"Of course, Spain is the best place in the world," he stated, beaming.

"How were your holidays?" I asked.

"I had awesum Christmas. Jorge goes, no Jorge went to America. Yeah baby!" he replied, with a terrible attempt at an American twang.

"Lucky you! Where did you go?" I enquired, grinning and leaning back in my chair. Boy I had missed his infectious enthusiasm and ridiculous waffle.

"Da Big Apple, Jorge went to New York to visit friend. It was awesum. Totally rad," he burbled.

"*Mira*, look, I show you photos," he continued eagerly, as he whipped a shiny silver phone out of his pocket and I continued to laugh at his appalling American accent.

"Another new telephone? Good effort!"

"Yes, is important. It has new fitchers. You turn in, no, turn on with this finger and for English is *muy* useful because there is voice translator. I show you," and he opened up the app on his screen.

"*Por ejemplo*, I no know what means this word effort you say. I no know the word, so I say to phone EFFORT... and...she tell me..."

"Translate FUCK," replied a computer-generated female voice.

My laughter did nothing to divert his determination as he fiddled about with the phone.

"No, I try again…EFFORT"

"Translate FUCK," she responded flatly.

"Ok, ok, we try different word," he muttered sheepishly, scanning the worksheet for another example. "Ok, here. I no understand the word borrow. *Qué significa* borrow?"

"It means to…" I stopped when he jerked his hand up in the air. "No! You no say me. I use phone. This time it give answer on screen."

"Ok! What does it say?"

"BORROW" he articulated clearly into the microphone.

Two seconds later the word *porno* flashed up on the screen.

He had one final attempt before admitting defeat and shamefacedly closing the app.

"Show me your photos anyway," I prompted, curious to see what he got up to on his holidays.

Leaning over the desk I cooed enthusiastically as he flicked through a series of pictures of him posing artfully outside American landmarks. The final one showed him in a backwards baseball cap and sunglasses outside an American shop, posing with a huge Wonka chocolate bar.

"Look, is from Charlie and *fábrica*, how you say *fábrica?*"

"Factory?"

"*Sí*, is Charlie and the Chocolate Factory. It's me with a Willy Wanker bar."

Uncontrollable giggles took hold of my body and I buried my face in my hands.

"What, what I say?" he asked innocently, as I continued to convulse.

"Nothing, nothing, but be careful with your pronunciation

of Wonker," I articulated clearly, avoiding all eye contact.

"What I say?" he replied, still clueless.

"Don't worry, let's move on to some work," I said, flicking through the book and determined to at least attempt a proper class.

"Ah, here we go. The next chapter is called *Holiday Friends*. It covers phrases like keeping in touch, getting home OK etc. I think it might be too easy for you. Shall we leave it and move on to the next chapter?"

Ever the diligent student he responded keenly.

"Noooooo, I like the book. We do it fast and then next chapter."

"Okey, dokey, chapter 6 it is," I said reluctantly, moving to the questions in the warm-up section. "Ok, so do you ever make holiday friends?" He chortled heartily, the warm, deep sound making me blush profusely. So much for the end of my crush.

"Well, last summer I went to Cádiz. There was a friend Paco, and we walked along the beach *cogiendonos de las manos*. You say taking hands? *Sí*. We was holding hands. The sun was leaving, was going down and it was very romantic." Wistfully peering out of the window, he carefully avoided eye contact.

"We had romantic dinner on the beach with candles. It was all perfect. He was a good friend."

OMG. The penny dropped. I CAN'T BELIEVE IT. He's gay. Could he really be gay? Could I really have wasted so much time thinking about him when he was gay all along? Noooooooooooo.

"Do you keep in touch with Paco now? Did you see him again?" I asked, incredulous.

He looked crestfallen, and turned his eyes back to the window.

"Is difficult. Paco lives in Morocco," he whispered.

"But he can still come and visit, no?"

"He doesn't have papers. He can't get papers. He lives in Morocco and works in an *alfombra* shop. In carpet shop." His voice cracked, and my jaw dropped down towards the desk.

My brain whizzing and whirring, I frantically tried to process these revelations. GAY. But of course. It makes so much sense. He's very good-looking. He dresses so well. He makes such an effort with his appearance. *Of course he's gay.* Hell, the other day he'd been late for his class because he'd gone for a face peel. How many straight men have face peels, let alone own up to it?

Silence hung in the air, when suddenly his hand smacked down on the table and a peel of hearty guffaws erupted from deep inside his abdomen.

"*Es broma*, is joke, *es broma!!!*" he announced gleefully.

"What?" I replied, dumbfounded.

"Is joke! I is joking!" he repeated.

"What? I don't understand – you mean there is no Paco?"

"Noooooooooooooo!" he cried, mortified, "I am not a gay gay!"

"Gay GUY," I corrected.

"But...but..." I stuttered, bewildered, "you looked so sad when you were talking about Paco."

"Haha, you estupid! You believe me! But is not true story – of course I'm not a gay gay. I am actor very good," he declared, puffing out his chest with pride.

I began to laugh so much the tears flowed down my cheeks and my body shook.

"I take your hair, you say in English? *Tomar el pelo?*"

"What? You can't have my hair! *Tomar el pelo* means to *pull someone's leg* in English. You were pulling my leg!"

"So have you ever even been to Morocco?" I asked, attempting to restore order.

"*Sí, sí,* many times. Is easy from Spain. And you?"

"I've never been to Africa," I replied.

"Don't you like black people?" he laughed. "You should go Morocco, they make good cake there. You try hashish cake?"

His loud barrel laughs still echoed in my ears as I left their offices, and I smiled at the realisation that my new professional attitude in his classes hadn't even lasted an hour.

13

Pride exudes from every pore of Spaniards. Since returning to Madrid post Christmas I had become even more aware of how it influences all aspects of their lives. I asked my students where they had been over the holidays and almost without exception they replied, "*I go my village.*" Ignoring the grammatical error, I found it fascinating how no one actually named their village, it was simply *my* village, regardless of whether they had ever lived there, or if in fact it was just where their family originally came from. With further probing they would disclose more details; they weren't from Spain, they weren't even from Andalucía or Asturias, Seville or Segovia, they hailed from Veguellina de Orbigo, Laguardia, Zestoa or some other place I'd almost certainly never heard of. A strong rivalry existed between the areas and they went to great lengths to persuade me their landscapes, food and people were the best in the country.

What a contrast to my own attitude. Whenever a Spaniard asked me where I came from I automatically said London, for two reasons. Firstly, everyone's heard of London and I couldn't be bothered to try and explain where Essex is, let alone the real name of the teeny tiny hamlet where my parents live. Secondly, Essex-girl jokes had haunted me throughout my life, and although barely anyone over here would have a clue about the connotations, it was deeply engrained in me not to mention it. Ridiculous, I know. Their pride and confidence in their villages, their country and themselves left a deep impression on me. I noticed it walking down the streets – people look up, they look around and they don't trudge along, gazing at the ground, their shoulders drooped, like people in England. Maybe it's because they like to look. I'd been in Spain quite a while now and I still hadn't got used to the staring on the metro, in fact to the staring everywhere. And the funny thing is that they don't even have a verb "to stare" in Spanish. Instead they say *mirar fijamente*, to look intently, and boy do they like to look intently.

***

The mechanics tried my patience more than usual in the run-up to their exams, and I couldn't wait for the distraction of my second date with Raul. He bounded up to me by the metro and kissed me warmly, his bristly cheeks tickling my face, before we linked arms and pottered down Calle de Alberto Aguilera. We stepped into a typically old-school *taberna* with VINOS written in swirly gold writing above the door, and blue and white patterned tiles lining the walls. A smell of vinegar, olive oil and stale alcohol hung in the air as we perched on high stools by the bar, chatting away.

"So, tell me about your work Eebee Fuller, how is it going?"

"I've had such a long day," I sighed, leaning on the bar and resting my head on my hand.

"*Pobre*," he sympathised, rubbing my thigh. "The boys were bad?"

"I can't control them at all and I don't really have a clue what I'm doing."

"I'm sure you are a great teacher," he assured me, with

more leg patting, his kind words making me feel tearful all of a sudden.

"Thanks, but let's not talk about them. No more mechanics chat tonight!"

"Ok, it's a deal. *Trato hecho*," and he stuck out his hand.

"Great," I replied, shaking it but keeping my eyes focused intently on the grubby floor tiles.

"I have something for you, something to help with your espanish," he said, grinning, as he whipped a brown paper FNAC bag out of his pocket and proudly handed me a flat package.

"You got me a present!" I exclaimed, "That's so kind." I excitedly pulled back the paper and unwrapped a bright orange hardback book entitled, *Mi primer diccionario en imágenes.*

"Is perfect for you. You like it?" he asked, eagerly.

I looked at the little red house, tree and balloons brightly depicted on the cover. A children's picture dictionary. My shoulders slumped as the penny dropped.

"Is my Spanish really terrible?" I asked, offended. I flicked through the pages, past body parts, furniture, animals and a whole host of basic vocabulary.

"Here, look," he said, taking it from me and showing me a handwritten message on the first page, "*Evie, espero que te ayude a mejorar tu español, un beso grande, Raul*" * followed by an unintelligible scribble. He smiled and waited expectantly for a response as I tried to decipher the words.

"What does this say?" I asked, pointing to the scrawl.

"Whaaaatt," he squealed, sounding more than a wee bit like a high-pitched Mrs Doubtfire as he rocked back in his chair and slapped his leg. "You really don't know what it

---

* Evie, I hope this helps you improve your Spanish, a big kiss, Raul.

means…?" He sucked his teeth and stared at me with pity. "Your espanish urgently needs my help."

"Well, what is it? The problem is your writing, not my Spanish – I can't even read it!" I retorted, my cheeks flushed and my pride wounded.

Laughing, he stroked his chin between his thumb and forefinger, in no rush to elaborate further. I shifted uncomfortably as his laughs echoed off the tiles, and heads turned in our direction. He leant over, his hand burning yet another hole in my leg, and whispered, "It means fuck, it's our first fuck." Oh god, is that what he was expecting tonight? I studiously avoided his stare and twiddled my hair round my finger, wanting nothing more than to pull it into a curtain I could hide behind. Instead I buried my burning face in the book again pretending to read, when he pulled another package out of his pocket.

"*Es una broma, una broma,* don't worry, the book is a joke! This is your true present," he chuckled, as he handed me another package and I unwrapped a slim, green paperback titled *Siddhartha* by Hermann Hesse.

"You know it?" he asked.

I shook my head. "I've never heard of it."

"Is very famous. Go on, read it. Read some to me," he said enthusiastically, as he sipped his *caña.*

Reluctantly I opened it and scanned the first page, my heart sinking as I realised I could barely understand a word in the first paragraph.

I gulped, "You're so kind, thank you. But I think I'll save it for later."

"Go on, read me some," he pleaded, looking disappointed.

I shook my head firmly, "Not now. I will next time. Thank you though, and I promise by the time I next see you I will have read lots."

Conversation thankfully soon moved away from my dismal Spanish as we pottered arm in arm around the streets of Malasaña. He wasn't a typical Spaniard by any stretch of the imagination and he loved to press for opinions on usually untouched subjects and to be antagonistic for the sake of it – something I usually thought immensely irritating but for once found rather refreshing. The streets buzzed with folk popping in and out of all the different bars and we weaved our way through the throng until we stumbled upon Plaza Dos de Mayo. A sea of people were merrily drinking in the centre of the square, wrapped up in fur and coats, many swaying their hips to an impromptu jam session. We continued out the other side, past vermouth bars full of aged, jowly men, hipster cafés with bicycles hanging from the ceilings and down streets decorated with colourful graffiti. Before we knew it we found ourselves outside Carmencita.

"Shall we go here?" he asked. "My friend has told me is nice."

"Sure, I love this place," I answered, pulling open the door. "The owner is a friend of mine."

We perched up on white stools by the bar, and when Miriam emerged from the kitchen she greeted us with a loud shriek, "Oh look, if it isn't one of my favourite people in the world. Eebee, are you on a DATE?!" she cried, giving me a massive wink and clapping her hands together. "How exciting! Juan," she shouted through to the kitchen, "*cañas* and *nachos* on the house for the lovebirds over here!"

Chuckling, Raul headed to the bathroom, hitching up his jeans as he went, while Miriam leant conspiratorially over the bar and continued with her interrogation, "SoOoOoOo how's it going? I must text Molly and tell her you're here. I can't believe you're on a date. This is too exciting!"

"Will you calm down," I chuckled, "I never would have come here if I'd known you'd be so embarrassing!"

She laughed and clapped her hands together again with a grin on her face. Raul returned and we spent the rest of the evening chatting, eating and drinking, with Miriam constantly eavesdropping in the most unsubtle of ways. When the bar closed he walked me home and lingered on the doorstep. "I've had a really good time tonight, thank you," I said, softly. And it was true. My cheeks ached from smiling, and all my earlier tension and stress over the mechanics was a distant memory.

Overwhelmed with gratitude and an undeniable wave of attraction I leant forward and lightly kissed him on the lips. He pulled my face to his and hungrily kissed me back. The touch of his rough lips made my body quiver and as I melted in to him I felt his heart pounding through his jacket. His hands moved down, slipped under my top and squeezed my waist, their cold electrifying my warm flesh.

"Let's go up," I whispered, my pulse quickening as he ran his thumb under my bra.

"Are you sure?" he asked, cupping my face in his hands as desire flooded his eyes.

"*Claro*," I replied with a smile, turning to unlock the door, taking his hand and leading him up the stairs.

***

Familiar, yet surreal, my life still felt like a film. It was in the early mornings I was most conscious of the fact I was living in a foreign country. The sunlight-dappled shuttered windows, the wrought iron balconies, the small, diagonal patterns of the paving stones and the beeping that accompanied the traffic lights had so recently been unfamiliar to my English ears and yet now, in those early mornings, with the pavement cleaning machines chugging by, I felt totally at home. Euros no longer felt like Monopoly money and the laminated tourist map had been happily put away for sporadic moments of exploration rather than everyday use. Time was whizzing by and I couldn't believe I felt so settled in Madrid already.

We soon welcomed the month of February. Freezing temperatures had taken hold of the city, and the still leafless trees cut dramatic silhouettes against the blue sky. So much had happened in the last six months, but this gorgeous, expansive cobalt sky had remained a loyal companion throughout.

The Spanish pride was rubbing off on me and I felt particularly chuffed with myself. Teaching was bloody exhausting and it was turning me into a complete bore who moaned about being tired all the time, but this was the first Friday night in a month I had managed to stay up past 9pm, which definitely called for a celebration. What was the point of living in a city famous for its nightlife if you weren't making the most of it?

I skipped down Fuencarral to meet Paige and Caitlin, two American girls who had been in my Spanish classes back in August. We'd learnt that there are more bars in Madrid per person than anywhere else in the world, so we'd decided to visit as many as we could over the next few months. First off we headed to El Tigre which had been recommended as something of a rite of passage for all *guiris*. Feeling slightly sceptical, we were locals now after all, but too happy it was the weekend to care, we headed straight there. Crowds of people flooded the pavement outside the door and I was on the brink of suggesting we looked for somewhere quieter when a waiter beckoned to us, seized my arm and towed us through the throng to the back of the room. He installed us around a wooden barrel, took our drinks orders and returned in a flash with three pint glasses. Actual pint glasses, each more than three quarters full of *vino tinto* and a huge plate of *huevos rotos*, a *madrileño* classic, precariously balanced on the top. Consisting of chips with *jamón* and fried eggs on top, all cut up and mixed up, it's a tasty heart-attack on a plate.

"Uff, sorry," cried Paige as she stumbled and split some *vino* over the barrel. "It's impossible to stay upright in this place." I nodded in agreement as a rogue elbow jabbed into my ribs. The place seethed with students, both foreign and Spanish, all taking advantage of the cheap drinks and generous *tapas*, and watching the football on the huge screen taking up most of the back wall.

Suddenly Caitlin grabbed my arm, laughing and said, "Do I spy *Fifty Shades of Grey* in your bag Miss Fuller? You're not reading that garbage are you?"

"Haha, I hate to admit it, but yes. Did I ever tell you about Raul who I've been seeing recently?"

"No," she replied, intrigued. "Is he one of your grease monkeys?"

"No!! I met him at a friend's party last year. Anyway, he is obsessed with getting me to read more in Spanish and last week he gave me…"

"He gave you *Fifty Shades of Grey*?" she interrupted, "he's clearly got plans for you!!!"

"NO! Haha, no, he gave me a random book called *Siddhartha* by some German guy."

"I think I read that at school. Pretty intense isn't it?"

"Yep, I think so. I'm sure it's a great book but it's flipping impossible to read in Spanish. I mean the language is totally archaic. It's so poetic, waffling on about withered branches and weather-beaten skin. I literally look up at least five words in every sentence and even then I'm not sure I've really got the gist."

"Doesn't sound ideal," agreed Caitlin.

I continued, raising my voice over the loud hum of the crowds, "So, anyway, my lovely new flatmate Rebeca saw me struggling with it the other day and a few minutes later she came back, saying she had a much better book to help with my Spanish and she proudly presented me with *Cincuenta Sombras*," I laughed. "I was sceptical, but I thought I'd give it a go and you know what, the language is pretty basic and repetitive but I'm learning a lot!"

"I bet you are! That's so funny – is it giving you some handy tips to try out with your mechanics?" asked Paige. "How's it going with them anyway? Any gossip to report?"

"I can unequivocally state there will never be any type of *Fifty Shades* action with any of them!" I declared, holding up my right hand in a mock solemn vow.

"Anyway," I continued, "Let's not talk about them. I don't want to be one of those teachers who bangs on about their students all the time. So dull. What about you guys, how's it going with the hunky *intercambios?*" Both of them had been dating men they'd met through language exchange websites.

"Ditched," they glumly replied in unison. "I'm so fed up with Spanish men," moaned Caitlin, "I mean they are just so *young* and *precious*. I hate to make generalisations, but they're all so super arrogant and only interested in hook-ups."

"Spaniards are so different. In so many ways," chipped in Paige. "Look at this place. It's fun for sure, and maybe we're just a bit old for it, but I don't remember any time in my life when I would have loved crowds like this. It's as though they all have serious FOMO – they can't bear to be some-where quieter in case their friends are all having a better time elsewhere."

"They have a pack mentality thing going on, they stick with their same old tight-knit group of friends their whole life, from childhood to old age," added Caitlin.

"The fact they are so closed about it is what bothers me, it's bloody impossible to break into their friendship circles," Paige said as she finished her glass of *vino* and frantically waved at the waiter for another round.

"I know what you mean. On one level they're super friendly and they'll always be happy to hang out and do stuff one-on-one, but in terms of cracking into a group it's pretty much impossible."

"I'm so relieved you feel the same. I'd been worrying about my chat and blaming my dodgy Spanish!" I replied.

"Not at all," said Paige, "I even found the same with Esteban's friends when I first came over here."

A deafening roar rose up from the crowds as someone scored a goal in the on-screen footie match, and a cold dribble of beer snaked down my neck as a fan cheered and whooped next to me, spilling most of his drink in the process.

"Are you still in touch with Esteban?" I asked, tentatively, when the noise calmed slightly. Paige had moved over from Denver six months earlier to be with her boyfriend, only to be unceremoniously dumped five weeks later.

"No, but I think it's better this way. I still feel so angry and upset with him, space has to be a good thing. I'm focusing on myself right now. Fate bought me here and I'm going to make the most of this opportunity as long as I can."

"We need to find some new men, guys. What are you up to tomorrow night? My flatmate is organising a party so you should come," Caitlin urged. "The way to get over a guy is to get under the next one, right?"

The giggles subsided and I said, "I'm actually going to a football match tomorrow, sorry. Party would have been fun."

"Now I know I don't know you too well, but you sure don't strike me as a soccer fan," replied Paige.

"I'm most definitely not, but Raul wants to take me and I reckon it's one of those things you have to do once in your life. New experiences and all that."

"Raul, hey? Sounds like you could be in for some *Fifty Shades* action after all," Caitlin giggled and elbowed me with a wink.

***

Raul had been horrified when I'd recently admitted I had absolutely no interest in football and had never been to a match, and as my self-appointed Spanish tour guide and cultural ambassador, he insisted it was essential for my education and well-being. Why the hell not, I had said at the time, yet on Saturday night I headed up Castellano towards the Bernabéu feeling anything but enthusiastic about the whole idea. The Spanish say the wind in Madrid is so piercing it can kill a man, yet so gentle it can't extinguish a candle and I pushed my hands deeper into my pockets as it bitterly enveloped me. Despite the Michelin-man-style duvet coat Carolina had leant me, my teeth chattered uncontrollably and I could easily believe it was capable of murder – the cold had entered my bones and flowed like icy water through my veins. The driving rain didn't help the situation either. I waited at the bus stop for Raul, feeling uncomfortably tall and female amongst huge crowds of drunk and leery short Spanish men. My bottom was firmly perched on the cold seat having been roughly pinched by one of said examples and I hoped this wasn't a sign of things to come. I finally spotted Raul striding towards me and felt disproportionately pleased to see a familiar face amongst the crowds. His arms wrapped me in a tight hug and he leisurely gave me *dos* stubbly *besos* on the cheeks, followed by a lingering kiss on the lips, his hands clasping my neck. The butterflies in my stomach came alive. What was it about this guy? Things had been going well but he confused me. He was so intense, so unfamiliar and so different to the usual guys I dated, I sometimes caught myself wondering what I was doing but for the meantime I'd decided to just give in to the chemistry.

Anyway, back to the football. We elbowed our way through the crowds towards our *vomitorium* – yep, that's right, that's what they call the tunnels to the different sections of the stadium – and wrestled further still through the sea of fans before finally locating our seats. Clouds of weed smoke hovered above us, adding to my light head and happy thoughts.

"You do know I am totally clueless about football don't you?" I confided in Raul as we settled into our seats.

"So, first thing you need to know is the Rayo Vallecano fans are famous for their craziness," Raul leant over as he began to share pearls of wisdom on the third team of Madrid, "and here we are sitting in middle of them!"

"Are they any good?" I asked.

"Weeellll, Real Madrid should win easily, but *nunca se sabe*. You never know. Is unpredictable game football."

The players began to line up on the pitch below.

"Have you tried *pipas?*" he asked, shoving a large bag of sunflower seeds into my hand. As I shook my head he continued, sternly, "*Pipas* and beers are essential for all matches."

"Ahhh, so that explains all the husks on the floor everywhere."

"Husks? What is husks?"

"You know, the outside part of the *pipas*."

"Ahh, *sí*. Now, is important you learn how to do this properly. You see, you put it in your mouth, between teeth *así*, with a little pressure you open it with your teeth, you eat the seed and throw down the, how do you call…husk? Easy. You try."

I tried to copy this manoeuvre, but his powerful gaze distracted me and I ended up spitting stringy bits of saliva-covered husk over my chin and onto my scarf. He greeted my inelegant attempts with wild guffaws and thigh-slapping.

"Haha, *me encantan los extranjeros* – the foreign people, you know, they never can do it. Keep practising!"

"I hate how you're always laughing at me," I moaned, frustrated by my ineptitude and embarrassed by the dribbles. Ignoring the game beginning below, I started to munch my way through the bag, concentration etched on my features.

Twenty minutes later the match was well underway and I had given up. Stylish *pipa* munching was not within my grasp.

"It's too much effort – it's not worth it," I groaned, throwing in the metaphorical towel and handing the bag back to him.

"Don't worry. You are still perfect to me *guapa*, even if you can't eat them right." With a wink, he put his arm around my waist and pulled me close. "Are you happy here?"

"Of course I'm happy," I replied, keeping my eyes firmly focused on the pitch as his stare burnt holes in my cheeks.

"I mean are you happy now? Now, in this moment?"

The silence pregnant with meaning, he turned my body to face him and his intensity made me shiver.

I gulped and whispered the truth.

"Yes, I am."

A slow smile spread across his face.

"I'm glad. You make me happy," and he edged closer to kiss me. I closed my eyes and waited for his lips to meet mine when a huge roar rose from the crowd and the man next to us jostled into me and sent me stumbling into the large woman in the row in front. Suddenly 40,000 people were on their feet jumping up and down, whooping, cheering and screaming like maniacs. The Rayo Vallecano fans definitely deserved their reputation.

1-0 to the crazy ones.

When calm resumed we stood rather awkwardly, both focusing intently on the pitch. I was still lost in thoughts on my feelings towards him when Michu suddenly seized the ball for Rayo Vallecano, dodged a series of tackles and headed directly towards the goal below. The noise levels rose with every step he took.

"Ooh, he's going to score, he's going to score, come on, *vamooooooooooos*," shouted Raul, letting go of my hand to leap up and punch the air with his fist.

Michu dodged several defenders before shooting, but the huge, muscly goalkeeper caught the ball expertly and hugged it to his chest. The fans around us grimaced, their thug-like faces contorting with disappointment as they swore in frustration. Moments later the whistle blew for half-time.

We sat down and Raul squeezed my hand.

"You are happy right?"

"Yes, I said yes," I tittered, a blush stretching up from my neck on its way to my cheeks. I could smell the beer and *pipas* on his warm breath.

"I am happy with you Eebee Fuller. I want you to know I am serious about you."

A lump rose in my throat. How long had I waited for someone to say this to me, and yet his words sent a wave of discomfort through me. I willed the players to come back on the pitch and provide a distraction as I fumbled around in my mind for something to say.

As we've discovered, talking about my feelings had never

been easy, so to dispel the tension and return to our usual easy chat, I leant back in my seat and asked, "Soooo, how is your work going? Have things improved with your boss?"

"No, but it no matter," he shrugged. "Why you look worried?"

"I'm not worried, but I am feeling very confused about what I'm doing with my life. I was invited to apply for a job in London this morning."

His ears pricked up immediately.

I continued, "It's a similar job to my last role, but with a considerably higher salary and in a much better company."

Fear and concern flashed across his features.

"But you love Spain. You are happy here. Why do you want to leave?"

"I do love it here, but, you know. It's difficult." I sighed.

"No, is not difficult. Is easy. Stay," he snapped.

I twisted and contorted my increasingly clammy hands in my lap, keeping my eyes glued on the husk-strewn floor.

"I adore the lifestyle here – the quality of life is incomparable with London. I feel happier here than I think I've ever felt, but at the same time it doesn't feel real. It's like I'm coasting along on holiday and at some stage I need to face the inevitable and get back to reality."

"Pah," he spat, "is terrible excuse. If it's so good why leave? It no make sense."

"It's more though," I continued, wishing I hadn't started this conversation, "I enjoy teaching, but if I'm honest I can't see myself doing it long-term. I need to use my brain and find something more interesting…" I trailed off, unsure how to explain all my conflicting emotions and totally clueless as to what I needed or wanted right now.

"Why? Why *should* you use your brain? Why you *have* to have a better job? *Los Arabes*, the Arabs, they focus on *being,* for them the best thing is to *be*. Not like us who want to *have* all things. *Have* knowledge, *have* power, *have* possessions. They know best I think. We should just *be* and stop to want more all the time."

"But that's easy for you to say, you like your job," I retorted.

"Pah, no, my job is boring, I no like it, but is no problem. I do it ten years and you only teach for few months."

He shrugged.

"Ten years!" I exclaimed. "How can you stay in a job you hate for ten years?"

"I have work and a salary, I can't complain. And the important thing is my free time. I work to live. My priority is family and friends. Keep your heart happy," he said imploringly. "Is the most important thing."

"But it's not so simple. I can't do something I find boring every day of my life. I want more – I NEED more."

"Well, look for a different job here," he pleaded, "what is it you want to do? You can find different job here. I can help you."

"I don't know what I want," I cried, hands flying up in the air as tears trickled down my cheeks, "that's my bloody problem." My heart pounded like a drum, as football fans filed past us on their way to the bar for more half-time drinks.

"How can you be so certain of yourself?" I asked, quietly. "Don't you feel like there is something more interesting out there for you? That you should achieve more?"

"Should? Why *should* I do anything I don't want to? I listen to my heart and no one else."

"How can you put such faith in your heart? I'm not sure I trust mine. I mean…" and before I could finish he grabbed the back of my head and drew me towards him for a rough and hungry kiss that melted my insides and left me weak at the knees.

"What does your heart say you now?" he asked breathlessly, his eyes clouded with desire.

I kissed him again, raw desire for him to possess me pushing all thoughts to the back of my mind.

"We go now," he said, taking my hand and pushing past our neighbours towards the exit. Back in my flat I let myself give in to passionate oblivion as his hands tangled in my hair, our ragged breaths and bodies united as one and we fell, entwined, into a blissful slumber.

**

"*Joder*," he muttered the next morning as he looked at his watch and turned over in bed, dragging the duvet with him. "Is very late. I must go or my boss kill me."

"Argh, don't go," I groaned, pulling him back and cocooning us in the duvet, marvelling at how my milky skin contrasted with his olive tones.

"*Sí*, believe me I would prefer to stay all the day in bed with you *guapa* but I must go," he said as he leant over, cupped my face in his hands and his lips grazed mine in a gentle, soft kiss. "But I will be back, *seguro*."

14

Absence really does make the heart grow fonder. After all my dithering over Raul, he'd now been whisked off to America for work and I struggled to focus on anything else. All thoughts of leaving Madrid were completely forgotten as I eagerly awaited his return. As my train trundled along to Charmartín, my thoughts turned to Ramón who'd been in touch, thanking me profusely for going to his opening, telling me off for having left without saying goodbye and urging me to join him for more mushrooms as soon as possible.

Rather than attempting any grammar, I'd decided to start with a fun lesson for Sofía and after a coffee at the bar with her colleagues we headed to the office to get down to work. We looked at different ways to offer advice and I pulled out a board game, a dice and some coloured counters. Her eyes lit up and a smile spread across her face,

"Oooh, I love the games," she exclaimed, clapping her hands together gleefully.

"Ok, so written on each square is a problem or an issue. They are all MY problems," I explained. "When your counter lands on a square you give me three pieces of advice for the problem using the structures we've talked about, ok? So things like *if I were you...have you thought about...you should...*etc. Ok?"

Nodding, she rolled the dice and moved the blue counter to a square reading *I think I'm ugly*. She responded enthusiastically,

"No is true. You is not very ugly Eebee. But you must. No, you have to go to the beauty place and do treatments. Always better with treatments." Narrowing her eyes and sizing me up, she continued, "You should cut hair and go for face treatment. Paint the nails too. Always important have *manicura*..."

I zoned out as she listed many more treatments I needed. It was enough to give a girl a complex.

"Ok, great. Excellent," I praised. "Let's roll the dice again."

She moved the counter on to the square, *I'm in love with Beyoncé*. "Ok, so you like girls. I not know this! *Claro*, now I understand. Why you no tell me?" she asked, before continuing, breathlessly, "there are some nice lesbian bars in Chueca you must visit. Chueca is gay area of Madrid. My gay friend she tells me Club 33 is good one. I think it is the most old, *perdón*, the oldest one, but I ask her for you and here, I give you others." She pulled a pen out of her bag and started scribbling a list for me.

"Whoa, OK now, you do realise this is a game don't you?" I leant forward on the table to emphasise my point and she looked up, wide-eyed.

"You is not gay?" she asked, incredulously.

"No! I'm not a lesbian," I stated, before adding emphatically, "I like *men*."

"But you say they are your problems?"

"Not my *real* ones – it's a game from the internet! It's just a game, to practise!!" I assured her, and we both collapsed into giggles.

The next square she landed on read *I've been dumped by my boyfriend*.

"*Qué es* doomped? What mean this? Sound orrible."

"It's when your boyfriend ends your relationship. They dump you."

"Oh, is sad. Like I say you Eebee, we do casting for doomped people. We do casting for you."

"Great, let's do it!" I responded enthusiastically, wondering what Raul would make of all this.

She rested her chin in her hands and peered pensively out of the window, continuing, "Is a pitty I no know more single men. There is my colleague Javi, but he is divorcing now. He has two children. I think he will stay with wife in the end. *Es complicado.*"

"Thank you for the thought, but don't worry about it. I have been dating a Spanish guy recently, although it's early days."

Ignoring me she continued, "I will think more men. Oh but then there is Jorge."

My ears pricked up immediately.

"He's single? But I thought he had a girlfriend? I didn't realise he was single," I warbled, incapable of believing I had finally discovered he didn't have a girlfriend.

She looked at me strangely, "Is single. We talk about it at lunch yesterday. You like him?"

"Hmm?" I asked, burying my head in a textbook and attempting to look nonchalant. "What?"

"You no like Jorge do you?" she persisted, watching me like a hawk. "No, no, you must not like him. Jorge no treat girls good. I no trust him."

"Hmm? No, I err, no. Just curious, that's all," I said, trying desperately to breathe slowly and keep calm.

We carried on with the game, giggling and gossiping our way through the squares. It was the perfect distraction, and what a discovery. After all those months of dreaming, Raul was instantly forgotten and Jorge leapt to the forefront of my mind. This new knowledge of his bachelor status didn't remotely change anything, but I felt elated nonetheless.

***

After such an overdose of male company at the Institute, I loved spending time with Sofía and Rebeca, but unfortunately it transpired another girl was about to enter my life too. Fernando called me to let me know a new teacher from the Native English Teaching Assistant programme would join the Institute until the end of the year. A huge wave of jealousy instantly boiled up inside me and I felt wildly territorial of a job I had been desperate to leave only months ago.

The following day, attempting to stifle my negative feelings towards her, I marched into the Institute determined to be friendly and positive. Fernando was nowhere to be seen, so I headed to class and began to unpack my files as the boys filtered into the room.

"Hi guys."

"*Hola* titcher, what we study today?" replied Carlos.

"Lots to do today," I replied. "We're going to look at pronouns, so I hope you're ready to learn."

"Yes, yes," sighed Rafa. "We always hardly work. I need hardly work today because I have exam of English next week."

"Sorry," I asked, distracted by the noise of the others joking around.

"I say we hardly work," he replied.

"You work hard, you mean."

"It's what I say!" he exclaimed, crossly. Someone was in a bad mood today.

"We *hardly work* means we do a little work. We *work hard* means we do lots of work. Big difference," I laughed, writing both phrases on the board.

The noise levels rose and I turned around to see Ander showing the others a video on his phone.

"Ander, can you put that away please."

"But titcher, is video of Ander on YouTube," piped up Rafa. "He does parkour *muy bien*. Come see titcher."

Curiosity got the better of me and I peered over their shoulders to see a younger, adorable version of Ander, with a dodgy mullet and a t-shirt five sizes too big, running around the city, leaping from wall to wall, swinging over bars and clambering over bridges.

"That's actually pretty good Ander," I praised.

The door opened and in marched Fernando, accompanied by a very glamorous girl clutching a large, green smoothie. With legs up to her armpits and glossy blonde locks reaching down to her waist, a patterned crop top revealing a perfectly toned stomach and an exotic tattoo, she was very stylish and irritatingly pretty.

"Eebee, boys, this is Madison. New teacher. She is from California and she here for to end of year. She speak perfectly espanish but please speak only English with her."

The boys whooped and wolf whistled and a hideous wave of jealousy instantly engulfed me. I wasn't sure why I felt so protective of my position when the boys had spent the last few months traumatising me at every opportunity, but it made me realise how much I had come to relish my celebrity status as the only girl in the building.

"Catch ya later Evie," she said in a lazy drawl as she flicked her long locks over her shoulder and sashayed out of the door with Fernando moments later.

"OoOoOohh, new titcher gorjoice," cooed Rafa. "And

she speak espanish. Better than you titcher. You need learn espanish."

"Enough," I said firmly, shuffling the papers on my desk, "let's start with pronouns."

The class proved a success and so feeling positive I invited Madison for a coffee in the *cafetería* at break time. When she tore herself away from flirting with José behind the bar, we sat down at the grey teachers' table and the verbal onslaught immediately began.

"So, shall I tell you a bit about myself?" she asked. "I've been working in Marañon Instituto – it's like one of the biggest *institutos* in Spain. I mean, it's like, huge. I loved it though, but all the *alumnos* are away on their *practicas* now, so they told me I'd have to come here for the rest of the year. It's ok, and everyone here seems like they're nice, but it's like a nightmare to get here, and my body is literally like, *so* tired I mean I'm not sure I can like handle any more work. And *las horas* are so strange – I mean I have to stay here at the *instituto* till like 7pm three days a week and I don't have any classes most of the time. Oh well, it like gives me time to do lots of other things. I'm working on my businesses and all my other *trabajo*."

Shudder. Her habit of dropping in random Spanish words made my hackles rise. Did she think she was a native? Or was she just trying to hammer home the fact that her Spanish was infinitely better than mine? I smiled sweetly as she continued, hoping my face betrayed a friendlier expression than I felt.

"So, *los consejeros* told me I need to help you with your Spanish," she said, chuckling loudly. "How is your Spanish? Haven't you found a Spanish man? I've had like a bejillion Spanish men and made so many friends – they call me the Queen of Malasaña as I like know everyone in the *barrio*."

Neighbourhood, I screamed silently to myself, it's not a *barrio,* it's a *neighbourhood.* Oblivious to my increasing and irrational rage, she blithely continued.

"You know, I just love it here. I've been here nearly three years and I love the culture, I love the people – I mean I've like fallen in love here soooooooo many times. I've banged SO many hot Spanish men in *mi cama.* I like want to raise my children here, I love the society here, I love the sun, but I think I need to get back to California and like get started on my career so I can settle down and have children before I'm thirty, cos like, everyone knows life like ends at thirty really, doesn't it?"

She paused for the first time with this and sat back in her chair as if contemplating the miracle of life.

"I'm thirty," I muttered.

"See," she replied without a second's hesitation, banging the table loudly, "you know exactly what I mean!"

Where did this trollop come from? I was already feeling self-conscious about my "advanced age" (as David, my boss at the agency, constantly referred to thirty). I really didn't need her making me feel even more geriatric.

"Talking about men, have you like banged any of the guys here yet?" Were we even talking about men? She launched into a description of her own tangled web of lovers before I had a chance to reply,

"My love life is so *complicado* I don't know where to start. First there was Paco. I met him in a cute little place in Malasaña ..."

The American tidal wave began to drown me and I desperately needed to escape. For the first time in ages I felt mateless and lonely. Raul wasn't going to be back in town for ages now his work in America had been extended for at least another month and he had been very off-ish on the phone recently. Jorge kept cancelling his classes and even Ramón had vanished from the radar since our last dinner. I needed to find an alternative option to occupy my thoughts.

I breathed a deep sigh of relief when the bell rang and we had to head to class.

***

At the end of the day I trundled off to Huertas to meet Belinda. We'd planned to check out the Decor Acción design fair and then, for a change, indulge in some *tapas* and *cañas*. Despite Madison bursting my confidence bubble that afternoon, the sun on my face had a restorative effect as I wound my way south through the city.

We met on the corner of Calle León where the huge lizard of CDs had been joined by some baby lizards made of rolled-up magazine sheets stuffed into chicken wire. Huge swathes of red, white and blue ribbons dangled from the building next to the Trinitarian church and fluttered prettily in the breeze. Vintage stalls lined the streets and we ambled along under a hanging creation of shoes and boots, browsing pots, paintings and all sorts of artistic creations. We hooked arms and sauntered around while I off-loaded about Madison and she responded with suitably supportive comments, before settling down in the sunshine for some drinks.

"By the way, there's some sort of English event thing going on tonight near Príncipe Pío if you fancy checking it out? My student Sofía gave me a couple of tickets and some drinks vouchers."

"You know me, never one to turn down a free G&T."

"Ace. It sounds random, but it could be fun. I love the Spanish view of all things British."

"Yep, a bright and shiny, sanitised version of Portobello, Camden and Buckingham Palace rolled into one just about sums it up," she laughed.

"Sofía was also very proud of how British the band are. I have no clue who they are, and I told her they looked like a pretty generic bunch of teenage boys to me. You know, checked shirts and dirty, messy hair etc., to which she replied – exactly, so British, all British people have bad hair!!!"

"She probably has a point. We're not exactly known for our style are we?" she mused, popping an olive into her mouth.

"Speak for yourself!" I retorted, staring through my pink sunglasses at my denim shorts, silk top and glittery, silver espadrilles. "Look at this," I exclaimed, gesticulating wildly up and down my outfit, "Elle Macpherson eat your heart out…"

Giggling, she replied, "Ok, cool. That sounds fun, so let's head there in a bit. But I warn you I must be home by 9pm. I've got a hot date with series 8 of *Grey's Anatomy.*"

"Are you serious?"

"I know, I know, but I'm knackered and I've got an endless stream of visitors over the next few weeks," she sighed, knocking back the rest of her *caña.* "My actors were so demanding today they've sapped all my energy."

"How's work going?" I asked.

"Actually really well. We've got a couple of people into some good films recently and a lot of castings lined up for the next few weeks. The agency is really taking off which is great, but it does mean longer hours and more work."

"Exciting though," I replied.

"Yep, it's all good, but I'm beginning to realise how demanding and diva like actors can be. It's *almost* enough to make me miss the lovely businessmen from my teaching days!"

I laughed. "Let's go for a bit of a wander and then head to London town!"

A couple of hours later we arrived at the large entrance gate, flanked by two massive Union Jack flags. Dotted around on the huge space in front of the deserted train station were endless shipping crates covered with yet more blue, white and red decorations and endless posters of the Queen. They housed pop-up bars, vintage clothes and jewellery shops and all sorts of food and drink stalls. There weren't many people, but then again it was only about 8pm, massively early by Spanish standards, but it gave the whole place a rather underwhelming impression. Jessie J blared out of the speakers as girls in red and blue tutus with promotional t-shirts and knee-high socks skipped around taking photos and Union Jack-covered tuk-tuks circled the 'streets', turning at signs pointing to Leicester Square, Portobello and Piccadilly Circus.

"Let's get some drinks," I said, spotting a bar along the back wall. "Seems a shame to waste the freebies." We pulled two stools up to the bar and perched there, surveying the scene while we nursed two pint-sized G&Ts.

"By the way, you never told me what happened with Raul?" she asked.

"Well," I sighed. "I managed to get my over-analysing mind under control a bit and was beginning to really enjoy being with him, but then some sort of disaster happened in their American office and he's been stuck there for a while now. I have no idea when he'll be back."

"Shame. Although I have to say I wasn't too sure I could see you with him," she admitted.

"I know, we don't really have much in common, but we had fun and I'm not sure I'm ready for it to end when it was only just beginning. We were in touch when he first left, but after a while he stopped replying to my messages so it looks like that's it. It's amazing how much more you want something when you can't have it." I studied my glass and made swirling patterns in the condensation with my thumb.

My thoughts were interrupted when I heard a loud and familiar voice say, "What's cooking, good-looking?" Jorge stepped round the corner and embraced me with two big, bristly kisses. "Titcher, how are you?"

Disorientated by his sudden arrival, I was incapable of stringing a sentence together.

"Hi, I'm Belinda," my friend announced, leaning over to introduce herself and giving him an eyeful of her cleavage.

"Yes you are *linda*, Belinda, very pritty indeed. It's nice to meet you," he replied suavely, "you are from England too? I am Jorge, the best student of Eebee." Chortle, chortle.

Belinda's eyes glazed over as she chattered away, the gin clearly taking effect. A wave of jealousy rose up inside me, but I was still incapable of articulating anything coherent, so I stayed quiet.

"You girls are having a good time?" he asked, returning from the bar with more drinks.

"Oh yes," we chorused, tittering like teenagers. "This place is great."

"So, do you enjoy your classes with Evie? Is she a good teacher?" Belinda asked, wobbling around on her feet.

"Oh yes, she the best," he replied, putting his arm around my shoulders and pulling me close. "I learn a lot with her classes."

My knees went weak with a combination of exhaustion, alcohol and the sheer thrill of being in such close proximity to him. He smelt divine and he radiated raw masculinity.

The banter continued until he suddenly announced he had to leave.

"Good to see you titcher, but I must now go to a dinner. I buy you girls one drink more and then I go."

He presented us with more two ice cold glasses and bade us farewell.

We admired his back view snaking through the crowds to the exit and Belinda admitted, "I *totally* get what you've been going on about all this time. If I was into men you'd have serious competition there."

We merrily abandoned all thoughts of an early night and headed to Whitby, my new favourite bar that served little bowls of penny sweets with drinks, for one last *copa.*

After wrestling our way through the throng, the bar provided welcome support when we reached it. A few moments later a tall, friendly-looking guy put his hand on my arm and inclined his head towards mine with a grin, "We are trying to decide what accent you have. Where are you from?"

"Guess!" I replied, laughing. I leant over to Belinda and whispered, "This place is a winner! I love how we've been here less than two minutes and we've already found some guys. *Adiós* Raul, I'm moving on!" I turned my attention back to the hottie, leaving Belinda at the mercy of his friends.

"Ha, I don't know. You are from England, but I don't know where."

He tried to guess, listing random English counties, while I unsubtly checked him out. His green and navy checked shirt was paired with jeans and Converse and he really made a rather attractive sight. Iñaki worked in a bank and had come to Whitby with some colleagues for a few drinks. After twenty minutes of drunken flirting, my heart sank when he announced he had a birthday party to get to, but his friends had no intention of leaving so we waved him off and knocked back another couple of rounds before the idea of a trip to Gabana cropped up. By all accounts one of the most pretentious clubs in Madrid, I'd heard about this place for months and leapt at the opportunity to see it for myself.

The guys were hilarious. I think. To be honest they could have said anything and I would have laughed; I was well on the way to being a giggling wreck. Santi was a bit older, in a battered leather jacket and with flecks of grey hair around his ears, whereas the other one was tall and drop-dead gorgeous. I mean *hot*. He had thick, wavy brown hair to die for, and a tanned, muscular chest peeking out of his crisp blue shirt. His English wasn't so great, but then again I don't think mine was by that point either. They ushered us into the club, bypassing queues of models and C-list celebrities and I realised that yet again my Spanish life had taken on a surreal, dream-like quality.

The rest of the night passed in a total blur. We stumbled out onto the pavement at 6am where I flagged down a taxi and announced I was heading home. The urge for sleep was so overwhelming this was not remotely intended as an invitation, but I can't say I protested when the hot guy jumped in to the cab and we kissed all the way home.

***

Beep, beep, beep, beep...

The alarm continued relentlessly, echoing painfully in my head. My limbs ached, my lips felt bruised and my blurry eyes struggled to open, let alone focus. With a lot of effort I turned over and my eyes fell on the smooth, supine body of a fine specimen of a man. Who the hell was he? I pulled the duvet over my body, ran my fingers over my cracked lips and racked my brain for clues. My memory flashed purple, blue and purple.

"*Soy muerto, soy muerto,*" he muttered moments later, shaking his head and gazing forlornly at the floor as he dragged himself up and pulled on his clothes. "I'm dead." With his slumped shoulders and exhausted expression, he looked like a zombie.

"I can't believe I go party now. *Soy muerto,*" he repeated, followed by more despondent head shaking. He tucked me up under the duvet and crept out of the flat, slamming the door so loudly he would have woken a hibernating dinosaur. Anyway, he'd gone, thank god. I felt wearily smug he had to take an hour and a half bus journey to Toledo for a friend's birthday, while I had zero intention of moving from my bed for the rest of the day. After nearly twenty-four hours of consciousness my weary, alcohol-flooded body could finally get some proper sleep. I turned over to snuggle down and close my eyes when a stab of pain shot through my left jaw bone.

"Ahh!" I shrieked, moving my hand to my cheek where the left side of my face felt tender and sensitive. I clamped my eyelids shut and tried to ignore the pain, willing sleep to come. Unfortunately, the need to pee wasn't going to go away so I heaved my body out of bed and stood up. A terrible idea. I sat down again instantly and put my head in my hands, causing another jarring pain to fire down the side of my face. I hadn't had a hangover like this for a very long time, if ever. I slowly stood again and shuffled my way to the door, leaning heavily on the wall for support while toxic levels of booze pulsated through my veins.

Like a dirty tramp, I crept naked to my bathroom and predictably, Rebeca chose that very moment to open her bedroom door.

"*Buenas,*" I feebly muttered, putting my head down and trying to cover my modesty as I stumbled past, ignoring the thumping pain in my head growing stronger by the second.

"Eebee, *JODER!*" she shrieked, a horrified expression plastered on her face as she reached out and grabbed my arm. "*Qué pasa con tu cara? JODER.* Eebee! What happen to you face?" Now, describing her as melodramatic on a normal day is an understatement, but the strength of this exclamation seemed excessive even by her standards and in my shocked, bewildered and semi-functioning state it was too much to take. She reached out to my cheek and I violently shuddered at her light touch. Tears started to well in my eyes and I dashed to the bathroom.

Oh god. OH GOD. WHAT ON EARTH HAD HAPPENED TO ME? Large red and purple bruises covered a huge chunk of my left cheek, neck and arm. Were they bites? *Quiero comerte.* Oh NO – I remember him saying *quiero comerte* – he wanted to eat me. Eat me? Did people actually do that? I desperately scrabbled around in the depths of my memory trying to decipher details of the night, when it all came rushing back like a tidal wave. I fell into a heap on the floor.

"*Eebee, estas bien?* You ok?" Rebeca asked, knocking on the door.

"Yes, yes, I'm ok," I replied, trying to keep my voice strong. "Don't worry – you go back to sleep."

There was no way I could face further interrogation. Images came flooding back and I remembered him biting me in the club and on the street outside. These must be love bites. URGH. An involuntary shudder of shame ran through my body. Was he some sort of animal? Weren't love bites something only hormonal teenagers did? I stared at my reflection in disgust and barely recognised the drained face staring back. The huge purple stain spread from my neck over the jaw bone and across half my cheek as all the marks grew and merged into one large bruise.

I couldn't bring myself to look upon this horrendous reflection any longer so I retreated back to bed and buried myself deeply in an attempt to retreat from reality. Despite squeezing my eyes tight shut, the rapid-fire series of flash-backs had started and nothing could stop the pieces of the previous night falling into place.

I'd gone to the loo in Gabana partly as an excuse to be able to sit down for a couple of minutes. By the time I'd had a little power nap and re-emerged, the others had vanished. A few solitary laps of the dancefloor produced no results, when suddenly he appeared out of nowhere (I have to call him 'he' as shamefully I couldn't even remember his name… was it Bartolomeo? Or maybe Marco?) and we sat on a sofa, where the first kiss happened. Minutes later he took my hand, led me to the exit and we pottered round the corner. He-who-cannot-be-named was so drop-dead gorgeous I pulled his face down to mine and kissed him excitedly. He hoiked me up onto the large windowsill and we couldn't keep our hands off each other. With remarkable skill he managed to whip my top off in one swift movement and I found myself lying on my back on the windowsill. I erupted into laughter – what the hell were we doing? All of a sudden I heard voices and stifled my giggles by burying my head in his chest – admittedly not the worst place to hide, despite minimal levels of cover. Shame and laughter alternated in a crazy, spinning whirl in my head, as I realised this was the complete antithesis of the chic *madrileña* behaviour my New Year's resolution had demanded.

Urgh. I shook my head and returned to the present. Cringing at the memories I burrowed further under the duvet in more vain efforts to escape them when suddenly I sat up with a jolt. Shit. I had so many lessons on Monday – how on earth would I explain the bruises to my students?

They wouldn't fade for several weeks, and I seriously doubted any make-up would successfully hide them. I racked my brain for possible excuses. No one would believe I'd been paintballing – they all knew how lazy I was. I was also a terrible liar so I couldn't pretend I'd been mugged. Vampires? Mutant mosquitoes? What else could I say? I frantically googled *how to get rid of love bites*, still periodically shuddering heavily as I waited for the results to load. Yahoo answers suggested slapping on a load of toothpaste as a miracle cure, so I crept back to the bathroom and covered half my body in a thick layer of the stuff. Mission accomplished I crossed my fingers and retreated back to bed yet again with a minty, tingling face, neck and arms when I thought of ice. That's what I need. Surely ice would help? I snuck off to the kitchen and fished a bag of frozen peas out of the freezer. A short, fitful doze later I woke to find toothpaste liberally spread all over the pillow and sheets, along with a number of soggy, defrosted peas. The escapeas had managed to get everywhere, the bed squelchy from their thawing. Absolutely revolting.

The tidal wave of involuntary cringing began to wane by Sunday afternoon and I summoned the courage to leave the flat, not least because I was dying of hunger and the cupboards were bare. Unfortunately, the bruises didn't seem to be subsiding, in fact if anything they were getting darker. My face resembled a rather puffy, dirty piece of popcorn after a heavy plastering of make-up, but I didn't have the energy to worry as I strolled to the supermarket marvelling at the sweltering heat of this early spring heatwave. Lingering by the frozen food section and lapping up the cool breeze, I suddenly heard, "Evie, Evie, is you?" Carolina rounded the corner from the vegetable section. "How are you?" she asked, giving me a tight hug.

"How is everything? You've been out so much recently and I have stayed so much with Antonio we've hardly seen each other since Christmas," she continued, holding me at arm's length and studying my face intently. "Are you ok? Your face looks quite, how you say, like big balloon?" She puffed out her cheeks widely.

"It's fine, it's fine," I tried to assure her, shaking my head down a little in an attempt to cover my face and neck with some hair. "I want to hear all your news. How is everything?" I asked, desperate to keep the focus on her.

"I have just returned from the north where we visit Antonio's family. It was super-beautiful!" she said. "I will have to show you all the photos, but are you sure you're ok? You're talking in a way quite funny." She reached out to rub my arm kindly as she closely studied my face. "I go Antonio's house again tonight but we must catch up."

"I'm fine, I promise you – I've just had a busy weekend and I'm totally exhausted!" I laughed, desperately trying to sound chipper. "I've got to run now, but let's have a drink and a proper gossip tomorrow. I'd love to hear all about your trip and Antonio and everything," I burbled, dashing to the cashier and sprinting back to the safety and anonymity of my duvet at top speed.

15

My shoulders slumped as Madison spied me across the *cafetería* and waved; I really wasn't in the mood for one of her verbal assaults today. Knackered and still sensitive about the bites when the bruises looked worse than ever, I wanted nothing more than to blend into the wall and disappear.

"What happened to your face Evie?" Madison asked, as she appeared at my side, put down her tray and pulled up a pew. "Everyone is like asking about your bruises."

I sighed. My attempt to disappear into the corner of the *cafetería* had failed.

"It's nothing," I replied, sheepishly, staring at my plate and taking a large gulp of water. "I had a few too many drinks at the weekend and fell over. Nothing to worry about. How are you? And what are you drinking? I kept meaning to ask – you're always carrying one."

"Oh this?" she asked, pointing to the cup of viscous green gloop. "It's a kale, avocado and broccoli smoothie. Essential clean eating. But tell me what really happened to your face, it looks baaaadddddd."

"It's nothing, honestly, don't worry," I said. "What's going on with you? Any developments in the fiancé / ex-fiancé situation?" She'd glossed over this the other day and I was intrigued to discover if it could be as *Hollyoaks*-like as I'd been led to believe. I'd happily enthuse about anything right now, as long as it didn't involve the bruises.

"We had a really, really, really big talk. On Sunday night, I didn't like sleep at all. I actually didn't come in on Monday. I rang in on Monday. But I *was* sick though, I was like really sick, but I didn't sleep also because I tossed and turned *todo la noche*. We talked about us, how much we mean to each other. This and that. But he got back together with his ex and I was like but you didn't even give us a shot first, you just got back with your girlfriend."

"How long has he been with her?" I asked.

"Almost a year now. And he broke up with her for me and then he got back together with her and I was like but you didn't try with us. Like you didn't try. And now you're telling me you love me and you wanna be with me and you want our dreams to come true and you wanna do all this stuff, buuuuuut, come on. Like you wanna have kids with me and if we'd stayed together we'd be going to California together now, this summer, to like see my family. I mean what? And the problem is I love him. I really do. And I wanna be with him buuuut…" she trailed off, twiddling the tips of her hair round her finger restlessly.

"He's Spanish?"

"Um, hmm. He's Spanish." Genuinely sad, she put her head in her hands. "I don't know what I'm gonna do."

A wave of guilt crashed over me; she really wasn't so bad and it's always awful being dumped.

"So he's still with this other girl?" I gently probed further.

"Yep, and she doesn't even live in Madrid. She lives in *Holanda* – she's half Dutch, or Dutch or something. It's just fucking bullshit. Like, I'm just mad. At him. The problem is also, on my part, he knows that he like has me, he has this great *amor* with me and it'll always be there. But when it gets too scary and it gets too up and down then he still has her. And she's a safe bet. She must be more stable than I am. Because I'm not very stable. Jeez, I know that. Soooo, he just like has me there.

"I totally don't understand why it has to be so hard," she continued, "I mean when we're together it's perfect. It's heaven and we like genuinely believe together we can change the world and make our dreams come true."

"I'm sorry, he sounds frustrating," I replied, distracted by a message on my phone.

"Evie, it was fun to meet you on Friday. I hope you have a good rest of the night? How about a beer after work one day? Iñaki."

My heart skipped a beat as I racked my brains to remember Iñaki until the penny dropped. Ahh, the friend of the biter. Why the hell not, I thought, turning my attention back to Madison.

"Yes, but then there is this other guy and we were supposed to go out yesterday but he was sick. And then because he was sick and he was gonna go home to Malaga this weekend anyway, he was like I'm sorry, I'm sick, blah blah. And I was like urgh, I'm so disappointed. I was like you owe me big time next week. And he was like fine, I'll buy you like double the drinks or whatever. He was like I'll call you at 8 or I'll send you a message at 8 when I get off of work and right at 8 he sends a message and he sends a picture of the train schedule and he was like I've just got two days off and I'm really sick and all I wanna do is go home."

Tying her hair up into a bun on top of her head she continued.

"Anyway, that's it really, so we're supposed to be having a date next week, but hmm, I dunno. I'm on vacation from boys." With this she erupted into maniacal laughter and shouted, "I'M GONNA GO ON VACATION FROM BOYS!"

I smiled as Celine Dion's heartfelt ballad blared from the radio, "Near, far, wherever you are, I am here in your heart and your heart will go onnnnnn…"

"My whole body is just like so totally exhausted. I just came from Metropolitano. I crossed like the whole fuckin' city."

"Who do you teach up there?" I asked.

"*Clases particulares* with businessmen…except today my alarm didn't go off so I went all the way out there for like an hour. It's normally an hour and a half so I get like 30 euros, and so it's not bad, it's worth it, but my alarm didn't go off and I woke up at like 9.15 and I had to leave at like a little before 9.30 and I was like I'm gonna be late, but then I could only do an hour and it was like a really long trip for 20 euros. But whatever I guess…"

***

I entered Carmencita for their weekly *intercambio*, a sort of social evening where anyone can go and informally practise their English and Spanish, but I predictably lost the urge to speak Spanish as soon as I crossed the threshold. David, who I'd met there previously, bounded up to me, still banging on about Depeche Mode and how I must love them as they are from Essex too. Exhausted by the chat, heat and noise, I started to make a beeline to the door when I spotted Chloe pushing through the crowds. Chloe. I'd almost forgotten what she looked like it had been so long. She gave me a massive hug and we started chatting. "Hang on a minute," she said, clasping my arm and raising it nearer her face, "what the hell is that?" She lowered her voice slightly and continued, "Is that from a man?" I looked sheepishly at the floor – I *really* didn't want to talk about this anymore. Unfortunately she took my silence as agreement and let out a massive whoop, "Hey, check this out Miriam," she shouted across the room, "Evie's into the biting thing too!" Suddenly I was the centre of attention and surrounded by sniggers. COULD THE BRUISES JUST GO??

Feigning weak laughter I focused on holding back tears. "Let's change the subject. Much more importantly I want to hear all your news. Tell me all!"

"Don't be silly, there's nothing exciting to report from me," she retorted. "I want to know about the man who gave you these," she laughed, pointing to the teeth marks on my arm.

"Oh God, don't. Honestly, I can't wait for the bloody things to disappear. If only it wasn't so hot – I'm dying to wrap up in scarves and jumpers and hide the damn things."

"Convert to Islam and wear a burqa," she suggested, "that'd sort you out."

"That sounds a little extreme, but I'm seeing Jorge tomorrow and I know he'll be a nightmare about it, so maybe it's not such a bad idea after all."

"Maybe the bites will drive him wild with jealousy?" she joked. "Are you still drooling over him?"

"Believe me, I've come darn close to pouncing on him recently," I replied, scrutinising the bubbles in my *caña*. "I just need to get over it though. It's never going to happen."

"T-shirt! T-shirt!" A voice rang out over the crowd and I smiled as Andrés waved wildly and barrelled towards me.

"T-shirt! Long time – why you not call me?" he asked as he kissed my cheeks and squeezed my muffin-tops in both hands.

"Andrés! It's been ages. Why haven't you called me?!" I asked, happy to see him again. "This is my friend Chloe,

Chloe this is Andrés. His grandmother lives in my building and funnily enough his brother Rafa is one of my students at the Institute too."

"Rafa?" she laughed, "I've heard all about Rafa."

She flicked her long hair over her shoulder.

"Hey Andrés, good to meet you. Are you here for the *intercambio?*" she asked, batting her eyelashes and stroking his arm as she leant closer.

He turned his eyes to her and his mouth fell slack.

"Um, *sí, sí, es verdad.* I need practise my English," he stuttered, lost for words. "You is *guapísima* Chloe."

"*Gracias,*" she replied, smoothly, "let's get some drinks and I'll teach you a few things." She continued batting her eyelashes as she guided him over to the bar. Since her relationship with Dave had ended she'd been a bit down, but I watched her in full-on charm mode, glad to see her back in her stride.

***

A long and boozy lunch with Molly at Casa Mingo, followed by a manic afternoon of classes meant by the time I got home it was too late for the extended siesta I had been planning. These little afternoon kips, such a cliché of Spanish life, had become an essential part of my daily routine. I dragged myself off to Café Comercial wondering if Iñaki had any idea what his friend had done to my face. I checked out his WhatsApp profile photo and felt reassured to see a nice-looking guy, albeit with a rather big nose emerging from his face of stubble. Not that I could judge noses, possessing a rather distinguished beak myself. As I arrived at the Glorieta my phone buzzed with a message "Evie, I only leave the office now. Sorry. I arrive in ten minutes." Typical

Spaniard! I leant back on the railings trying to deduce whether the nerves or the numerous glasses of cider at lunch were making my tummy tickle, and chuckling at how I'd met Raul in exactly the same spot only a few months earlier.

The first thing I noticed when Iñaki approached me was his deep, crinkly eyes, almost swallowed into his face as he smiled nervously and kissed me on both cheeks, but above all what struck me was his gentle aura.

"So tell me about your day Evie, how was it?" he asked, easily.

I could have kissed him then and there as he pronounced my name perfectly. Carolina was the only other Spaniard I knew who reliably said it correctly and I loved it. I grinned as we headed towards Plaza Olavide and started wittering away.

"I've had the funniest day with my students – you wouldn't believe what happened in one of our exercises this afternoon…" He reached out and grabbed my forearm.

"I'm sorry Evie, I need maybe ten minutes to change my switch in English. To switch to English. Can you speak more slow?"

"We can speak in Spanish if you prefer?" I offered timidly, dreading the idea in the midst of a low-confidence-in-my-Spanish phase.

"No, no is problem, I like to speaking English. I just need ten minutes to change my head," he repeated, looking sheepish.

As always Plaza Olavide reverberated with life but we managed to bag a table under one of the big trees, the shade a welcome respite from the warm evening sunshine.

"*Qué quieres Evie?*" he asked, switching back into Spanish as the waiter appeared by our side.

"*Una clara con limón porfa,*" I replied, opting for a shandy.

"*Nos pone una clara con limón y la cerveza mas fría y mas grande que tienes por favor?*" he asked the waiter, with a smile. I sat back and smiled as they joked in an easy manner.

I have no idea what we really spoke about and the time flew past in a blur. Boy did he know how to talk. A lot. And he obviously relished the opportunity to practise his English. Not for the first time since arriving in the country did I feel a little like I was being used for my language skills, but I was giggly enough to enjoy the evening, let him witter and simply offer the occasional interjection.

"I am going to order a wine now," he suddenly announced, motioning to the waiter, "would you like a glass too?"

"Sure," I agreed. Why the hell not?

"What do you prefer, Ribera or Rioja?" he asked, in a loaded fashion. "Is an important question."

"Ribera, of course. I love Ribera," I pronounced smugly, knowing it to be the choice of the locals, while tourists opt for the better-known Rioja.

His face fell, "Oh no, we cannot see each other again," he stated glumly. "Is impossible."

"Why not?" I asked, leaning over the table, wondering how I'd clearly committed treason.

"You must have Rioja. It's the greatest," he ordered, sternly. "I am from Logroño in the Rioja region and we are very proud of our wine." He smiled as he said this, but I was well aware wine and pride were no laughing matter in Spain, so I hastily changed my mind.

Two drinks later he announced he needed to get home.

"I am not here this weekend and then I am off on holidays on Friday, but maybe we could meet on Thursday night if you are free?" he enquired cautiously before adding, "and next time I help you with your Spanish too of course."

"Sounds great," I replied, realising I would have said yes

to anything at that point. I added, "I'm off on holiday to Granada for that long weekend too, but Thursday is a plan."

"Ahh, Granada is wonderful place. What you do there?" he asked.

"My flatmate Rebeca is a flamenco dancer and she's in a show there, so a few of us are going to give moral support. It should be fun."

As I wound my way through the streets filled with the lightness of a new crush I realised he hadn't asked me about the bruises. What a hero.

16

The turquoise dress? Or the green one? I stared into the mirror and wondered if I appeared more Spanish on the outside, for I definitely felt a Latino vibe was taking hold of my soul. Perhaps it was simply confidence, yet the two were inextricably linked in my mind now. I was a bit more tanned for sure, but you'd be hard pushed to call it brown. Forget my pale skin tone, when I finally made it out of the door after five outfit changes I felt like a true *madrileña* and I sauntered down the street with a swagger in my step. I turned the corner to see a white church gleaming in the bright evening sunshine and my eyes fell on Iñaki perched on his motorbike under the shade of a tree. James Dean eat your heart out.

"I arrived sooner than the British. I thought you were known for your punctuality?!" he said lazily, pushing his hair back from his face and fixing his smooth brown eyes on mine as a languid smile spread across his face.

"You must have driven too fast," I quipped back, "and anyway, I'm Spanish now so I have to arrive late for everything."

My mouth felt dry and a blush crept up my cheeks, not helped by the blazing sun.

He cleared his throat, "So, I was thinking. There is this

bar. It is very British. Well, maybe not so British for you, but it has gin and tonics. It's effectively Friday today for me as tomorrow starts the holiday, so I feel like a gin and tonic. What do you think? It's called the Bristol Bar."

"Sure thing, sounds great. I think I've seen it – does it have red and black writing?"

"Yes, it's near Alonso Martínez."

"Perfect. I love Alonso Martínez and I went to university in Bristol so I'm sure anywhere with the name must be good!" I mentally kicked myself at this lame comment.

"Do you want…" and he trailed off, waving his hand at the bike.

"Of course," I said, gulping nervously. "I haven't been on a bike before, but *vamos!*" I warbled, over-enthusiastically. That fire in my cheeks was really blazing out of control now.

He unlocked the seat and took out a helmet. I pulled it over my head and fiddled about ineptly with the chin strap, fumbling like a child.

"Here, I help you." As he swiftly fastened it his dark eyes bored down into mine and I didn't know where to look. Unlike any eyes I had ever seen, they were deeply set back with low lids, and their surprising intensity made my hands go clammy. I hobbled on behind him ungracefully and put my arms loosely round his middle as he turned the key in the ignition and revved the engine.

"The only thing you need remember is not to try and balance the bike. If I move to the side, you move with me. Ok? And you can hold me, but try not to take advantage of me," he said, chuckling. "If you prefer there are handles behind."

I tittered nervously and instantly moved my hands onto the handles, my knuckles tightly clenched. *Of course* there were handles at the back. Why hadn't I thought of that?

Everything looked different from the perspective of a bike

and as we zoomed through the streets I was immediately submerged in the familiar warm wave of total contentment. Despite all the ups and downs of the last nine months I felt more carefree and happy than ever before and I wanted to let out a yell of happiness.

We took a scenic route to the bar, and as we drove I thought back to my first few days when frankly I'd been pretty unimpressed with the city. I couldn't believe I'd ever thought like that when now I felt such overwhelming love for the place and all its quirky details. The warmth of the sun had turned the buildings a gorgeous, golden hue against the cloudless blue sky, a perfect backdrop to the everyday street scenes below. Chic women in pyjama-style trousers, sandals and silk tops wafted down the streets holding leads attached to little rat-like animals pretending to be dogs. The Bangladeshi man at the *fruteria* waved as we passed and I recognised the creepy guy from the *locoturio* at the next corner. On evenings like this Madrid was the most stunning place in the world. I knew this not to be true architecturally or artistically, but I must have been blind to miss its magical and understated charm at the beginning.

My romantic daydreaming ended abruptly as we ramped up onto the pavement and came to a jerky halt. I wobbled off the bike – balance, elegance and grace never having been my strong points, even without the unsettling addition of a good-looking guy added to the equation. He smoothly removed my helmet, took my hand and led me into the bar.

Conversation flitted between many subjects and we talked about his love of surfing and his childhood, and his desire to move abroad struck a chord. On paper his life sounded perfect, with a warm and loving family, a good job in a bank, a great-sounding group of friends and an awesome flat, yet he was dying for an escape. Craving an adventure and feeling restricted and confined by all the things he was blessed and lucky to have. I poured out my heart on the emotional ups and downs which had accompanied my Spanish adventures.

"If you want to go abroad you *must* do it," I advised. "Honestly, I know it's hard to make the decision, but once you've made it then everything just happens and it's really not difficult."

He looked at me disbelievingly.

"You really think so?"

"Iñaki," I said, plonking my drink down on the table for emphasis, "I can *promise* you won't regret it and if it doesn't work out you can come back and you'll find nothing will have changed."

I paused for dramatic effect and added, "Moving out here is THE best thing I've ever done in my life. Fact." The words came out with a force that surprised me and I was shocked to realise I whole-heartedly believed it.

He looked pensively into the bottom of his glass and I thought it was time to stop preaching and lighten the mood.

"So does everyone call you Iñaki?"

"Always my friends call me Iñaki. Although some call me Nacho too," he grinned.

"*En serio?!*" I asked, laughing.

"*Sí,* is common nickname for Ignacio."

Conversation moved on to a discussion about relation-ships. He admitted that after several long-term girlfriends, he'd been single for over a year now.

"Like, is easy to date girls, but now I want a real connec-tion. I want something more than I had in past," he tried to explain. "Is difficult to find, but I am hoping." Did he think we had that connection? I felt so content in his company, not to mention the jolt of electricity that ran through me every time we touched, I most certainly did. As we drained our glasses and ordered more drinks I sat back.

His laid-back attitude and comfort in his own skin exuded from his every pore. I suppose it's a typical outcome when you're the only son in a close family. I had come across many men where this undiluted parental attention had resulted in a spoilt, arrogant man, but if it existed, I hadn't yet seen that side of Iñaki. From time to time he pushed his hair back from his eyes in a smooth, lazy movement that made me want to lean over and kiss him right then and there.

"I'm sorry Evie, but I think we must leave now. I need to collect the car from my parents for my trip tomorrow."

"No problem, I should do my packing too," I smiled to mask my disappointment.

We strolled outside and hopped back on to the bike. "Now I have drank one gin and tonic and one wine you can take advantage of me if you want," he said with a cheeky grin.

I laughed and gave him a friendly squeeze round the middle before putting my hands firmly back on the handles.

After another exhilarating journey we pulled up outside my flat and loitered in the setting sunshine, chatting about his plans for his surfing weekend in Portugal. I couldn't stop smiling as he stared at me intensely but he didn't make a move.

Someone had to take control.

"I must let you go now," I said firmly. I put my hand on his shoulder and went to kiss his cheek when suddenly his mouth found mine. Soft and gentle, his kiss matched his personality and I pulled him closer. Opening one eye I surveyed his face, his adorable face.

I wanted time to stand still as we stayed there laughing, kissing and chatting for what felt like hours. Finally I reluctantly pulled away, saying coyly, "Have a great holiday and..." but before I could finish his lips found mine again and I happily surrendered to more kissing. His hands slipped around my waist, under my top and their warmth made me quiver with delight.

A few moments later it was his turn to pull away.

"I really should go now," he muttered, before adding playfully, "but I don't want," and lowering his lips onto mine once more.

"Ok, you must go," I asserted, "but enjoy the surfing and send me some pictures!" I laughed, pulling away but leaving my hands in his and gazing into his eyes.

"Right, I must let you go. Have an amazing time," I repeated.

"So, I arrive back on Wednesday night and we talk then?"

"Great, yes. Have a wonderful time," I replied. God I was getting WAY too repetitive, "*y vamos hablamos – pero la próxima vez hablamos solo en español.* I think you've been using me for my English!"

After one final kiss I walked to the door and as I climbed the stairs my phone buzzed with the message "*besas muy bien* ☺" The butterflies in my stomach came back with a vengeance – he didn't kiss so badly himself!

17

Iñaki: Hey Evie! How are you? When are you going to Granada?

Evie: Yo! *Estamos en camino ya!* Are you there yet?

Evie: I had fun last night – thank you!

Iñaki: Yes! We've landed and are now at the hotel getting ready for the beach.

Iñaki: I had fun too!

Iñaki: Do u know what to see in Granada?

Evie: I am staying with some friends who have a house there so I am leaving them in charge of everything.

Evie: All I know is I want to go to the Alhambra and we are going to see a friend dance some flamenco!

Iñaki: You are so touristic!

Iñaki: You will love it. You can send me pictures if you want!

Evie: Haha, ok, but only if you send me a photo of you standing on a surfboard!!

Iñaki: Haha, I'll try.

Chloe's family had been seduced by Granada when visiting years ago and had bought the house in the hills outside the city on a whim, then and there. As I pushed open the wooden shutters of my room and filled my lungs with the deep, fragrant air I totally understood; beyond the riotously bright flowers of the paved courtyard, snow-sprinkled mountains filled the window frame in a breathtaking display of dramatic peaks.

The terracotta tiles felt wonderfully warm on the soles of my feet as I padded across to the pool, the scent of the oranges from the neighbouring garden loitering in the air. Stretching out on a lounger, I joined Rebeca, Chloe and Belinda and we dozed and gossiped in the sunshine, life in Madrid already a distant memory. Awoken from a heavenly slumber by my phone, I reached out and fumbled around under my clothes for it. *Iñaki has sent you two images* and two slightly fuzzy shots came into focus. It was him all right, standing on his board and riding a wave. Not exactly Keanu Reeves, but he looked pretty cool nonetheless and I couldn't help but grin. Beep, beep and the phone flashed with another message: "Here are photos for you. Your time next. I wait for your pictures! How is your trip so far?" Oh god, I hated this sort of thing, particularly when my budget phone couldn't take selfies.

I dithered over my response before typing, "Looks amazing – great pictures!! We are staying in valley outside Granada – it's sooo beautiful", and attaching an arty photo of my feet against the backdrop of the pool and the distant mountains.

Seconds later he replied: "It's very nice even though the purpose of receiving the picture was seeing you", then a winky emoji.

Was there no placating him?! After more banter I could avoid it no longer, so I sneaked into the kitchen and begged Chloe for help.

"Oh I LOVE this sort of thing!" she exclaimed merrily, clapping her hands like an excited toddler. "Where shall we start? I think you should be sitting by the pool."

"Um, ok," I agreed, meekly. "Whatever you think – you're the artistic director, but let's get it done quickly. I hate having my photo taken."

"Gimme your cup of tea," she grabbed the mug from my hand and set to opening a bottle of rosé. "You'll look better with a glass of this in your hand."

"It's not going to look too posed is it?!" I ventured.

"Not at all. Leave it to me. He'll be eating out of the palm of your hand in no time."

"Come on, give me your best smile," she cried from the other side of the pool. "Look happy! Have another swig of the rosé. Maybe put your other leg in the water too?"

I meekly followed her instructions, much to the amusement of the others and half an hour later the cringeworthy photoshoot was over. I selected one of the pictures to send him and then decided to turn off my phone for the afternoon. Enough of that for one day!

As we lounged by the pool, the conversation inevitably turned to future plans.

"So have you decided what you're going to do next year Evie? Are you staying in Madrid?" asked Chloe.

"Oh god, I don't know. I'm allergic to the very idea of plans. I adore this idyllic Spanish existence, but my old boss emailed me about a great sounding job in London the other day and I have a niggling feeling it's time to get back there to normality sometime soon. On the other hand I know I've only just met him, but Iñaki is so lovely I quite want to see where that could go."

I paused to take a large swig of wine.

"What about you? Are you looking forward to getting back to London?"

"Not really," she sighed. "If I had the guts I'd move down here permanently, become a writer and spend an inordinate amount of time in this exact spot."

"That's not a bad plan. I think I'd have to come and join you," Belinda chipped in. "This is total bliss."

"Anyway, FAR more importantly, tell me about Andrés! I bumped into his granny yesterday and she told me he'd been on a few dates with an English girl called Chloe!" I exclaimed, sitting up in my lounger. "I can't believe I knew nothing about that!"

"Well," she replied coyly, "all I can say is he has an amazing body."

I leant on my arm to turn and peer at her through my shades.

"No way!" I squealed, "Was this after the *intercambio* at Carmencita's?"

"Yep, he took my number and we've met up a few times," she nodded. "After that disastrous trip to New York I was so miserable, but Andrés makes me feel good and the sex is out of this world. As Ethan would say, he sure knows how to use his spanner!"

"I'm so happy for you," I laughed.

"When do we get to meet the charmer?" asked Belinda.

"Soon," replied Chloe. "You'll meet him soon."

***

"Guys, we're going to be late," shrieked Chloe, as we put the finishing touches to our make-up and rushed out to the car. "I don't know exactly where this place is so we need to leave now if we're going to make it in time."

Half an hour later after endless wrong turns, we pulled up outside a traditional-looking tavern, the ochre and deep red façade decorated with dark wooden beams and dominated by gorgeous rambling flowers. We ran in and grabbed some drinks, settling round a low table onto rickety stools. As our eyes acclimatised to the smoky atmosphere I made out a cavernous stage and locals huddled round barrels and tables drinking *copas de vino* and *rebujitos*, a sort of sherry spritzer.

Rebeca had been excited for days in the build-up to the show and her enthusiasm was contagious. Her family had been flamenco dancers for generations and she took the tradition very seriously. They'd all cut their teeth on this stage and many of her ancestors featured in black and white photos lining the walls. I shifted on my stool, anxious for the performance to begin, but my patience was rewarded when Rebeca emerged on stage in an utterly mesmerising whirlwind of claps, stamps and twirls. Her hair was slicked back into a tight, glossy bun with a large red flower peeking out from behind her ear. A black and red dress clung to her body, dipping at the back to reveal tense muscles between her shoulder blades, and the endless ruffles on the skirt and sleeves swayed with her every move. Gold hoop earrings swung violently as she flung her head back and forth and her black-heeled shoes passionately struck the floor in time with the music. A hunched man with straggly dark hair sat at the side of the stage accompanying her with his guitar and haunting voice, hypnotic in his emotional intensity. Every sinew in her body was taut as she moved in time to the melody and every pore exuded pride, sexuality and passion. I couldn't take my eyes off her and my feet tapped uncontrollably to the rhythm.

"I feel cheated to have been born English," Chloe whispered to me, tears glistening in her eyes. "My soul is Spanish. I should have been Spanish." I was relieved I wasn't the only one enthralled by the performance.

More dancers joined the stage and by the time they ended, exhausted yet elated, it was as if we'd danced every step with them. We clapped, whooped and stamped for hours and didn't wind our way back to the farmhouse until the sun was rising.

***

Sofía gave priceless insight into the Spanish fashion sense. Very attractive, she obviously spent a lot of time and effort on her appearance. While we worked through some conversation cards focused on fashion and shopping, her face lit up as she described her favourite shops, designers and dresses, but her brown eyes widened in shock as they read the question, *do you ever wear second-hand clothes?*

"Never," she retorted, "I would NEVER wear second-hand clothes," looking at me in disgust and shaking her head.

"Never?"

"Definitely, never, never," she asserted emphatically.

"In Spain, nobody wear, *perdón*, nobody wears second-hand clothes," she continued.

"How funny. In England there are lots of charity shops and there's no shame at all in buying clothes there."

"*Pero los ingleses*, you English, you are not known for your style," she laughed, looking rather too pointedly at my stripy skirt and strappy top.

The subject of the crisis (pronounced *creeseees*) never strayed far from anyone's lips in Madrid, yet it surprised me how they seemed incapable of cutting back on their spending in certain areas. Yes, they searched out cheaper gas or electricity deals, and perhaps they bought fewer designer clothes, but whatever they did buy remained designer. I would have thought all restaurants were struggling, but to the contrary, the newspapers reported that *tapas* bars were flourishing. People may not be able to afford to go on holiday, but they weren't prepared to cut back on their socialising. Life out and about on the streets, *livin' la vida loca* and laughing with friends over *cañas* and *tapas* was far too engrained in their blood to be sacrificed, regardless of the economic climate. Laugh as I may about this, I loved how they prioritised living over working and put their families and fun before money and jobs. You couldn't pretend all was rosy here, and yes, the homelessness, the desperation of the beggars, and the number of people trawling through bins on the street depressed me at times, but the general optimism and positivity of people was equally humbling. The buskers on the metro were tirelessly upbeat and creative in their attempts to earn loose change and the generosity of people to both the buskers and the beggars warmed my heart.

***

"Ok, boys, I've been thinking and as all you seem to want to do is flirt I've got a special lesson for you today. We're going to practise speed dating! Have any of you ever been speed dating?" I babbled, so excited by this flash of inspiration, the words came tumbling out at top speed.

They shot me bemused looks. "Titcher, what is speed dating?"

"You know," I said, over-enthused as the idea took shape in my mind, "when you go to a bar and sit at a table. Maybe there are ten men and ten girls. A girl comes and sits with you, you chat for ten minutes and then you move round and chat for ten minutes with the next girl and so on. You know, this will be great practice for flirting with English girls!!"

"Winston wants to flirt you teacher," said Rafa, grinning.

"Let's not start this again," I replied sternly, determined to make this lesson a success.

Taking a deep breath, I continued, "So, who wants to be a girl? We need half the class to be girls and half to be boys."

"Sebo does teacher, Sebo is a big girl," muttered Carlos, moodily.

"No, make Winston a girl. He is pretty hair," added Rafa.

"Marcos has girl face. He sings with girl voice," shouted Jesús from the back of the class.

I sighed.

"Ok!! Quiet!! It's hard to believe you're not twelve years old when you talk like this. I will choose," I stated, grinning at the prospect of making the most obnoxious little upstarts girls for the afternoon.

They shifted the tables around and we began.

"So, give me some examples of questions or expressions you might use," I asked, struggling to keep a straight face. What was I doing? I couldn't help but think back to my interview with Alba and her strict instructions on being a good cultural representative. I'm not sure this was exactly what she had in mind...

"Come on, what do you say when you go and talk to a girl in a bar?"

"Titcher, Sebo ask me to seeing my chest mountains. Is rude, no?" Rafa shouted across the room.

"Yes, Sebo, that's not the best word for them. What did you say?"

"I want to seeing them. Is wrong? What you call them teacher? Teets?"

"We've talked about this, remember? If you ask to see a girl's chest mountains I *promise* she will laugh at you. Boobs, breasts or tits are the most common words. But baps, jugs, melons, bazookas, norks...I dunno, there are hundreds of others. Call them what you like, but chest mountains is *not* a good expression."

I took a deep breath and continued, "Now, *enough* of that, focus on your flirting. Oh and I forgot to say, I'm going to come round and give you all a card with a personality adjective on it and I want you to try and act like the word when you are flirting, ok? A bit of revision for all the adjectives we learnt the other day."

I clapped my hands and looked at the clock. "Ten minutes starts now!" I exclaimed and I wandered over to the first table to see how they would get on.

"So Hector, you're the boy, yes?"

"Not boy titcher, I am man," he pronounced proudly, thumping his chest, "and Winston is a girl."

Winston grinned sheepishly at me as they picked out two cards from my pile and read them.

"So titcher, are you doing anything tonight?" asked Hector, pushing back his chair and coming to stand next to me. Tall and dark with a strong jawline, and a winning smile, I found his close proximity unnerving.

"Um, what?"

"Are you doing anything tonight?" he repeated.

"No, why?" I replied quietly.

"Maybe we have dinner with how you say, um, with candles and music? What you think?"

"Are you serious?" I asked, perplexed, a blush creeping up my cheeks. He hummed a slow song as he edged closer and took my hand. Chairs scraped as the rest of the class turned around to see what was going on.

"No titcher, have dinner with me," interjected Winston, as he leapt to his feet angrily and roughly pushed Hector away from me. "You *gillipollas*. I fight you!" he shrieked, shoving Hector again so hard he stumbled over his desk and fell onto the floor.

"Boys!" I exclaimed, jumping between them. "We are

NOT having a fight in the classroom. What the hell is wrong with you?"

They erupted into guffaws and slapped each other's back.

"We good actors titcher, like Brad Pitt! You believe us!" cried Hector.

"Yes, we is acting our adjectives. Hector have romantic card and I have angry card."

"Ahhh," I sighed in relief, "you had me there! Good work boys."

"Now back to the speed dating!" I moved on to listen to Rafa and Jesús.

"What do you call them again titcher? Titties?" asked Rafa.

This boyish waffle still made me giggle, but I couldn't help but feel disheartened. I'd been teaching these guys for over six months now and it appeared they'd barely learnt anything useful for general conversation, let alone technical English for their course. Through their lessons and my own struggles with Spanish I'd become painfully aware of just how much time it took to master a language.

Iñaki. Iñaki, Iñaki, Iñaki. On repeat, at top speed, he whizzed through my thoughts nonstop as I desperately restrained myself from messaging him. I knew he had returned from his holiday and I couldn't help but check my phone every two minutes for a message. Finally, my patience was rewarded.

Hey Evie, how was your trip?

Morning! It was so much fun and I LOVED Granada… why do holidays always have to go so quickly? How was Portugal?

Jaja, I don't know why…my trip was awesome…do you feel like meeting today after work?

So, minutes later, it was all planned. He would pick me up from the Antonio Valdes offices at 8pm, with the added thrill Jorge might see me leaving with him.

***

What a change from when I used to hang off every word out of Jorge's mouth. I struggled to focus in his class as the hands of the clock ticked ever slower through the session. The second they reached 8pm I leapt up, waved goodbye and skipped out of the office.

I perched on the wall, feigning interest in my phone and attempting, unsuccessfully, to look nonchalant. Out of the corner of my eye I spotted a white motorbike approaching and a wide smile spread over my face. Iñaki hopped off, removed his helmet and oozing confidence he strode towards me for a protracted kiss.

"How are you?" he asked shyly when we finally pulled away.

"I'm good, I had a funny lesson with my student."

"Excellent. We go have a drink and you can tell to me about it."

"Great," I nodded enthusiastically.

"Shall we go to my area so I can show it to you? And also, it has the bonus we can first go to my flat to search my wallet? Do you mind? If it is not there I don't know where it is."

"Sure, why not. *Vamos!*" I said, "but first…" I pulled him close for another kiss.

I clambered onto the bike in my usual inelegant manner

and as we sped off towards Metropolitano I marvelled at how familiar the city now seemed. As we headed into the underground parking lot of his building a sudden panic hit me that the whole *I've lost my wallet* story had been a ruse to get me to his flat and I'd been a complete mug to fall for it. My overactive imagination never failed to get the better of me and a voice in my head told me to wait with the bike while he went upstairs, but curiosity got the better of me. I trailed after him into the plush and hotel-like cream marble lobby fully aware that if I was about to be raped and murdered then I was a horribly willing victim.

"*Buenas Nico,*" he chirped to the porter, giving him a wave as we passed his desk and headed into the waiting lift. We trundled upwards to the nineteenth floor where the gleaming silver doors opened to more expanse of marble floor. Around the corner he unlocked the door to 1918 and I timidly followed him into his pad. The door swung back and revealed the most incredible, expansive views of the city. Through the huge windows opposite, the vastness of Casa de Campo spread out to the west, the Faro de Moncloa stood proud and prominent in the centre and you could even see the Teatro at Opera peeking through two tall buildings. There was a small terrace with a hammock strung up across it and a table and chairs covered with his drying wetsuit and towel, but I couldn't tear my eyes from the view.

"It's like a painting," I muttered.

"*Sí*, I am very lucky."

"Which direction is this?" I pointed out of the window.

"Is south."

"Nice, so your terrace is sunny all day. How do you ever stop looking at that view? It's magical," I gushed.

"I take time in the morning when I take a coffee to just

look at it. My room at my parents didn't have much light so I very appreciate it."

I finally moved my eyes away to take in the rest of the flat. "I can't believe how tidy you are!"

He shrugged nonchalantly. "In small flats you have to be."

A skateboard peeked out from underneath a large cream leather sofa, and a well-used surfboard leant against a bright orange armchair in the corner. Clearly sporty. I carried on snooping and deduced he loved his music too. A pair of large speakers dominated the shelves, *Rolling Stone* magazine lay on the table next to a well-thumbed copy of *1001 Records You Should Hear Before You Die*. I liked his style. Laid-back and unpretentious. A modern TV sat in the corner, in comic contrast to the cracked brown, yellow and white retro tiles on the kitchen wall.

A large cityscape photograph enhanced with vivid strokes of paint dominated the wall opposite the windows.

"Is one of my younger sister's works," he said, following my gaze. "Shall we take a beer here? And I can show you more of her art?"

I nodded enthusiastically, too preoccupied to answer now the view had distracted my attention once more. He whipped a couple of bottles of Mahou from his fridge and cleared some space on the terrace. As we settled into conversation I wondered why I'd ever been nervous; he was warm, relaxed and the conversation flowed easily. Clicking through his sister's website, he proudly talked me through endless examples of her arresting works of art.

"This is one of my favourites," he said, showing me an image of a classical marble statue flying through the centre of a bright, mad and chaotic dancefloor. The sense of movement and speed was striking and the contrast of the old and new intriguing.

"This is a club my sister worked in when she went on Erasmus to Buenos Aires." He pointed to some figures in the foreground, "and these are her friends. They are espanish too."

"I love it!" I gushed. I really was impressed and his pride in her work was touching. When he'd mentioned she was an artist I had imagined some average watercolour landscapes – a far cry from these scenes which wouldn't look out of place in a New York gallery.

Hours passed as the sky turned velvety black and lights flickered on all over the city. Suddenly he pulled me to my feet and kissed me gently.

"Let me show you El Escorial," he said. I leant over the wall and he wrapped his body around me. "Here, you look to the right," he whispered, taking my hand and pointing into the distance. Following the lights on the road, I could see the twinkling of the small town in the distance, nestled in the foot of the mountains.

A rumble from his stomach prompted us to order some pizza which we devoured hungrily the moment it arrived, barely tearing our eyes from the mesmerising view.

"Look what I have finded," he shouted triumphantly from the kitchen. "Do you like these English chocolates?" he asked, returning to the balcony with a box of After Eights.

"I love them," I chuckled. "Have you ever played the After Eight game?"

"Game? No. What is that?" he asked, a perplexed expression crossing his face.

"It's so funny. Here," I instructed, taking the box and pulling a chocolate from its black wrapper. "You tilt your head back and put the chocolate on your forehead, like this."

"Then you wiggle all the muscles in your face to get the chocolate into your mouth without it falling on the floor." I began stretching and contorting my face, shifting the chocolate down over my eyelid and onto my cheek.

He stared wide-eyed at my bizarre movements and my cheeks began to burn, the chocolate started to melt and I belatedly wondered why I had suggested this game. After an agonising few moments, I coerced the mint into my mouth with my tongue, well aware a chocolate-smeared face wasn't exactly the most attractive look, but triumphant nonetheless.

"You English are so strange," he laughed, stepping in to kiss the chocolate off my cheeks and sending my pulse racing, "but it is a good game!"

"So, your turn now?" I laughed, passing the box over to him.

"I have a better idea," he muttered, taking my hand and leading me to his bedroom.

18

Nine months of winter and three months of hell describes the Spanish weather, according to an old proverb, and, now the thermometer constantly flickered around 38 degrees and a creeping lethargy took hold of the city, I could understand why. After frequent cold showers I lay naked on my bed craving autumn and the need to pull on jeans and a woolly jumper; yet within thirty seconds I was dry and another thirty later I began to sweat profusely again. Whoever said that pigs sweat, men perspire and women merely glow had clearly never been to Madrid. To make matters worse, in England the warmer temperatures brought out a flurry of podgy, white flesh and cellulite, but here the Spaniards flaunted their flawless, tanned legs in minuscule shorts while skimpy crop tops revealed horribly toned stomachs. They managed to stay effortlessly cool while foreigners such as yours truly wilted, turning ever deeper shades of pink and dripping with sweat, like potatoes roasting in the sun.

Ever since I spotted the first pair of *pantalones cortes* back in April I had developed an unhealthy obsession with staring at men's legs. Shaved or hairy, stubble or smooth? Do so many of them really wax? I had seen beautifully smooth legs, chests and even arms on men and I was having to radically redefine my ideas of masculinity. Or was I? I couldn't decide if it was a perfectly understandable development when you live in a hot country, or whether it was yet another reflection of the excessive vanity of Spanish men. Their devotion to their appearance was admirable, if unsettling; the young boys immaculately dressed in mini-chinos, V-neck sweaters and with perfect glossy curls; the lanky teenagers in sleeveless t-shirts and shorts who keep their endearing baby faces throughout their teens; the thirty-somethings of *barrio* Salamanca with their slightly high-waisted jeans, shirts and perma-tans, even the middle-aged businessmen in their somewhat shiny suits, highly polished shoes and neat comb overs. There is just something a little too perfect about all of them.

***

The Mercado de Motores took place in a train museum to the south of the city. Stalls laden with leather wallets, funky vintage jewellery, furniture assembled from recycled objects, industrial light fittings and mountains of cheese, honey and chorizo were lined out alongside the trains, underneath an expansive iron roof. Delicious smells of paella and BBQ burgers wafted through the air from the food trucks behind the museum, where a local band belted out Latino tunes in the blazing sunshine.

"Why don't we head out and get some food?" suggested Belinda.

"Good plan. Far too many people in here," moaned Chloe, huffing and puffing as she pushed her way towards the far end of the building. "At least the English apologise if they step on your foot or elbow you, I can't stand how the Spaniards are totally oblivious to the concept of personal space."

We nabbed a table in the shade and tucked into *paella*, *jamón* and *tortilla* as conversation turned to the horse races. Belinda was being taken by her friend Jaime the following day and I'd managed to invite myself along too.

"What are we going to wear?" Belinda asked. "I mean I have no idea if this is like Ascot and we need to be smart, or if it's more of a scruffy point-to-point kind of thing."

Chloe laughed, "I don't think the Spanish really do scruffy, do you?!"

"You're right, we should probably be smart. I think it's high time I started to dress to impress anyway."

"Always a good idea," agreed the ever-glamorous Chloe.

"So what's Jaime like?" I enquired, intrigued. Belinda had been introduced to him through a tenuous link via distant cousins, neighbours and a friend, or something along those lines. She'd met him a couple of times recently, but other than that I knew little.

"He's very traditional and Spanish, but good looking in a Euro way. He's tediously obsessed with horses, but he's been very kind to me with some work introductions. He's surprisingly well-connected in the film world."

"He might be the man of your dreams Evie!" exclaimed Chloe gleefully.

"He might indeed, although I have to say Iñaki's filling that spot perfectly at the moment," I admitted coyly, a soppy smile creeping over my face.

"I thought we hadn't seen much of you recently as you'd been working hard," Belinda teased, prodding me in the ribs. "Is it really because things are going well with him?"

"Haha, yes, sorry, I've been spending a lot of time with him. I know it sounds cheesy, but I'm not sure I've ever felt so relaxed and happy with someone. He's totally dreamy," I replied, grinning like a Cheshire cat. "Although it's so ironic he comes along just when I'm beginning to think about moving back to London."

"What?!" they screeched in unison, Belinda dropping her fork.

"Are you serious?" she asked, open-mouthed. "You're really thinking of leaving?"

"Well I was," I played with the bright yellow *tortilla* in front of me and took a deep breath.

"I am," I asserted. "But the whole Iñaki thing is really making me have second thoughts and I'm completely torn," I admitted sheepishly, twirling my bracelet round and round in my fingers.

"Wowzer, I had no idea that was even on the cards. Is it because I'm moving soon and you can't bear the idea of Madrid without me?!" joked Chloe.

"Of course! No, I don't think I've consciously admitted it to myself before, and I've never said it out loud, but on some level it's been a long time coming. I adore Madrid – you know how much I love everything about this ridiculous place, but I'm just not sure I can keep kidding myself I love teaching."

"I can see that," agreed Chloe, gently.

"It's great in some ways and I feel so much more confident than I did at the beginning. You know I get such a kick when my students get the hang of something, but in the grand scheme of things I don't really feel like I'm teaching them much." I paused, continuing to fiddle manically with my bracelet, my eyes focused on the remnants of the *tortilla*. "I get fed up with the travelling between classes and the constant cancellations and changes, but most of all I miss being part of a team and feeling like I'm getting somewhere with life."

"Are you sure leaving is the answer? If you were stuck in an office again I bet you'd crave the freedom and flexibility of your life here," said Belinda, wisely.

"True. The bloody grass is always greener. I can't stop changing my mind and I feel totally paralysed by indecision."

"I also met this really lovely old English lady on the bus the other day," I continued. "It was totally random but we ended up going for a coffee and she told me her life story. She married a Spaniard when she was nineteen and over here to study Spanish, a bit of a whirlwind thing. Sadly he died quite young, but she chose to stay here for her children and grandchildren etc. She speaks perfect Spanish and is effectively Spanish really, but says she still feels like an outsider; people take one look at her and it's clear she's English so they treat her like a muppet tourist, but yet when she goes back to Devon she says she feels even more out of place. She really made me think and I'm not sure I could cope with that feeling long-term."

I continued to push the remains of my food around my plate with my fork and sighed, "Oh what shall I do guys? It's seems teenage to stay for a guy when things are at such an early stage, but at the same time would I be totally mad to chuck it away?"

"Let's be pragmatic. How does the idea of moving home make you feel? Happy or sad?" asked Chloe.

"Pretty depressed if I'm honest. I've never been good with the whole concept of change and I have no idea what I'd do back home. At least here I know I'll have teaching work as long as I need it. Nearly all my students have said they'd like to continue their classes next year for a start."

"Well, there's your answer then. You should be where you feel happiest, and you've said before you're happier here than you ever were in London," she said earnestly.

"True. Moving was undoubtedly the best thing I've ever

done, but it does all feel like a dream. I'm sure it would be better if I had a more settled, office job here but I've been looking for a while and it's impossible."

"Well it's not like you need to decide now once and for all. You'll always be able to find teaching work, so why don't you just stay a bit longer, see how things pan out with Iñaki and think again at Christmas," Chloe suggested, sensibly.

"*Poco a poco,*" she added with a wink, laughing.

"Yep, I know, but the thing is it all slightly came to a head the other day. I got another email from my old boss about this great opportunity back in London. They still haven't found anyone, and he said he'd put in a good word for me if I was interested." Making exaggerated speech marks in the air, and putting on his American drawl, I continued "*If you haven't become a professional bullfighter by now…*I hate to admit it, but the job sounds amazing. The deadline is soon though, so I need to step on it if I'm going to apply. AND, a great friend from uni just posted a thing on Facebook saying she's looking for a new flatmate, so if I am going to go back it feels like now could be the right time."

"But you weren't so happy in London were you?" said Chloe.

"No, I wasn't, but maybe things would be easier now. I feel so much more confident and I mean, if I can cope with the mechanics surely I can cope with anything now?!"

"Have you talked to Iñaki about it?" chipped in Belinda.

"No, I know I should but I don't dare bring it up."

"Would he ever come to England with you?"

I shook my head vehemently, "it's waaaaaay too soon, and I doubt it anyway. He's a real sun worshipper at heart, and having only ever visited Slough he has a seriously dismal view of the UK. I can't imagine him enjoying it there if I'm honest."

"Urgh," shuddered Chloe, "why would anyone want to go to Slough?"

"Have you spoken to your parents at least?" Belinda asked, tentatively.

"Briefly. I know Mum wants me to go home, get a proper job and settle down, but then Dad always tells me he envies my freedom and adventures and thinks I should make the most of them while I can." I added ruefully, "It's easy to see where I get the two sides of my personality from.

"Anyway, let's change the subject. Chloe, aren't your parents coming to visit soon?"

"Shit, yes, they're arriving today. I've got to run if I'm going to make it to the airport in time!" She leapt to her feet.

"They're only here for a couple of days, so let's do something on Wednesday," she kissed us goodbye, swung her bag over her shoulder and raced towards the exit.

***

I set off bright and early the next morning to pick up Belinda before walking to meet Jaime on the corner of Calle Velázquez and Calle Juan Bravo. I spotted a shiny, navy Polo and knew it had to be him. A typically charming Spaniard, although a tad unforthcoming, he was kitted out in a Schoffel gilet, burgundy jumper, checked shirt, brown chinos and polished brogues, seemingly oblivious to the already high temperatures and blazing sunshine.

"*Cómo estás?*" Belinda asked, greeting him warmly.

He shook his head gravely.

"I have been very ill. A serious flu," he sighed. Belinda and I exchanged a glance, stifling giggles at his gravitas.

"Oh no," she replied, "are you sure you should be going? Would you prefer to be in bed?"

"No, no. Is ok, I show you the races and then I sleep this afternoon," he said as we got into the car and sped west through the city, out of the Arch of Moncloa and soon arrived at the racecourse.

The sun shone and I was giddy with excitement to be somewhere totally new and different. Not to mention the fact I'd always had a penchant for gambling. The place could have been Latin American; with its adobe style architecture, arches and colonnades it would have made the perfect hacienda for a Mexican drug dealer in a film. There was a large open space in the centre where people lounged, drinking beers and soaking up some rays with music streaming out of a nearby building, and it was 10.30am. Only in Spain.

In all honesty, we didn't pay much attention to the races. Other than making a few misguided bets, we ended up drinking beer and chilling out in the courtyard with Jaime and his friends.

"Eebee, I can't believe you've been here nearly a year and your Spanish isn't better," he proclaimed loudly, bringing a flush to my cheeks. "Why is that?"

"I'm not a natural linguist, but I'm getting there," I retorted, bristling and I doggedly devoted my attentions to loudly addressing his friends in my best Spanish for the next hour or so. Javi and Ana were lovely. An architect and engineer, they were recently married, effortlessly cool and within moments had invited us to join them for a late lunch and drinks at Entre Caceres y Badajoz, their local joint in *barrio* Salamanca. Coughing excessively as if on death's door, Jaime set off home to rest and indulge his man flu.

Distinctly merrier and poorer than we had been that morning, we arrived to find the restaurant heaving with people and overflowing onto the streets. Jovial laughter, shouts and chat hung in the air as I turned to Javi and Ana.

"It looks packed here, shall we try somewhere else?"

"No, no, is fine, follow me," Ana replied with a grin as she determinedly barged her way past the crowds to the bar and we shoved through in her wake. She easily made space where I could have sworn there was none and we installed ourselves in a prime spot round a large wooden barrel by the bar as she shouted drinks orders at the barman. With every new round of vermouths came more plates of *tapas*, including a deep saffron-yellow *paella* with four little forks, silky octopus with golden mashed potato liberally smothered in olive oil and steaming plates of tender beef, peppers and onions on bread, dripping with yet more olive oil. Chaotic, rowdy, fun and loud, the afternoon passed in a blur of food, drink and new faces. How could I, in all seriousness, be thinking of jacking this in and moving back to Fulham?

***

I turned off my phone and closed my eyes, desperately craving a good night's sleep and a break from my worrying but a rising chorus of enthusiastic shouts, grunts, yells and screams rang through the air every few minutes. Spain were playing the Netherlands in the World Cup, so as with any football match the entire city had come to a standstill. Every other man I'd passed on the street that day sported a Spanish football shirt and even some immaculately dressed grannies had football scarves neatly tied around their necks.

I tossed and turned and attempted to ignore the sweltering heat and raucous post-match celebrations, as well as banishing thoughts about the future from my mind. Sleep was not coming and I couldn't stop thinking about the job in London and wondering what the *right* thing to do was. At 3.30am, after hours of internal debate I leapt from bed, switched on the light and turned on my computer. In a moment of clarity I realised I *had* to apply for it. It wasn't as if that meant I would definitely move home, but it kept my options open and clearly all this umm-ing and ahh-ing proved I would regret it if I didn't at least apply. It *had* to be better to know, and it took the decision out of my hands. Obviously if I didn't get the position then the question of leaving could simply be forgotten, and if I did get offered it? Well, that bridge could be crossed as and when. I'd spent so long recently being negative about London in comparison to my sunny life in Spain, denying the reality that I did miss my friends and family and the feeling of going somewhere, of getting on with life. Teaching had many perks, but I didn't want to commit to doing it for the rest of my life and couldn't face explaining the difference between the present perfect and past simple tenses for another thirty years. Having completed the brief application form and attached my CV, my hand hovered over the *send* button for several minutes before I took a deep breath and clicked submit. I retreated back to bed, clamped my eyes tight shut and prayed for the zz's to arrive.

19

Iñaki had been working in Bilbao and the ten days since we'd seen each other had dragged more slowly than a slithering snail. Perched model-like on his bike under the tree, the scene had lost none of its initial impact and my heart skipped a beat as I turned the corner and trotted over to meet him. He stood up and planted a prolonged kiss on my lips, his hands snaking down my hips and pulling my body to his.

"Oh god I've missed you," I murmured breathlessly. "I know it's only been ten days but..." He raised his finger to my lips.

"No more talking, we go," he decreed, and we retreated back to his flat under a darkening velvety sky.

***

"There's a storm coming," I announced as we lay entwined in his hammock, surveying the city shimmering with lights.

"*Seguro,* and we will have good view here," he agreed. "Now, come, we put clothes on and we prepare the *gazpacho*. If you love it so much you must know the best way. My mother she teach me and is the only thing I know."

I opened the antiquated, buzzing fridge and searched between the beer and the beef.

"So what do we need?" I asked.

"Tomatoes. First, you start with the tomatoes. Cut them and we put here," he instructed, pointing to the blender.

"Yes sir," I laughed, giving him a mock salute and setting to work.

"I cut the peppers and then we need garlic, oil, vinegar and a little *pepino*. How you say *pepino* again? Oh yes, is cucumber." He continued assembling the ingredients and putting away the washing up while I chopped, constantly bumping into me due to the cramped space and distracting me with kisses.

"You should be proud you know. I show my friends in Bilbao the English way to eat After Eights," he joked.

"Did you really? That's hilarious! I'm not too sure you should really call it the English way though. I suspect it's only my weird friends who do it."

His face fell, "Oh, I tell everyone is an English traditional game."

"Well you never know, it might be and wherever it came from we will just have to turn it into a global phenomenon."

"Haha, ok, I will try to spread it all over Spain."

The vegetables were soon whizzing away while I unwrapped some *jamón* and cheese and put it on a plate. Iñaki cracked open a bottle of Rioja and we settled on the balcony for the quintessentially Spanish feast. The cool *gazpacho* was perfect – its simplicity so refreshing and I marvelled my skin hadn't taken on a tomato-coloured hue recently when I'd been living off a diet which was 90 percent made up of the stuff.

A bolt of lightning flashed across the sky and we clambered back into his hammock. I stretched out against his warm, lean body and let out a sigh of contentment as we watched the storm take hold across the city.

***

I awoke to a hand gently running up and down my spine and I could feel his stare boring into my back.

"Morning," I muttered sleepily, turning over to face him and running my hand through the smattering of soft, dark hair on his chest.

"Morning *guapa*," he replied, smiling and rubbing his eyes and leaning over to kiss me. "Normally I suffer in the mornings, but it's OK today as you are here. It will be more hard to get up though."

"Well, it's Saturday so no need to get up any time soon."

"Good point. What do you feel like doing? Shall we have a brunch and pool day?"

"Perfect," I agreed. "Although an hour or so more of sleep would make it even more perfect. You didn't let me get much rest last night!" I joked.

"Hmm, I can't resist you," he laughed, as he nuzzled into my neck, covered my chest with kisses and distracted me from sleep yet again.

It was a glorious day with a lovely breeze taking the edge off the rising temperatures. We indulged in a mountain of delicious pancakes and coffee and made our way to the roof of his building to be greeted by yet more stunning and expansive views of Madrid.

"Here, let me show you." Draping his arm across my shoulders, he guided me to the edge and pointed out endless sights while I surveyed the city in wonder. We strolled round all sides of the building, before we lathered on sun cream and settled on some loungers by the pool. Heaven.

"You haven't told me about your work. How is the teaching?" he asked.

"The mechanics are as odd as ever, but I do feel like a few of them are really improving," I sighed, "but some of my other students are another matter altogether."

"Oh yes?"

"I've been doing a few substitute classes for a friend with this guy Marcos, a super-arrogant stockbroker from Seville. Yesterday he asked me to call a high school in Kentucky where his son studied last year, to get some paperwork from them. It was a total farce."

"What is farce?" he interrupted.

"Something ridiculous and stupid," I explained. "Anyway, I didn't understand exactly what he needed, and the several women I spoke to had no idea and weren't inclined to be very helpful at first although we did sort it out eventually. In the end I was completely torn between feeling glad to be useful and yet majorly irritated at being treated like a glorified PA."

"That is not right," he said, turning on his lounger to face me. "You should not be teaching people like that. Maybe is better you find new students."

"Yep, well luckily I only have one more class with him and I won't be sad to say goodbye! Most of my classes are finishing soon for the summer so I can't really complain."

There weren't many other people on the roof except for a drunk teenage girl flirting with the pool attendant, and we spent the rest of the weekend in a blissful haze of swimming and sunbathing, retreating to the hammock on his balcony whenever the afternoon heat got too much.

***

As I wound up my last class of the year with Sofía a few weeks later I had a heavy heart. Antonio Valdes had been such a sanctuary of fun over the last year and my students there an endless source of amusement and support. The idea of a two-month break over the summer when the whole place pretty much shut up shop, let alone the potential possibility of never returning, was too much to bear. As we packed up our things, Sofía pronounced proudly,

"Before you leave, we have some boobs and present for you."

"You mean booze! I thought we'd been over this – there's a big difference!"

"*Sí, sí*, of course!" she laughed.

She rushed to the office and returned laden with bags clanking with bottles, and accompanied by Jorge, Lopezones and the rest of the team.

"We gift you gin, wine, champagne and vodka – all your favourite things!" laughed Jorge. "Thank you for your classes, you are a very fun titcher."

"Yes, you are the best!" added Sofía, pulling me into a hug. "We see you back after summer or if you go to England in August maybe we come on office trip to see you! We go team trip to Oxford Street!"

Passed around the group like a doll, they all kissed me warmly. "Have a good summer and we keep in contact. We go for drinks soon. Kisses!" they chorused as they clustered around the doorway to wave me into the lift. I somehow managed to keep the tears under control until the doors closed, but the floodgates opened as I left the building and I wearily wandered down the pavement as they rolled down my cheeks. Why was it, when you felt sensitive, kindness tipped you over the edge into emotional havoc? I lugged my bags of *boobs* and surreptitiously tried to wipe mascara off my tear-stained cheeks as I rounded the corner to meet Iñaki by the metro.

"You ok?" he asked concerned, striding over and enveloping me in a huge hug.

"Yep, I'm ok," I stuttered. "It's silly. It was my last class of the year with these guys and they are so sweet to me. I'm really going to miss them over the summer."

I hiccupped and looked up into his eyes.

"Let's go back to my flat so I can change clothes," he suggested, wiping a tear from my cheek and giving me a kiss, "and then I take you for dinner. We could try a Mexican place near of my flat – I think you need a margarita."

"Sounds perfect," I replied, still hiccupping. I loaded all the bottles into the bike, hopped on and as we zoomed down the street my spirits lifted by the second. After a beer on his balcony I was almost back to normal and we headed off to the restaurant.

"Ahh, we have got here *un poco* too early. See all the children?" he commented, regretfully as we pulled up outside a brightly-coloured red restaurant decorated with plastic palm trees, sombreros and retro posters of Mexican wrestlers. Toddlers ran in and out of the tables while younger babes snoozed in their mothers' arms.

I looked at my watch and saw it was 9.30pm.

"Early?" I replied, incredulous. "Do you really call this early? I can't believe there are so many children here at 9.30pm. In England they would have gone to bed hours ago!" I responded, shimmying my shoulders gently in time with the cheesy Latino tunes floating out of the kitchen.

"I don't remember going to bed before midnight in as far as I can remember."

"Seriously?"

"Well, I never need to get up earlier than 8.30, so if I go to bed at 1.30, I still have seven hours and I don't need more."

"Where do you Spaniards get your energy from?! I could *easily* sleep for ten hours every night, if not more."

"What time did you have dinner as a child?" I asked.

"Normally 10pm, 10.30ish…"

"Ha, I don't think Mum let me stay up till 10pm till I was about sixteen!" I exclaimed, as we sat at a table by the window.

"I do love how long the days feel here though. Don't get me wrong, it took me months to get used to your hours, but I like it now. Everything feels so slow, in a good way."

"Sometimes is good. But the statistics, they say Spanish people spend more hours in the office than any other country, but at the same time we are the least productive workers in the world I think," he said, ruefully.

"Is your day that long?" I asked. "I thought you only had to be in the office at about 9.30am."

"Well, I arrive at the office at 9.30am. I don't do much work before 10.15 when all the department go to a café down the street for a half hour breakfast. This is written in our contract. Then when we return we properly start work at about 11. We work until 2pm then we have lunch break. Usually I come home, maybe swim in summer, have lunch and maybe short siesta and then return to the office to work until, maybe 7pm. Is a long day," he sighed.

Wide-eyed, I fell about laughing at this description.

"*En serio?!* That sounds like the best day ever!" I chuckled. "I don't think you would survive in a London office."

Shaking my head, my laughs drowned out his strong protests while we tucked in to heavily cheese-laden nachos washed down with a jug of chilled margaritas.

"You're loving those nachos, aren't you Nacho?!" I joked. "I think I'll call you Nacho from now on you know. I like it!"

"You no believe how many friends make the same joke during my life," he commented wryly, shaking his head as he scooped another pile of cheese into his mouth.

"Ha," I laughed, "What a great sense of humour your friends have!" My mood was soaring in direct proportion to my intake of a certain tequila spirit.

"You are such different persons when you speak Spanish and English. Is funny," he commented.

"How?" I asked, intrigued.

"In English you are much more self-assured which is good. I like confident women. But when you speak Spanish it's so cute and I feel like I need to look after you. I like it too." He smiled as he took another swig of margarita, his eyes watching me over the rim of the glass.

"Oh god, do I really sound like a child in Spanish?"

"Yes, but it's cute. *Suena dulce cuando hablas en español.* You sound sweet in Spanish. *Me gusta mucho*," he said, reaching across the table and taking my hand. "But in English you are more serious, like a teacher."

"You know what?" I sighed, taking his hand between mine, "I actually need to talk to you about something serious."

"Oh?" he looked up, "wait a minute, I ask the bill." He signalled to the waiter before turning his attention back to me. "What you want to say?"

"Actually, no, don't worry, it's not important," I mumbled, conviction deserting me and unwilling to spoil the mood with talk of my future.

Our stomachs full to bursting of tacos and chimichangas, we got back on the bike and zoomed off towards his flat.

"Do you fancy one more drink?" he asked when we stopped at traffic lights, his voice muffled by his helmet.

"Sure, why not?"

We skidded to a halt on the pavement outside a building with a neon sign reading Segundo Jazz Bar.

"This place is great and they always have *música en directo*," he reliably informed me as we walked in through a black door and down a dark red corridor. It was 11.45pm and the place was nearly empty.

"Are you going to tell me this is too early?" I joked.

"*Jaja*, yes, it is early still," he agreed.

"But it's a Tuesday?!" I was incredulous people would be out so late on a weeknight but equally aware my love of early nights and granny-like timetable in London was not something to be proud of. I scanned the room and noted we were the youngest by a long way; none of these lucky oldies would have to get up early tomorrow. The walls were dark red and lots of low, brown velvet-covered bucket chairs and sofas littered the room. We got drinks and settled on a sofa, and he was soon proved right. A younger clientele trickled in as a Cuban lady started crooning Ella Fitzgerald's *Summertime*. Iñaki put his arm around me and I snuggled into his shoulder as a wave of sheer contentment washed over me. All thoughts of England evaporated and in that moment there was nowhere in the world I would rather have been.

***

A slight hangover brought back the all-consuming doubts the next morning. I felt like a fraud as I bought a newspaper and settled in a café for a leisurely breakfast while properly employed people hurried to the office in their suits, stressed and determined expressions plastered on their faces. The security and purpose of their lives seemed so appealing and I resigned myself to the idea that maybe getting the London job would be the best thing after all.

Later in the day the factories and industrial wastelands flew past the window in a blur as the blue and grey bus made its way to the Institute for the last day of term and I couldn't bear the idea I might never make the journey again. Or that I was actually sad about it. Back in November it had been damn near impossible to stifle the urge to leap from the bus at every stop and head straight back to my blissful anonymity and hermit status in Calle Melendez Valdes. I loitered outside the entrance recalling the near panic attack I'd had when I first arrived, and all the embarrassing, entertaining and downright bizarre moments I'd had within the imposing red brick walls since then.

"*Hola* titcher," hollered Rafa with a grin as he walked past flanked by classmates.

"Hi boys," I waved, as my phone started to vibrate in my pocket.

"*Si*," I said, answering it.

"Eebee, it's Alba from the Native English Teaching Assistant programme. How are you?"

"Hi Alba, I'm good thanks. And you?"

"I'm fine. I wanted to say unfortunately it is not possible for you to continue at the Institute next year. We've put you on the waiting list for a placement in another school and we will let you know if something comes available."

"Um, ok," I gulped. "And when will I find out if I have another place?"

"I don't know, but at some point soon. I'm afraid I can't say at the moment."

After hanging up the phone I wanted to wail, *but I don't want another school – I want to go back to my mechanics!* Welling up, the idea of going to a normal school next year and an assistant role horrified me. It would be totally tedious in comparison and undoubtedly feel like a backwards step. There's no way I'd have the freedom I'd had at the Instituto and never again would I find myself discussing such enlightened subjects as boobs, breasts and tits. Pushing all thoughts of the future to the back of my mind, I walked towards the entrance with a smile, determined to enjoy my last day.

I finished up my reports on the boys and wandered the quiet corridors for a while, reminiscing. The clunky blinds in the classroom that failed to block the burning sunlight. The dodgy, archaic computers that didn't work, yet were a useful timewaster as we all fiddled with the buttons, projector and CD drive. The pervasive odour of oil and grime from the workshops.

"Hey Evie, do you like have anything to do right now? I was thinking of like going for a stroll outside to work on my tan if you wanna come too?" Madison shouted down the corridor.

"Sure, why not," I agreed and we sauntered out to the hideous wastelands surrounding the building. As we ambled I largely tuned out of her boy- and love-centred warbling and then she said, "This is going to sound suuuuuuuuper-hippy, but why don't we go and sit on a patch of grass over there? My friends always say I'm like super-hippy. Would you think I was strange?" she asked, slurping on yet another of her filthy looking green concoctions.

Masking my irritation, I threw myself flat out on the grass, slightly wary of what I might be landing on.

"I can't believe you drink so much of that green stuff. Is it really good for you?" I asked.

"You should try it. It's like incredible for your digestion. This one is like my best so far: kale, lettuce and cabbage." She sighed with contentment as I shuddered with disgust.

Full steam ahead she filled me in on every minute detail

of her love life as I struggled to keep my heavy eyelids open. She then moved on to telling me about her previous job in an academy called Armchair English.

"Do you still keep in touch with any of the other teachers there?" I asked, innocently, wondering how many friends the self-proclaimed Queen of Malasaña managed to keep.

She hesitated for a second, flicking her long hair over her shoulder, "Well, like, to be honest, they were just like jealous that I'm a naturally good teacher, because I'm naturally like very good at getting on with people. *Los escoceses no me caen bien* – I don't like the Scottish very much. I worked with lots of them in my old job – the men were like creepy and the girls were jealous. I think they like envied me for my looks too. I'm used to like a certain way of living – I don't go around saying like *tengo dinero,* I've got money, but they didn't like me because I'm rich. The men said like really inappropriate things to me, but I've had about a bejillion boyfriends so I'm used to men. Some of my co-workers couldn't deal with it though.

"They didn't like my tattoo either, I don't know why." I'd noticed her tattoo when she did her frequent, and unnecessary, stretches and yoga moves around the building. Every flash of her perfectly flat and tattooed stomach served to remind me how squidgy my own stomach had become. A diet of *tortilla* and *cañas* was not helping Operation Bikini.

"What does your tattoo say?" I asked, feigning interest.

"It's like Indonesian for love. I got it done in like the dark times and I'm not saying there aren't dark times any more, but back then they were way darker. It helps me. It connects me to my grandmother too."

After momentarily gazing into the distance, she changed the subject back to boys. Of course. Her favourite subject. "Did you have Alfredo in your classes? He was so good. He came to every class. He wanted me. *Obvio.*" She made a sweeping gesture around her face with both hands, "I mean look at this, all these boys like want me. It's exhausting sometimes. One day he came in early and waited for like two hours for class. I told him I'd been typing away in the *despacio*, in the office, and he should have come find me, but hey. He's a sweetie. And I think he just really liked me. Urgh. Have I put lipstick all over my face? I always forget when I put lipstick on. I bet it's all over my face right now."

Thanking my lucky stars when I heard Fernando calling our names from the door of the Institute, we dutifully trotted back into the building. The end-of-term lunch had enjoyed a build-up similar to that of the World Cup and the *cafetería* was full of huge trestle tables laden with *jamón, lomo, chorizo, tortillas*, salads, crisps, anchovies, *pimientos de padrón* and all sorts of other Spanish delights. Some of the students were helping out as waiters and Winston rushed over and pressed a glass of warm beer into my hand as soon as I entered, whispering.

"You have touched my heart Eebee and I will be missing you this summer."

His eyes misted up as he continued. "Can we go for dinner one day? Or I can cook you? I will be too sad if no see you this summer."

I scanned the crowds behind him hoping someone would come and rescue me. To no avail. I took a big swig of beer and cleared my throat.

"Winston, it has been a pleasure teaching you, but no, I don't think dinner is a good idea," I said firmly, shifting my weight from one foot to the other.

"I hope you have a lovely summer and good luck with your studies," I continued, heading to the group of teachers by the door where I let out a sigh of relief.

The next couple of hours whizzed by in a beer-clouded haze. Fernando gave me a big hug as I left and said, "I wish you return in September. I know is not possible but we keep in *contacto* and I be missing you. *Buen verano* Eebee *y mucha suerte.*"

"Thank you so much Fernando," I stuttered, wiping tears from my cheeks. "I have really enjoyed my time here and good luck with everything in the future. I hope you have a lovely summer too."

The boys queued up to bid me farewell.

"We like very much your classes titcher," said Carlos, and they all nodded in agreement.

"We miss you and your napples," said Rafa, swaggering around with his fingers on his nipples, to a raucous chorus of laughter from the boys and looks of astonishment and confusion from the teachers.

Time to leave.

"I will miss you all – thank you for everything and have a great summer!" I shouted over my shoulder as I walked out of the *cafetería* for the last time with a heavy heart.

20

The ginger light of the evening sun was warm and kind and crowds had flocked to the wide, open *terrazas* of Pintor Rosales to soak up the relaxed atmosphere and admire the view over Caso de Campo. The metal arm of the chair scorched my hand as I pulled it up to the table and joined Chloe, Lucinda, Molly and Ethan in skilfully bagging the only spare table in sight.

"*Hola,*" I smiled, waving at the adorable toddler beaming up at me from beside my feet, immaculately dressed in a blue floral smock dress with white lace edging to the sleeves, collar and skirt. Her wavy auburn hair was held in place with patterned gold clips, little gold balls glinted in her earlobes and blue leather buckled shoes completed the look. The glamorous mother could have passed for a model, her silk blouse adorned with gold studs, her glossy dark hair swinging in a long ponytail, and gold designer sunglasses wrapped around her face. Not to mention a whole heap of jewels making her glisten like an overloaded Christmas tree. The father completed the set in neatly pressed chinos, a checked shirt and a Ralph Lauren sweater casually thrown over his shoulders. The perfect Spanish family enjoying an evening out. Yet from their appearances you would have thought they were off to enjoy a three-course meal in a Michelin starred restaurant rather than crisps, *tortilla* and beer on a dirty table outside a slightly dodgy bar.

"So, *salud* people," smiled Belinda, raising her glass as she stretched out in her chair. "Isn't this fab?"

"Sure is," we all agreed.

"So Evie, tell me, how does it feel to have finished at the Institute?" enquired Molly, as she scanned the menu. "And more importantly, how's Winston going to survive without you?"

"Winston will be fine," I laughed, "I'm sure he'll find someone else to obsess over soon."

Ethan reached over and gave me a playful punch on the arm, "I think you're a disgrace. I can't believe you had five hundred and thirty men at your fingertips and you haven't shagged one. I bet they were all dying for you to shift their gear sticks?!" He slapped his thigh and guffawed loudly.

"I don't want to burst your bubble Ethan, but I feel I need to tell you that you really don't have a future as a comedian!" I laughed. "And sorry to disappoint but I'm not going to have another chance now," I replied. "They told me this morning I can't go back next term. I've been put on the waiting list for a normal school instead."

"Because you let them all look under your bonnet?" Ethan continued. "Now that's better isn't it?!" He held up his hand for a high five.

"Come on guys?!" he laughed as no one slapped his palm.

"They just get worse and worse," Belinda smiled, shaking her head and turning to Molly. "I can't believe you married this joker."

"Tell me about it," she sighed. "He saved up all his lines until after the wedding!"

"So why can't you go back to the Institute?"

"Apparently it's a bureaucratic thing and you have to

rotate on the scheme. Nobody can do two years in the same place."

"So have you decided anything about next year?" asked Belinda, tentatively, as she successfully speared two *bocarones* off a plate with a cocktail stick and popped them in her mouth.

"No! I ended up applying for the job in London, but I haven't heard anything. I'm trying to forget all about it and just focus on enjoying every minute here.

"What about you guys? What are your plans for the summer?"

"Well," said Molly, "It's a bit last minute, but Ethan's been given some time off work, so we're gonna go back to Canada for a month next week."

"A month? Wow, awesome!" chorused Chloe and Belinda.

Molly leant over and whispered conspiratorially, "and between you and me, I'm hoping I'll be able to persuade him to move back at the end of the summer. I'm gonna line up so much fun for the coming month he won't know what's hit him."

"Drumroll please, I have some news too," added Chloe. "With literally no warning, my leaving date has been changed for the hundredth time and now I have to leave tomorrow so I can be in the London office on Monday for the start of a new project."

"What?!" we shrieked.

"I know! After all this waiting, it's bloody irritating they're so shambolic, but sadly it's out of my hands." She shrugged.

"I just have to be Spanish about it and go with the flow," she added in a resigned tone.

"So does this mean tonight is our last night here together?" asked Belinda, "we'd better make it a good one."

"Let's have the night to end all nights," suggested Molly.

"We should go on a Malasaña bar crawl to all our favourites and then we can go hit up the dancefloor in Luna afterwards."

A flurry of calls followed and Iñaki, Gabriella, Miriam, Carolina, Rebeca all signed up to the plan.

A blush spread over Chloe's cheeks as she read a message on her phone. She cleared her throat and announced:

"So, guys, I have another mega piece of news too. I might not have told you but I have a boyfriend!" she blurted out, excitedly, "and he's coming to join us in a minute."

"Woah, I can't take in all this news!" Belinda exclaimed, "who is he?!"

"Weeeeeeeeell, it's Andrés, Evie's friend who I met in Carmencita a while back."

"Whaaaaaattttt!!" I shrieked, leaning forward in my chair, "I thought that was just a fling!"

"It was only a bit of fun at first and I never thought it would last, but what can I say, he's great and I think it's really grown into something. He's got some time off over the summer so he's going to come to London for a bit and we'll see what happens."

"*Poco a poco!*" she added, making us all laugh.

"Well cheers to Andrés," volunteered Ethan, raising his glass. "It's good to see you looking so happy *chica*."

"*Salud,*" we chorused, clinking our glasses together. "And here is the great man himself!"

"Hey t-shirt, hey guys," he drawled as he swooped down to give Chloe a smooch on the lips, his hands lingering on her face.

"*Hola mi princesa,*" he whispered to her as he pulled up a chair and slouched back with his arm across Chloe's shoulders, the pair of them grinning like soppy teenagers.

"I can't believe I didn't know about this. You're a dark horse!" I joked, playfully prodding his arm.

"I is not a horse t-shirt. Why you say that?" He looked perplexed as the others laughed.

"Don't worry," I reassured him, "it's a silly English expression."

"Is you jealous?" he teased, "You missed your *oportunidad* with me and you sad now I find another *princesa inglesa?!*"

I chuckled, "Can't wait to discuss this with your grand-mother!! Now do you want a drink here or shall we move on?"

"Let's go," suggested Belinda, "I know the Spanish nights are long and everything but we've got plenty of places to get to tonight so we should crack on."

At our first pit stop, the glossy and industrially decorated La Pescadería, we refuelled with pisco sours served in jam-jars, accompanied by *bienmesabe* wrapped in newspaper cones. The modern atmosphere couldn't have contrasted more with Bodega Ardosa, the old-school haunt where we later crowded round an old wooden barrel in the corner with vermouth, olives and *jamón*.

A heated debate over where to find the best *tortilla* in Madrid was put on hold when a broad, swarthy man waved at Iñaki and pushed his way through the crowds.

"*Tío, cuanto tiempo!*" he exclaimed, hugging his friend with much grinning and back-slapping.

"Evie, guys, this is my friend Javi. We was at school together since a long time," he explained, as Javi embarked on a round of introductory kisses. Slick, with luscious dark curls atop his head, sparkling eyes and a smattering of freck-les, he had caught the attention of most of the women in the bar.

"So, how are things Javi?" asked Iñaki, leaning on the windowsill, cradling his vermouth in his hand.

"*Bien, bien,*" he replied, "I had a great afternoon with the *toros* today."

"Evie, I should explain you, Javi is a bullfighter." As the words tumbled out of his mouth, us girls all swivelled our heads to gaze adoringly at the newcomer.

"Really?" I cried. "A bona fide bullfighter?!"

"No way," laughed Molly, swooning, "I've always wanted to meet a bullfighter!"

Lapping up the attention, Javi whipped his phone out of his pocket.

"*Sí, sí,* here, *mira,* if you like I show you pictures."

"Tsk," chortled Iñaki, dismissively, "girls is always the same with the bullfighters."

We cooed over an endless stream of photos showing Javi in an elaborate white diamante-covered jacket, dancing and prancing in a ring with some feisty bulls. We practically had drool dripping from our mouths as we admired them and hung off his every word, much to the disgust of Ethan, Andrés and Iñaki.

Finally, I'd met a bullfighter, I laughed, thinking back to my old boss John and his obsession with me falling in love with a *torero*. He'd be loving this if he was here.

After *unas bombas* in La Musa and more cocktails in Passenger and Kike Keller, we wobbled our way to Luna, passing some inebriated girls living up to the stereotype of Brits abroad, shamelessly flashing their boobs to every Spanish man in sight. The club was heaving when we arrived and we joined the queue, laughing as our new-found friends flirted outrageously with every man on the street, a great spectator sport. Ethan and Andrés had struck up conversation with a handsome man in the line when one of said girls, I think her name was Poppy, swaggered over, putting her finger to her lips as she pensively sized him up.

"You're gorgeous. I really fancy you," she decreed, leaning

forward and kissing him passionately on the lips. The girl at his side went berserk, taking aggressive steps towards Poppy and gesticulating wildly,

"*Qué haces? Es mi novio. Joder! Las inglesas...joder.* Is my BOYFRIEND!"

Poppy barely batted an eyelid at the news he was taken. While he stood rooted to the spot, the girlfriend continued to rant and rage, but Poppy simply flicked her gorgeous blonde locks over her shoulder and sashayed into the club, wobbling precariously in her heels.

We soon followed into the bar, and after a jaunt around the dancefloor retreated to the *terraza*, seeking respite from the hordes. Fairy lights, vines and lanterns dangled from the pergolas, with luscious plants dotted around the walls and an extremely well-stocked bar manned by two beefy barmen at the back. Armed with yet more drinks we settled round the tables and soaked up the ambiance, tapping our feet to the Spanish tunes floating out from the dancefloor.

Rebeca peered out from under her long fringe, staring deeply into Javi's eyes and he stared back, enthralled. Their bodies moved closer and closer as if pulled by a magnetic attraction and I couldn't help but laugh at the cliché of a bullfighter and a flamenco dancer. A hand grabbed my shoulder and I turned, distracted, to find Raul looking nervous behind me.

"Hey," I asked, surprised, "what are you doing here?" I jumped to my feet, kissed him hello and realised my body was covered in goose bumps. He hadn't lost his effect on me.

"I came to see you," he replied, shifting awkwardly from one foot to another and rubbing his stubbly chin with his thumb and forefinger. "Molly told me you would be here. I returned from New York this morning and I want to say you that I would really like it if I could take you for dinner again

Eebee Fuller. I have missed our times together and think in you a lot. You are a very especial person."

"Um, well, yes," I gulped, "it's good to see you. Come and join us. Do you know everyone here?"

"*Sí, sí*," he nodded, scanning the faces round the tables.

"But I don't think you've met my, err, Iñaki," I added, looking up at him tentatively, "he's my..."

"Eebee, *guapa, tanto tiempo!*" I was nearly knocked off my feet as Ramón burst into our group and threw his sweaty arms around me. "*Cómo estás?*" he asked breathlessly, slobbering over my cheeks and blindly ignoring the others.

"Ramón, hi! I know, it's been super-long time! Good to see you. How are things? What's your news?" I babbled, thrown and relieved by his appearance.

"All is very good *gracias*. Look, there," he pointed to a pretty, curvaceous girl by the bar. "See the girl *guapísima?* Is my girlfriend Lucia, I will present you shortly. I only want to apologise I have not contacted with you recently. I thought when met you I want girlfriend English, is *muy* in fashion now, but *en realidad,* Lucia is Spanish and we are much more good together. We have relation *complicado* but very passionate. We break up and make up *todo el tiempo, sabes* like in the films, and when we are together we are united in passion all the hours." He rubbed his hands together with glee.

"Say no more," I grinned, patting his arm, "I understand and I hope things work out for you."

He bounced back to Lucia and I laughed as they began writhing all over the dancefloor, his hands energetically exploring her body. I turned to see Ethan introducing Raul to Iñaki.

"Why didn't you tell me he was back in town?" I hissed at Molly, urgently pulling her to one side.

"Geez, I'm such a doofus, we've had a manic couple of days sorting things for Canada and it totally slipped my mind, don't worry though, it'll be totally fine."

"I know, but a heads up would have been nice."

I hesitated before taking a deep breath and walking over to join the guys.

"Is that the famous Ramón?" asked Raul with a smirk. "He is *exactamente* like you describe."

"So tell me Eebee, how are you? And how do you and Iñaki meet?" He rubbed my arm as he spoke, memories flooding back as his touch set my pulse racing. "Is good to see you."

"Err, well, we met in a bar and he's actually my boyfriend." As the words came tumbling out the colour drained from his face.

"Oh," he muttered under his breath, tugging at my arm, "I thought we had something special Eebee."

"Her name is EVIE," Iñaki interjected, stepping over to us. "Evie, who is this guy? Is something going on?"

"Calm down Iñaki, it's all fine. Just give us a minute," I implored, pulling Raul to a corner of the *terraza*.

"Listen, Raul, I'm sorry, but you can't seriously expect us to carry on where we left off?"

"Why not?" he urged, "we is good together Eebee. You know it too."

"I haven't heard from you in months!" I muttered, digging my nails into the palms of my hands.

He let out a ragged sigh. "I know, I am sorry. Was impossible in US, so much work and I am not so good at messaging. I never stopped thinking in you."

"Why didn't you say that?" I pleaded. "You can't expect me to read your thoughts. What was I supposed to think?"

Iñaki watched us like a hawk, shifting from one foot to another. When Raul cupped my face in his hands he could take it no longer and marched over, shoving him away from me.

"What you want?" he asked aggressively.

"To talk. Eebee and I have *historia* ok, we need to talk." Raul held his hands up in the air and looked at me beseechingly.

"EVIE, her name is Evie," he exclaimed.

"*Joder tío*," Raul swore, throwing his weight against Iñaki who stumbled back into the vine-covered wall, before running head first back at him. They wrestled and knocked into a table before falling to the ground in a tussle as I looked on in disbelief.

"Ethan, get over here!" shouted Molly, beckoning at him and Andrés, who rushed over to tear them apart.

"You're so ridiculous. You need to calm down." I shook my head and Iñaki winced as I pulled him close after the guys had dragged him and Raul apart. "Are you ok?"

"*Sí*, I is fine," he sighed.

"Wait here a moment," I asked. As the others crowded around him, I walked over to Raul, slumped on a chair with his head in his hands.

"Are you ok?"

"*Sí, sí*, all good," he replied, hanging his head.

"You are an amazing guy Raul, but if you like a girl you have to tell her. You can't expect her to wait for you if she doesn't know how you feel, ok?"

He nodded in silence, looking up at me as he gingerly touched his ribs. "I hope you is happy Eebee Fuller. And I hope we can be friends."

"*Trato hecho*," I agreed, holding out my hand. "It's a deal. Friends."

We shook on it and I returned to Iñaki's side.

The rest of the night passed in a blur of colour and dancing. When the sun began to rise we stopped for the obligatory *churros* and hot chocolate before tottering home for some well-deserved sleep.

***

I woke up the next day, my head pounding, to hear emails popping up on my phone left, right and centre. My hands shook as I scrolled through and spotted one from the art gallery in London with the subject line *Job application*, and also one from Alba. Gulp. Moving slowly, I lifted the duvet and as quietly as possible I climbed out of bed and snuck onto the balcony. Gently pulling the door closed behind me, I curled up in the hammock and closed my eyes. If I was to leave my future in the hands of fate, then this email from the gallery would be a big sign in one direction or the other.

My head ached, my stomach churned and my hands were shaking. Taking a deep breath I opened up my inbox and stared at the messages, too nervous at first to click on any of them.

With a deep sigh I summoned up courage and decided to read Alba's. Once opened it took my eyes a wee while to focus on the words.

Dear Evie,
Following our conversation yesterday, I am writing to inform you that a position has become available for next year in a secondary school in Villaverde Alto. The hours and pay would be the same as last year. If you would like to take up this offer please confirm in writing within the next forty-eight hours. I will then send you the contract to sign and the contact details of the Director for you to make plans directly.
Many thanks, Alba

I knew nothing about Villaverde Alto and couldn't believe I'd been offered a place. Oh why is there no one I can talk to properly about this? Despite drawing up endless lists of the pros and cons of my options, I'd arrived back at square one. My heart knew I should talk to Iñaki, yet I struggled to articulate my feelings in English and to do so in Spanish would be impossible. How could I expect him to get to grips with the crazy vacillations of my mind anyway, when they were such an enigma to me.

I clicked on the other email.

Oh god. Gulp.

It was a reality.

They'd offered me the job.

I squeezed my eyes closed, wondering if I deleted it quickly enough I could pretend it had gone straight into my spam folder and I'd never seen it.

Memories of the last year flashed through my mind. Who knew the window displays of knife shops could be so decorative and elaborate? That watching Spaniards eat doughnuts with a knife and fork could be so entertaining? That the Spanish expression for making a scene translates directly as mounting a chicken (*montar un pollo*)? Or even how so many Spanish men think it acceptable to shave their legs, chests and arms? Simple tasks like visiting the *fruteria* and registering at the doctor had become entertaining rather than a chore, and left me grinning for hours, despite taking twice as long as in England. The nerves as I approached a shop and loitered outside trying to concoct the correct sentence in Spanish gave way to an irrational burst of joy and satisfaction when the mission was accomplished. I loved the constant communication teaching required and never in my wildest dreams had I thought I would end up practising speed dating with a class of 18–40-year-old mechanics, let alone enjoying it. I'd built a great group of friends, found a lovely flat, somehow bagged a wonderful boyfriend and generally laid strong foundations for a life. It felt like home. A mad, chaotic and unpredictable home, but home nonetheless.

It was the Spanish version of me I was most terrified of losing if I went back to the UK. So much more carefree, brave, open and positive, I loved her and feared she would be swallowed up by the banality of London life, yet perhaps I should open myself to the possibility it would allow her to flourish further.

My inner warblings were arrested by Iñaki stumbling out onto the balcony and climbing into the hammock with me, rubbing sleep out of his eyes.

"You OK Evie?" he murmured. "You up very early."

"Um, yep, nope. Oh I don't know," I mumbled.

I shifted awkwardly to turn and look at him, my clammy hands fiddling nervously with my bracelet.

"Do you believe a person can have a second soul?" I asked.

"What are you saying?" he muttered, eyes closed and semi-conscious.

"I read a quote the other day – *to have another language is to possess a second soul* – and I get it completely. It's like there are two versions of me now and I'm torn between them."

"Hey, *cariño*, look me. Are you ok?" he tilted my face to look me in the eyes.

"Well, listen, there's something I should have talked to you about before." I paused, unsure how to continue.

"You see, the thing is, I've been offered a job back in London. A really good job and I don't know what to do." The words came tumbling out in one breath and my heart pounded as I gazed at him anxiously.

The hammock rocked precariously as he shifted his weight

onto one arm. "You leaving? You can't leave. You love Spain, you love it here, no?" he implored.

"Yes, you know I do, and I love Spanish Evie, but is it all just a holiday or a dream? It's too good to be true in many ways, but I need to do something more with my life," I whispered, tears flowing freely down my face.

"I no think is good excuse to leave. I have lived here thirty-three years and every day feel like a holiday. Is a good thing – is Madrid." He gently wiped the tears from my cheek. "You are happy. You should stay."

"But I will only ever be a menial English teacher here."

"You are much more than that to me and together we can find you another job if you want. I'm sure. Stay, for me," he pleaded.

"But you've just been saying how much you want to move away?"

"I wanted a change, something different in my life, yes, but you have given me that. We stay, and I no mind if I am with you. Please stay."

Gulp. This was one of those moments, the type of which come only a handful of times in life. Faced by a crossroads, I had no idea which way to turn. His chestnut eyes searched mine and my head and my heart battled each other; my head ordering me to go home, take the good, sensible job and retreat to the safe and familiar, while simultaneously my heart screamed *stay!* Take a risk! Throw yourself into his arms and STAY! As I'd waited thirty years to find a wonderful boyfriend, would I be a complete muppet to chuck it all in? For the sake of my sanity a decision needed to be taken immediately so I wiped my sweaty palms on my knees, took a deep breath and said...

Acknowledgements

Too many people have put up with my wafflings on all things Spanish over the last few years to be listed individually here, but my own Spanish adventures wouldn't have been half as much fun without the fabulous Lucinda Howells. *Muchísimas gracias* also to Angie Grossman, Maria Palacios Atienza, Carol Gonzalez Vives, Marianne Job, Jorge Onrubia, Margit Sperling, Maeghan & Ian Stocker, Jen & Andrew Barnes, Sam & Sarah Strang Steel, Grattam, Jane Masey, Lottie Gilbey, Begoña & Maria Hormaeche, Bea Sedano Cuevas, Inés Prieto Ortega, my students and all the other Spaniards who enriched my time in Madrid and provided me with so many magical *madrileño* memories and so much inspiration for this book.

Back in Blighty, special thanks to Amicie de Villenfagne, Matthew Paton, Tri Benton, Al Janvrin, Lucy Floyd, Camilla Webb Carter, Richenda Gurney, Katie Colony, Isabel Lamb, Anna Wright, Rebecca Crookendon, Chrissie Boyle and Sophie Montagne for their support along the way and their patience in the face of my fascination with obscure Spanish idioms, as well as to the Colton Arms gang for all the mechanical euphemisms that didn't quite make the final cut. And to everyone else who has been kind enough to let me indulge in nostalgic Spanish drivel so often, thank you.

Of course huge thanks are due to Sam Carter for his

advice, enthusiasm, help and patience, without which this may well have simply festered in a folder on my computer. Last but not least I owe a great deal to my long-suffering and wonderful parents. My biggest shout-out goes to you for being quite simply superstars.